Love in the Wrong Locker

Millie Lang

Contents

Chapter 1

I'm going to murder Jason.

Specifically, in his sleep. I'll choke the life out of him when he least expects it with one of his pillows and stuff feathers into his mouth as soon as he stops breathing.

Or, even better: I'll slip some hemlock in his water during dinner and he'll die in his sleep. But where could I get something that hasn't been used since Socrates killed himself a couple of millennia ago?

Regardless, I still want to kill my brother for using that damn Sharpie on my walls. I don't mind a little harmless prank now and then. This, however, was not harmless at all. Do you know how much rubbing alcohol I've had to use to get it off most of my walls?

A shit ton of it. And I'm not even finished with it, yet.

I don't even know how he managed to not wake me up when he was doing this. I could easily applaud him because I'm not exactly what one would call a deep sleeper—even a drop of a hat could wake me up. But how did I not wake up to the sound of a squeaky Sharpie over my bedroom walls is way beyond me.

I wipe my forehead with the back of my hand as I finish up one side of the wall, standing on my tallest tiptoes. I've been at it for a few hours now and I have one more left to do. I definitely have better things to do than deep clean my walls on Labor Day, after a long-ass three-hour drive from my aunt and uncle's house.

One extra hour, another emptied bottle of rubbing alcohol, and a folding chair later, my wall is free of the permanent marker. Take that, Sharpies! Guess you're not as permanent as you thought you would be.

I take one breath in and immediately walk out of my room coughing because now my room reeks of rubbing alcohol. I leave the door open to let some of the smell out and I head to the bathroom to wash my hands. I should probably take a shower but I don't have any clothes I can change into.

All of my clothes probably smell like the strong liquid substance that was used on my walls only an hour ago.

Screw it.

I turn on the faucet and step into the shower. As the warm water runs down my body, I start to think of ways I can get back at my brother for this little prank. We've been at this little prank war since I got him back on April Fool's Day earlier this year for changing the password on my laptop. I could have lost this big project I'd been working on that entire school year because of him.

So I added bright orange dye into his three-in-one while he was at practice as payback. He looked like an Oompa-Loompa until the next morning when he had used Dad's instead.

An idea finally comes to mind as I finish washing myself up head out of the shower and put on my bathrobes. When I begin to towel-dry my long, dark-ombre hair, I spot the tube of toothpaste still sitting right in front of my sink from when I used it this morning.

Then an idea hits me fast as I begin to towel-dry my hair.

I head in and out of my room to grab some clothes to change into, making sure I hold my breath the entire time until I head to the bathroom. After changing into them, I grab the toothpaste and rush downstairs to the pantry. Jason just happens to be running out of his family-sized pack of Oreos. I don't know how many are left because I don't really like Oreos myself but they could definitely use a little TLC.

So I spend my time removing the cream in the middle and replacing it with toothpaste. I'm thankful that my toothpaste is white so the cookies don't look so suspicious.

I head back upstairs to my room so I can open a window because just leaving the door open isn't going to cut it. It fucking reeks but I want to remain as innocent as possible in the case that Jason enters the house at this exact moment.

I spent most of my time this summer mainly going back and forth between reading a book that my bestie Amy had lent me the last time I saw her and writing ideas for my next big project in my school's animation club. So instead of sticking my nose into my sketchbook or laptop, I crack open the book that Amy had lent me. To All the Boys I've Loved Before by Jenny Han may no longer be as popular as it once was but I'm only just getting into the realm of reading outside of school.

And it's a good one. Fake dating, secret love letters, and Korean culture? I think I may have fallen in love with Peter Kavinsky already, too. I'm also definitely not Korean—I'm the most white-looking Cuban you'll ever meet—but I've noticed that interracial romances in YA books are far and few in between.

It's not until I reach chapter thirteen that I start to feel parched. I mark the page that I'm on and head downstairs for a glass of water. Just my luck, I hear the garage door open and just know that Jason is finally home. My Ryder radar is never wrong.

Knowing better than to stand in the middle of a war zone, I walk out of the kitchen and find myself a suitable place to hide. Far enough to where I could not be detected yet close enough to hear my brother's horror when he reveals the surprise hiding in those lovely Oreos of his.

I'm drinking my water when I hear footsteps. I wince when I hear more than one set of feet pitter-pattering around the kitchen.

"Hey, thanks for telling me this," Jason's voice rings as I hear the door to the pantry open. "I'm glad you came to me."

"I'm glad you didn't belittle me when I told you." Wait a minute, I know this other voice...

Derek!

Shit! He brought Derek over??

I give myself a mental facepalm before quietly sipping my cup of ice water. I can't do anything to give myself away.

"It's still crazy you've kept it for so long," my brother is saying. "When did you know?"

"Honestly? I think I've always known."

"Is that why you turned down Macy when she asked you out last month?"

"Yep."

What could they be talking about? The suspense is killing me!

But my question is never answered because only a second later, I hear an eerily quiet crunch before Jason practically shouts, "fuck! Bro, give me a napkin." I'm pretty sure he's spitting the toothpaste-filled Oreo out of his mouth.

"It can't be that bad," Derek's voice says before biting into another cookie. "Nope. It's worse. Yuck!" He spits the cookie out of his mouth too.

I'm only going by sound here but I can tell that both of them are a little angry—if not both of them then definitely Jason.

I really hope Derek's not angry.

I quickly run upstairs to grab my headphones and blast Taylor Swift's rerecording of her Speak Now album in my ears so that I act all clueless to the events happening and then walk back downstairs. This time, I direct myself over to the kitchen, where I grab a bag of jalapeño chips.

Just as I open the kitchen cabinets for a bowl, I feel a tap on my shoulder. Taking a headphone out, I turn around to find my brother's glare pinned right at me. His hazel-green eyes are seething with rage. "What happened to the Oreos?"

I cross my arms over my stomach. Not in insecurity—I'm wearing an oversized t-shirt—but to try to assert dominance. And because I'm no longer hungry. "Wow, no greetings? You just got home and all I get is your attitude. Tsk, tsk."

"You know damn well what I mean." He grabs a napkin from the counter and spits in it. "Ugh, that was gross. I'm gonna brush my teeth," he says to Derek. "I'll be right back."

As he heads out of the kitchen, I call out, "I hope they tasted fresh!" I try to hold back a laugh.

"Fuck you!" He shouts back and whatever control I had is relinquished as my head falls back in laughter. Man, did I get him good. I think it might be my best prank so far.

"Damn," Derek mutters as he watches the display. "What did he do to you?"

Wiping the tears from my face, I shrug and answer, "Sharpie all over my walls. It took me hours to clean it all up and my room still smells like rubbing alcohol."

He winces. "Remind me never to get on your bad side, Attie."

My cheeks turn a rosy pink. "You'd never get on my bad side, Derek."

He smiles in return. "Thanks."

"I'm sorry that you got caught in the crossfire."

Derek waves a hand over to dismiss it. "No worries. At least I wasn't the target." He gives me a warm smile and I almost melt right there.

I've been crushing hard on my brother's best friend since middle school. Yeah, four years of pining after someone who is somehow friends with my brother pretty much sucks. But I couldn't help but fall in love with him. I don't know exactly when it happened. Maybe I had always been in love with him, who knows?

But have you seen him? He's got the whole package. Tall and lean after years of playing volleyball, wavy brown hair, and smooth skin that is slightly sun-kissed due to the amount of time he's spent outside. And on top of all that, his eyes are just so pretty! Sure, they're brown, but they aren't dark brown. They're like a light, honey-ish color. Twelve-year-old me just couldn't help herself.

Where was I?

Oh right!

"So, Attie, how have you been?" He asks.

"Oh. Uh, just fine. A little tired after driving back from the Inland Empire last night. My prank was also a huge success." I start to feel warm again. And not in a good way, but as in a this-is-so-uncomfortable kind of way. I swear my voice just went up an octave or two because I'm rarely ever alone with Derek. Usually, Jason is a buffer or Derek's older brother is around.

He chuckles. "I can tell. Maybe I'll try that with Ian someday."

I let out a little giggle at the thought of it. Ian Bale is just about Derek's polar opposite. If you put them side by side, you wouldn't be able to guess that they were related.

"What are you laughing about?" Jason asks as he steps back into the kitchen, grabbing two soda cans. I try to grab one from his hand but he brings it out of reach. "Fuck no! Not until you apologize for the Oreos."

"Hmph. Then you have to apologize for the Sharpie on my walls that took me hours to get rid of."

"I didn't damage anything. Besides, you can paint over it."

"I wouldn't have been able to." I hold my hand out. "Keys, please."

Jason's brows fly up to his hairline. "I didn't hear a magic word."

The glare I give him could easily shoot lasers right into his pretty face if given the ability. "Por favor."

Sighing, he grabs the keys to our bright blue Jeep Wrangler from the pocket of his shorts. I take them with a pleased hum and head upstairs to grab my bag. As much as I would like to be around Derek today, I need a break from the testosterone, rubbing alcohol, and bullshit I endured this weekend. "Gracias."

When I head back downstairs and towards the garage, I unintentionally overhear yet another conversation between Jason and Derek.

"Wait, how am I gonna get home now?"

"Ask Ian. He can't be that busy right now, can he?"

"He still has football practice and painting the parking lot. And if it wasn't that, he's probably jumping off some cliff with one of his friends or something."

I roll my eyes at that last sentence. Ian is basically the all-American teenage boy you'd read about in coming-of-age stories. Tall, starting quarterback, blond Clark Kent look-alike with a hint of boyish charm and a slightly wild persona.

I've known him since he and Derek moved to Santa Barbara back in elementary school.

It doesn't even surprise me at the thought that he'd be doing something crazy. It's why I don't really hang out with him when he's around. I prefer to keep my distance. He's not a bad person—at least, not to me—he's just too spontaneous in my opinion.

But could you blame me? I'd like to live to see my high school graduation.

When I hop into the driver's side of the Jeep, I look out the open window and rest my elbow just above it as I press on the brake and turn the key. It's still crazy to me that summer is officially over—then again, it's Southern California, a state that looks like summer all year long—but it's nice to know I'll be getting back to a more familiar routine.

A safe routine, with no more crazy mishaps that occur outside of homework and obnoxious tests.

Chapter 2

"Okay, when did I say I would be doing all the work?" My best friend and team captain, Braiden James, asks as he spills a bucket of bright green paint onto his designated parking spot. I'm standing right next to him while my own parking spot dries. I had only finished the first coat and had a general idea of what I would be painting.

"You didn't," his girlfriend, Sophia Castro answers as she fans herself. Summer is the equivalent of hell's sauna, especially in Santa Barbara. It's worse because instead of the dry heat that surrounds Texas, it's humid as hell in the West Coast. But maybe that's because Santa Barbara is a beach town and beaches tend to be humid. At least it's only Labor Day.

Yet who's idea was it for us to paint the parking spots after school starts back up?

"Still." BJ wipes the sweat from his forehead and turns to me. "Kind of glad we didn't have a two-a-day, right Bale?"

I nod, grabbing a water bottle and basically chugging it. For someone who has lived in two of the hottest places in the country, I sure hate the heat. But summer means no school and making the most out of it.

And it's coming to an end. Thank GOD.

"Can you guys believe it?" Sophia asks as she hops onto the top of the trunk. "Senior year began a month ago. And you have your first away game of the season coming up."

"Yeah," Braiden says. "It's hard to believe that this is our last year."

"And that we still have so much to do. Like, pull the ultimate senior prank, set Ian up on an actual date, get nominated for homecoming king and—"

"Hold on there, Castro," I interrupt. "You lost me at 'set Ian up on an actual date.' Why the hell do I need to go on a date?" I've done crazier things in my time that I would not like to name but dating has been the craziest thing that I haven't done and probably will not.

At least, not randomly.

"High school is a matter of trial and error and this is literally the best time to start dating when you get the chance." She places her hands on her hips as an attempt to be assertive. "You know, for someone who is always up to trying new things, you seem so against it."

"Because dating is my one exception," I tell her. I've seen the fallout of dating and love—it's not pretty. Sure, BJ and Sophia are also the exceptions to this because I swear they've been giving each other puppy-dog eyes since they started dating, probably even before.

Grabbing my bucket of paint and a brush, I get back to painting my spot. "Besides, even if I was up for it, there aren't many girls who I'd be interested in."

"Man, your standards are too high." BJ isn't exactly one to sugarcoat things. "Besides, you can literally have any single girl you'd like."

Well, not everyone.

"I should set you up with Rue," Sophia says, brown eyes bright. "I can totally see you two together. She's just your type."

"What do you mean by that?" I raise a brow. Last I checked, I don't have a type. Sort of. And not having a type means that I don't have any standards. Wait, that's a lie. I do have my limits.

"She'd totally want to go out with you." She winks before grabbing a thick paintbrush and dipping it into the bright yellow paint bucket. "It's obvious to anyone with eyes."

Rue Barlow is one of Sophie's best friends and the co-captain of the cheer team. I've talked to Rue a few times, made out with her at a party or two but I've never been interested in going on a date with her. That hasn't changed at all.

"Guessing by the look on his face," BJ chuckles. "He didn't know. Are you sure your eyes are fine? You have four of them."

I flip him off, even though his back is turned towards me.

The sun's starting to set when my parking spot is completely dry. It didn't even take that long to finish but BJ and Sophia wanted this huge decal on their spot—they're always carpooling, which, I won't lie, is kind of adorable —so I mainly stayed to help them out.

"Sophie and I are headed to the beach to ring in the last day of summer," he tells me. "Are you down to join us?"

I'm about to respond when my phone buzzes in my back pocket. I check to find a text from Derek, my little brother.

Younger Nuisance: Can you pick me up?

Me: Why can't Jason drop you off?

Younger Nuisance: He doesn't have the car anymore. Attie took it.

I look back up from my phone. "Sorry guys. Derek needs a ride."

"We'll see you tomorrow," Sophia waves before they both crawl into BJ's truck and the happy couple drives off into the sunset like their own makeshift happily ever after.

I will never understand their incessant need to spend so much time together. Maybe it's because I haven't exactly found someone like that but I don't need to rush it. I'm only seventeen, after all. My parents didn't even meet until they were thirty and that didn't exactly go so well.

I hop into my old 2013 Toyota Camry and head into the direction of Jason Ryder's house. I've known the Ryders since Derek, Dad, and I first moved to California in elementary school. We've spent so much time at their place that I could drive there from my own house without my glasses.

It's not long before I pull the car into the driveway and cut the engine. I sit in my car for a few minutes and just as I'm about to text Derek that I've arrived, a loud carhorn is blasted into my eardrum, followed by the words, "get the fuck out of my parking spot!"

By a familiar, high-pitched voice.

I don't need to get out of the car to find a bright blue Jeep Wrangler parked by the curb to know who the owner of that voice is. And it isn't Jason Ryder.

It's his twin sister.

I do get out of the car anyway and find Attie's pale blue eyes soften when she sees me. "Sorry, Ian. Thought you were a random stranger."

I sit myself on the hood of my car. "Don't worry about it, princess."

Her face turns pink as she sips her smoothie. "Are you here to pick up Derek?"

I nod. "He said you had the Jeep. I could move my car—"

She waves her hand to dismiss me. "It's fine. You're not gonna be here long, right?"

"Not really. If Derek decides to get his lazy ass down here." I shoot a pointed glare at the two-story brick house in front of me.

I hear giggling come from my right. "You must have a strong vendetta on my house if you're looking at it that way."

I scoff. "That old thing?" I point to her house. "Never." It's not a lie either. It feels more like a regular home than my place.

"Well..." Attie turns to the house. "I should probably head inside. It was nice to see you, Ian." Before opening the front gate that leads to their backyard, she turns to me. "By the way, your glasses look like they're about to fall off."

Huh. I didn't notice that. I push them up the bridge of my nose and wave at Attie and just as she opens the gate, Derek exits, causing Attie to stop in her tracks.

"Hey, Derek. Leaving already?" Her voice is a little shaky and has gone up an octave.

"Yeah. I'll see you later, Attie." He heads towards my car and Attie disappears from my view.

"Yo, what up, you big nuisance?" I'm not sure if it's normal for brothers to have nicknames for each other but that's how Derek rolls. When we were in elementary school, I started calling him a nuisance (I was ten and didn't know what it meant) and he hit me with the most childish sentence to ever exist:

"I know you are, but what am I?"

"Is Dad home?" He asks.

I shrug. "I should be asking you that question. Why would I know that answer?"

Usually, I'm up and out of the house before Dad is even awake. Despite what happened to our parents back in Texas, Derek and I don't have a strained relationship with our father. But both our schedules mean that we hardly ever see him.

"So, is there anything going on with you and Attie?" I nudged his shoulder.

My brother rolls his eyes. "Why would there be anything going on?"

"You tell me."

Shaking his head, he answers, "no way. Even if there was, I can't break the bro-code. Honestly, Ian, she's more likely to end up with you than she is me."

I scoff at that. If only that was true. Unlike Derek, I hardly am ever around Attie Ryder. And she knows about my reputation—hell, the entirety of Santa Barbara High School knows. I'm not exactly known to stick with one girl for a long time.

Add that to the crazy shit I've done outside of school and you get the ultimate Attie Ryder repellent. Now available in stores everywhere!

All joking aside, I can honestly say—as his brother—that Derek has more of a chance with her than I ever would. In fact, he could have any girl he wants but as far as I know, he's never had a girlfriend. I used to think it was because he put volleyball and his studies before everything else.

Another part of me thinks that school has nothing to do with his dating life, or lack thereof. But I hate assuming as much as the taste of beer so I always keep those thoughts in the back of my mind.

I start the engine. "Okay, little nuisance. Less talking, more driving."

I could use some time at home right now. And that says something.

Chapter 3

J unior year is supposed to be the worst part of high school, according to some of the members of the animation club that I'm a part of. Ask me next June how it actually is because I'm still indecisive.

So far, the school has won all of this season's game, my honors math teacher gave us a quiz on Tuesday, and I'm still waiting for another masterpiece from Taylor Swift after listening to my favorite, 1989, on repeat for the past month. Another album cannot come soon enough but you can never tire of iconic songs.

"Hey, At-Bat, are you ready?" my best friend, Amy Pierce says as she's tapping on my shoulder. School had ended for the day but we're still in the computer lab even after hours because I have some work to touch up on.

"Almost," I answer as I'm stuck on Canva, a very popular graphic design website, working on the new logo for the animation club. After being nominated as the vice president, I took it upon myself to add a little bit of flair for the poster for the Club Rush happening on Friday. "Just need to add this one little detail."

She peers over my shoulder, her curly hair barely touching my shoulder. I'm never bothered with people looking over my shoulder. Can't be bothered with something when you do it yourself. "You sure about going black and white?"

I nod. "It's classy."

"It's a high school club." She sighs. "You can go as messy as you'd like."

"Well, I like this theme." I add one last little detail, save it to my account, and power the computer off. Standing up, I grab my bag and phone. "Okay, now I'm ready."

"Let's go." Amy grabs her bags (yes, I said bags) and walks out of the computer lab with me following behind. I usually get a ride from Amy after school to her house if I don't have the Jeep, like today.

I've missed hanging out with my best friend since kindergarten. Now that her boyfriend, Carter, is off at college, I basically get her all to myself. And thank God for that because there's always something about her boyfriend that has rubbed me the wrong way. Maybe I'm wrong and I really hope I am because I only wish for my bestie's happiness.

We wave goodbye to Mr. Ali, the teacher who's currently watching over the computer lab, before heading out to the student parking and into the sedan she borrowed from her aunt. Amy turns on the radio and turns the volume up when Harry Styles's As It Was starts up. I love Harry Styles as much as the next person, but this is one of my favorite songs of all time.

But there's no denying that this song is an absolute banger. We sing along to the music playing until we reach her two-story house which isn't that far from school. Once we enter, Amy and I are greeted by her aunt Mary and the smell of chocolate chip cookies. I may not be the biggest fan of chocolate but those cookies are my only exception.

"Mary! I thought you were going to leave as soon as I got back," Amy says.

She places the tray of cookies on the cooling rack before removing her apron and gathering her niece for a hug. Her aunt Mary has been more of a motherly figure to my best friend than almost anyone. Except my mother, of course. I don't know exactly what happened to Amy's mom—it's a sore topic.

Her aunt looks up and pins her green gaze at me. "Hey, Attie! It's been a while since you've been over."

I smile. "Nice to see you too, Mary."

Amy lets go of her aunt before dropping her stuff by the door and taking off her heels. Compared to my five foot six frame, Amy is very petite. The heels give her a slight advantage but they look painful to me. I don't know how she does it. But then again—it's Amy. Poised and stylish everywhere she goes. They probably don't even bother her.

"So," Mary says as the three of us sit down. "What's been going on with you, Attie? Any cute guys you've been seeing?"

My cheeks turn pink as I shake my head. "Nope. Still single."

"Really? But look at you." She gestures to me. "You're a total knockout. How has no one snatched you up?"

"She's still hung over Derek," Amy answers, which earns her a smack on the shoulder from me.

Mary raises a brow. "Who?"

"Derek Bale," Amy says.

"I know the last name. Is he the blond football player with the glasses? Always on the bench?"

I shake my head. "That's his brother, Ian." Though since Carter moved away, Ian has now become the starting quarterback from what I hear. What? I may go to a big school but people are still louder than humanly possible.

"Shame. If I was your age, I would have snatched him up faster than the claw at an arcade game. You're still prettier than him though."

"Thanks." Amy's aunt is kind of like a mentor to me as well. A big-sister figure to me and Amy, since she's not that much older than us. They even look like sisters, with their honey blonde hair that's pin-straight on Mary and curly on Amy. The only difference between them, aside from height, is their eyes. Mary's are a grassy green while Amy's are this deep blue that almost look violet but are really indigo.

I'm friends with such pretty people. It's kind of unfair but also an ego booster when one of them calls me pretty. I know I'm average at best, and I don't even mind it.

"So, then, who's Derek?" Mary asks.

I think back to the last time I saw Derek. Usually, he and Jason would sit with me and Amy at lunch and today was no exception. "He's tall, too, but no glasses. He's on the boy's volleyball team. He has wavy brown hair. Not light brown, not even dark, either. It sits in the middle. And his eyes? They're just as warm as him."

"Sounds like you only like him for his looks," Mary observes.

I shake my head. "No I don't. He's really kind, too."

"In other words," Mary adds. "The bare minimum."

Having a kind soul, especially in high school, isn't a bare minimum. It's a rare quality that you'll only find in a select few. In fact, the bare minimum for me is not smelling like Axe body spray and talking about how many girls you hit up at every party you go to.

"It's not the bare minimum," I mutter.

"Attie." Mary places her hand over mine. "You deserve more than the bare minimum. You deserve someone who would go above and beyond for you. A person who makes your heart flutter just by a single glance or a word. You deserve unconditional love."

"Wow, you really thought of that on the spot, now did you?" Amy smirks.

Mary's cheeks turn red. "I've thought of that for a while."

Amy whispers in my ear, "and I thought I was a hopeless romantic."

One of these days, Marilyn Pierce is going to get that love story you see in rom-coms.

"Does he at least know how you feel?" Mary asks. "This Derek dude. Not going to lie to you, Attie—his name makes him sound like a cocky douchebag."

"He doesn't and never will," I say, a little too quickly. "Why would I tell him?"

Amy and Mary stare at me as if I've grown two heads, or still taking in the very detailed information about all of Taylor Swift's exes. Bug-eyed, silent, and I swear I can hear the gears in both brains shifting.

"What?" Amy eventually breaks the silence. "You've got to be kidding me."

"Attie, you can't be serious," Mary says with surprise.

"You guys are saying I should tell him how I feel?"

"Yes!" Both girls say it at the exact same time.

"Hell, no." I would rather jump off a cliff than tell Derek Bale how I feel.

"Come on," Mary says. "What's the worst case scenario? He doesn't like you back."

"No," I correct her. "The worst case scenario is that he humiliates me in front of the entire school. I'd rather just keep my head down." I've been doing that for the vast majority of my high school career and I sure as hell won't stop now.

"Teenagers and their imaginations," she mutters.

"Well, Attie does want to be an animator," Amy quips.

Mary then pins her eyes on me. "Does an animator keep their head down?"

"Uh, yes," I tell her.

"Not literally." she rolls her eyes. "You smart-ass. Okay, I don't exactly know where I was going with this but I'm just gonna go straight to the point: you can't keep your head down forever. Eventually, you have to look up at what's in front of you. And right now? It's a chance to do something about those teenage hormones."

"They're not hormones," I say.

"She's right," Amy quips.

Thank you, Amy.

"It's been like that since before puberty," she continues.

Nevermind.

"Jesus," Mary mutters. "I'm gonna check the mail." She gets up from her seat before freezing in place, her eyes lighting up. "Hey, wait a minute. Why don't you write him a letter?"

"A letter?" I wonder aloud.

Amy gasps. "Oh my gosh, yes! Like Lara Jean. You can write a letter about how you feel and instead of hiding it in a box, you can just leave it in his locker."

"I'm only halfway through the book," I tell Amy. "Don't those letters eventually get out or something?"

"Well, yeah. But you don't need to put his name on it. No one else is gonna see the letter but you and me. And Derek, of course." She starts pacing back and forth, like Sherlock Holmes trying to solve a mystery. "Just write everything—you're a good writer, so that shouldn't be so hard—and slip it in the locker vents when no one's looking."

I run my hands over my face. That doesn't sound so bad but... "Again, what if he humiliates me in front of everyone?"

"Derek's not a douchebag, Attie. He would tell you privately, right?"

He would. I see him at my house a lot anyway because of Jason. If he didn't like me back then he would keep it a secret. From my brother and his, too.

"Besides, getting those feelings out in the open can help you move on from him. You have been trying to get over that stupid crush for a long time now."

Holding back an eye roll, I sigh in defeat. "Alright, fine." I stand up and grab my backpack. "But let's do homework first."

"Yay!" Mary grabs the keys and opens the front door. "I'll see you girls later."

We head upstairs to Amy's room, where she has a big enough desk for the both of us. On account of Amy's amazing sense of style, she dreams of going to fashion school once we graduate. Her big desk is mostly used to accommodate for the sewing machine that now rests inside her closet.

I take out my physics textbook and open it to the page our homework is on. Right then and there, Amy slams it shut. "Nope. You are writing that letter first."

"Amy! I can write it at home."

She shakes her head. "I know you. I know for a fact that when you get home, you're gonna think 'fuck this' and do a full one-eighty. It's one letter. I'm not gonna tell you how to write it. I'm only going to watch you write it and seal it."

I raise a brow at those last two words that came out of her mouth.

"You left your wax-seal kit here the last time you came over." She waves it off. "Now, take a piece of notebook paper and write."

Taking a deep breath, I grab my notebook and rip a piece of paper out from the very back and write. At first, I'm very hesitant to put my bright blue mechanical pencil to paper but as soon as the first paragraph is done, I manage to write the rest. And all it takes is melting some blue and silver wax to seal the letter shut and I am done.

I know that crushing on your brother's best friend is the most cliche thing to do. Ever. Possibly more than write a song about said crush. Because the former isn't in any way achievable. Maybe Amy's right about one thing: I can possibly move on after this.

Once I've stamped the seal with a heart, I stash the letter in my backpack with a small yet content smile on my face. It's not much but it's one small step towards that little goal I set for myself back in sophomore year—and one that isn't likely to burn in hell. Even though he might not actually read it immediately and I might not send it to him tomorrow, my heart is out there and chances are, nothing's gonna change that.

Nothing at all.

Chapter 4

My friends think I do this every week to check on my brother but the truth? I just wanna be humbled for once. The day before our first away game is always a little stressful for me and I don't want to be surrounded by people who could increase my ego. I just want my head out of the stars for a moment and on ground zero.

So I wait by our lockers right before lunch begins. I don't open it until I see Derek walking in my direction. Looking at us side by side, you wouldn't believe we were actually related. Derek takes after Dad in almost all ways when it comes to appearance. Same brown hair that I'm so used to and the same eyes. I may take after Mom with my lack of perfect vision, among other things, but I did inherit Dad's towering height and love for football.

"Hey man," Derek says as he opens his locker. "So, Jason finally asked out that girl from last week's pep rally."

I raise a brow. "Which one? Brunette, or blonde?

"Blonde."

When the school year started back up, we had updated our bet on how many girls Jason is going to go out with by his high school graduation. He's a serial dater to boot, probably worse than me. At least the girls I get with know what they're getting into—which is not a relationship. But Jason's dated around... see, I lost count as to how many girls.

"Did she say yes?"

Derek nods. "That means girl number 9. What number did you say he would reach?"

"Twenty." I smirk.

"Psshh. That's a lot, even for Jason," Derek says. "I'd be surprised if he even reached fifteen by our senior year. He's too selective."

I shrug as I open my locker. As far as middle school, Jason's made it to the talking stage with way too many girls and has gone on a date with at least half of them. Derek and I have been betting on his dating life since his best friend got his first girlfriend back in middle school. It started out with how long each relationship would last but by sophomore year we both knew each girl would only have a month at the most. So we just updated it to how many girls he would date within our grade school lives.

Once I enter my locker combination and open it, a piece of paper floats down and I follow it with my eyes right until the moment it reaches my red Jordans. I bend down to pick it up and find a glittery blue wax seal with a heart in the middle, keeping it closed.

Derek looks over to me. "Is that really for you?"

I shrug. "I don't even know what it is."

"Dude, you're having a blond moment right now."

I roll my eyes. "Okay then, Sherlock Holmes. Tell me what it is."

"It's obviously a love letter. Do you see the heart?" He points to the wax seal.

A heart doesn't always mean love. Right? Besides, who's dumb enough to write me—of all people—a love letter?

I pocket the letter. "I'll figure it out later. Let's go eat."

We head over to the cafeteria and after grabbing food, Derek leads me over to the table, where Jason and Attie are arguing over which bear is more dangerous. From what I hear, Jason thinks it's the polar bear while Attie argues the black bear.

"You wouldn't need to attack a polar bear!"

"That's because you'd be dead before the thought ever crossed your mind. Duh."

"I will never understand why they argue these things," Derek mutters as he sits himself down on the bench. "It's so random."

Jason grabs an apple from his tray. "Kelly brought up a movie that her uncle was a part of, and it has to do with a bear on drugs."

"Who's Kelly?" I ask.

"It's his flavor of the month," Derek answers before uncapping his water bottle and taking a sip.

"I would pay good money to watch that movie," Attie says. "Oh hey, Ian."

"Sure it wouldn't scare the shit out of you?" Her brother teases.

Rolling her eyes, she grabs a napkin from her tray, crumples it into a ball, and throws it at Jason, hitting his face. Princess has a good aim, I'll give her that. "First of all, I've walked into the kitchen to find you making out with some random chick one too many times. If that doesn't scare me then I don't think anything else will. And secondly, the idea of a bear on cocaine sounds so stupid that it's hilarious."

I have to agree with that last statement. "When will that movie come out? Or is it already out?"

Jason shrugs. "Didn't ask. And where's Amy?"

Just at the moment, a tiny girl with curly blonde hair approaches our table, with a small Tupperware box of cookies in one hand and her bag on the other. "Made it. Took a while to convince Dad since I knew he wasn't going to eat them all. Hi, Ian."

I only know Amy because her boyfriend, Carter Bruick, was the starting quarterback last year. Now, that mantle has been passed onto me. "Hey."

"Ooh, are those chocolate chip?" Jason's eyes light up.

When Amy nods, he opens the box and takes two. "Your aunt is a savior sent from the fucking heavens."

"I'll let her know you said that." She laughs as she sits down on the only empty spot next to me, starting a conversation with Attie. That leaves me as a fifth wheel. A little left out in this tiny group. A senior—fifth wheeling a group of juniors.

Oh how my life has become.

I reach into my front pocket, hoping to find my phone but instead I grab the mysterious letter by accident. I did say that I would take a look at that later.

It is later.

While the others are talking, Amy peers over to me and sees the letter in my hand. Her eyes squint for a moment, but whatever she's staring at causes her eyes to widen. "Uh, Ian. Where did you get that?"

I try to put the letter back into my pocket but the tiny girl has crazy reflexes. "Why? Is it yours or something?"

"No," she answers too quickly. "I mean—"

"What are you guys looking at?" Jason leans over the table. "Hey sis, isn't that your seal?"

"What?!" Attie leans over the table as well and her long dark hair spills onto the table. When she sees the letter, I'm too slow to stop her from grabbing it out of my hands. She pretends to look over it but something in her eyes tells me that she has something to do with it.

"Uh," Attie hesitates to say anything but eventually leads with, "not mine but I know who it belongs to." Right then, she grabs her backpack and stands up. "I'll return it to them. See you later, guys."

She practically runs out of the cafeteria, abandoning her food and leaving everyone else more confused than when we started. And she took the letter with her.

"Is something up with her?" Derek asks. "Or did I just imagine all of that?"

"Nope," I say.

"She definitely ran away from us," Amy adds. Then, turns to Jason. "Don't you know what's wrong with her?"

"Don't look at me." Jason holds his hands up in surrender. "Our twin telepathy is rusty as shit. I wouldn't know what's wrong with her even if I tried." But the look in his eyes say otherwise. "Besides, you're her best friend."

The four of us are silent as we ponder this. Well, I'm at least pondering this because a little voice in my head is telling me that the letter was actually from Attie Ryder. I've known her and Jason since I was in the fourth grade and not once has the idea of Attie having feelings for me ever crossed my mind.

Not until this moment. But I don't like not knowing. So right now, there's only one thing I can do.

Grabbing my bag and tray–making sure to take the one Attie left—I stand up from my seat. "I'll go check on her."

"She's probably in the computer lab," Jason points out.

"And I thought your twin telepathy was rusty," Amy teases.

"It is, Tiny," he retorts. "But anyone who knows my sister would know that she spends too much time in the computer lab, working on whatever art project she can. At least, lately she has."

"Thanks," I tell Jason. "I'll see you guys later."

I throw away the trash and head out of the cafeteria in the direction to the computer lab. I've only been inside of there once or twice in the time I've attended Santa Barbara High, so I have more of a general sense of where it's located.

When I arrive, I look at the windows to find the same head of dark hair hunched over a computer. I can see only half of her face but there's a little tear falling down her cheek. This is the first time I'm seeing her cry and it almost breaks my heart to see her this way.

I quietly open the door and knock three times to get her attention.

Chapter 5

"Got any room?" A familiar voice says from the other side of the room.

I quickly wipe the one tear that managed to escape my eye before turning my head to find Ian leaning against the door frame. The soft smile on his face accentuates cheekbones that are so prominent it's almost unfair.

"Come on, princess," Ian says. "Are you going to leave me hanging here?"

Of all the things that make me blush, it just has to be the nickname Ian gave me all those years ago.

I let out a quiet laugh and gesture to the seat next to me. Ian heads in and makes his way over to me as I exit out of the animation software I was just on. I don't let people—not even Amy—look at my individual projects.

"Are you okay?" He asks me once he's settled himself into his seat.

I nod, my cheeks turning even redder than they already were. When I'm embarrassed, it's obvious on my face. My pale skin means that you can easily tell how I feel. Nauseous, embarrassed, excited—you get the gist.

"You sure? Because you ran out of the cafeteria faster than the speed of light the moment you saw this." He points to the folded-up piece of paper sitting right on top of the keyboard.

The letter.

I forgot to hide it because the only people in here when I arrived were me and Mr. Ali, the physics teacher that everyone either wants to be or wants to fuck. He had gotten roped into computer-watching, yet again.

"Speaking of, I was wondering what you were going to do with it," he continues. "My bet was on lighting it on fire."

I chuckle at the thought. Not because I find burning paper sacrilegious but because Ian's trying to put a smile on my face. And it's almost working. Almost.

"Can I see it?" He doesn't wait for an answer before he lifts the letter off the keyboard and is so close to opening it when I come to my senses and snatch it out of his hand.

"Wow," he replies. "Okay. I mean, I get it's a love letter to me and all—"

"Where did you get this?" I ask. I sound timid right now but I don't care. I need answers and I need them now.

"Uhh, it was in my locker." He just stares at me with confused blue eyes resting behind his framed glasses. "I opened it. It fell out. I picked it up, put it in my pocket and the rest is history."

I basically let him take it back. But he doesn't open it. Instead he just places the letter in his right pocket. "You know, princess, if you wanted to declare your undying love for me—"

"Nope. That letter wasn't even supposed to be for you." The words are out of my mouth before I can even think better about it.

Ian stops in his tracks, his mouth still open as if he was still speaking. Which, to be fair, he was when I had interrupted him. Do I care? Not really, because the one thought that passes through my mind and makes a pit stop at the front is the fact that I thought it was Derek's locker this entire time.

I facepalm myself. How did I not think that it was Ian's? I see him and Derek hanging out by the locker almost all the time when I enter the building and I just always thought that it was Derek's. Ian never struck me as someone who goes straight to his locker every morning before class.

"I'm sorry, what?" Ian raises a blond brow at my statement.

I can't really lie to him, not after basically shouting to the rooftops that I didn't write him a love letter. "The letter wasn't supposed to be for you," I finally admit, lowering my head to my lap.

"Then why was it in my..." He trails off and I can only assume that he put the pieces together. "You thought your crush's locker was mine?"

I don't need to respond. But all I can say right now is, "please don't tell anyone."

"Why would I?"

I look back up to Ian. His face doesn't show any sign of laughter. So he's serious.

"I-I just thought that would happen."

Ian pushes his glasses up the bridge of his nose, muttering something I can't really hear before saying, "you thought I would joke about getting a love letter that wasn't meant for me? In front of other people? No way, princess. I may seem like it at times, but I'm not a douchebag and it's not my business to joke about shit like that." He puts both hands on my shoulders. "This will stay between us, alright? That you can be sure about."

He seems so certain that nobody will know. But I don't want to think about that. Ian isn't someone who's lied to me in the past. I don't think he would lie to me right now. I can tell in his eyes. His bright, ocean blue eyes that I never realized were so vibrant even behind his glasses. They don't hide fibs.

"Alright," I finally answer after a moment of silence because I got so lost in his eyes that I couldn't speak. "I believe you."

The bell rings less than a second later. Ian grabs my bag from the floor as well as his and stands up. "Here," he says, handing me my backpack. "I'll walk you to your next class."

I smile a thank you as I grab the bag, remembering one thing. "Can I have that letter back?"

He shakes his head. "I better keep it."

"What?" I try to reach for his pocket but his reflexes are too fast. Stupid quarterback skills. "Why not?"

"Well, it's better safe with me so that you don't place it in the wrong locker again." He winks. "Besides, it's a memento. It's not everyday that Attie Ryder gives you a love letter that isn't meant for you."

I roll my eyes before stopping at an open door. "This is me. Thanks again, Ian. For agreeing not to tell anyone."

He shrugs and makes a zipping motion over his lips. "Tell what, princess?"

Smiling, I wave goodbye and head into my honors math class. I'm glad that I don't share the rest of my classes with Amy, Jason, or Derek. I actually don't have any classes with Derek at all, so I'm free until after school when Jason and I go home for the day.

Right next to me, a very tall brunette sits right on top of the wood desk itself instead of the chair. She narrows her eyes at me, as if she's trying to solve a puzzle.

I know Rue Barlow. Or, at least, know of her. A senior on the varsity cheer team, she's the stereotype of every cheerleader in whatever movie or teen coming-of-age story you can think of. Peppy and bright on the field but treats everyone else like shit. There aren't really a lot of cheerleaders like her at Santa Barbara. At least, not in this school.

"So, what were you doing with Ian?" She asks, twirling her long hair.

I don't even know what the hell she's doing here. This is a junior's class and there aren't any seniors in this period.

"Why?" I can feel my face twist when she asks.

She shrugs. "Just wondering."

Does this girl have eyes? Ones that work, at least? Because she definitely could use glasses. But I don't want to deal with whatever bullshit she has concocted in that pretty head of hers so I just wave her off. "Nothing you need to worry about. Just talking."

"That didn't look like talking to me," she says. Rue is dragging this conversation out to the point of annoyance.

"Well, I don't know what it looked like to you," I tell her. "But whatever it is, you're wrong."

I can hear her scoff and mutter, "you juniors are so fucking useless, sometimes," before hopping off the desk and storming off, basically pushing my friend Sierra out of the way as she stomps out. Sierra Haynes is the one friend I have in the animation club. In fact, she's the president to my vice president this year.

"Damn, there goes the Grinch," Sierra mutters as she fixes her wavy red hair. "What did Rue Barlow want with you?"

I shrug and shake my head. "What does Rue Barlow want with anyone in our grade?"

She laughs. "Good point. But seriously, what did she want? I don't think I've seen her this angry since Evan's party last fall."

Sierra's older brother Ethan is on the lacrosse team with Jason and he throws these huge parties when their parents are out of town, which is pretty often. I was at the one he hosted last fall, when Carter finally had the guts to ask Amy out on a date. Not too shabby for her first party. I, however, try to block that evening out of my mind whenever Amy reflects on it.

"She just asked about Ian," I tell her. "And then stormed off like something was at her feet."

I thought she would laugh too but instead, Sierra's eyes practically bulge out of their sockets. "Ian Bale?"

I nod.

"She asked you about Ian Bale. Why?"

I shrug. "Who knows. I was walking with him to my class and she thought something was going on."

Sierra gasps and basically grabs onto my hand. "Is there? Oh my gosh, I would die if there was."

"Why would you die?"

"Because you would be the first person to tie him down," she answers, as if it's so obvious. "Do you know how crazy that would be?"

I let those words settle in. She's got a point. Ian's dating life lacks one thing: dating. He has hookups, instead. Ones that girls would talk about the next day. Jason, Amy, and I are in a class that consists of mostly seniors—which is basically a gold mine for my brother—so I've heard more about his "conquests" than about Newton's Laws of Physics in the past month.

"It would be crazy," I reply. "But Ian doesn't do juniors. Or anyone younger than him."

"Again. You'd be the first. Haven't you known the guy longer than most girls?"

I nod again.

"And do you like him?"

"I can tolerate being around him, if that's what you mean."

Sierra rolls her eyes. "Okay, smart-ass. But are you dating Ian?"

Before I can tell her that nothing's going on, Ms. Lang smacks a ruler onto the white board so she can command our attention and begin today's lesson. Out of the corner of my eye, SierrA mouths "you better tell me" before our teacher can catch her.

I don't need to tell her anything, because there's literally nothing to tell. Ian and I are friends, or at least friendly. That's what we've always been and that's what we'll always be.

Chapter 6

Cheer practice lets out at the same time as football practice every single day. And every single day after leaving the locker room, I find Rue Barlow standing right next to the doors. I know she's waiting just for me because I have to deal with the same routine over and over again.

A new routine, sure, but it's been going on all fucking month and she has yet to take a fucking hint.

I avoid any eye contact with her but to no avail. She trails after me as I walk towards the senior parking lot.

"Hey, Ian!" Rue is basically running towards me. She can't really run with those high heeled boots on, putting her at eye level to me. I don't really care about height but if she's trying to seduce me, then she's doing a shit job at it.

It's not to say that I don't have a type—everyone has a type, whether they deny it or not—but even I could point out that Rue is objectively good-looking. A lot of football players would, if given the chance, go out with her, fuck her, all that jazz. I can't say the same thing anymore.

I keep walking at a steady fast pace to my car but she's still behind me, like a lost cat wandering the streets at night. "Ian!" She eventually is right by my side, twirling her long brown hair in her hand and I have to stop walking. Guess it's time for another round of rejection.

For her, not for me.

"Finally," she says, catching her breath as she slows her pace and comes to a stop after reaching me. "I've been meaning to ask you something. So, do you know—"

I turn to face her. "Rue. I don't want to sound like a jerk but I've got something really important to do in the next few minutes." I check the clock on my phone. I need to be at home pretty soon if I'm going to make it in time.

"Don't worry, it won't take long." She starts to fan herself. "A friend was asking if you were busy after the game tomorrow."

I raise a brow. "Is that friend you, by any chance?"

She scoffs. "No. Do you really think I would name drop? You should know me better than that, Ian."

Despite having gone to the same school as Rue for the past three or more years, I don't really know much about her. We're not close, if you can count Enzo Rivera's party last July where we may have locked ourselves in a room together. On purpose. But nothing other than kissing occurred.

I just know that she's one of Sophia's best friends and co-captain of the varsity cheer team. We've had no classes together—at least until this year—and I've felt no other attraction other than a passing moment. But she should have known what she was getting into that night.

"Sorry, Rue," I tell her for what seems to be the fourth time this week. "Even if I wanted to, I can't. Need to be on my A-game this year."

"You can do that with a date," she says, taking a step closer to me. "That hasn't stopped you before."

Well, it sure as hell is stopping me now. Senior year means I need to learn some self-control. I love jumping off the rocks as much as the next person, and I've definitely pulled many harmless pranks on Coach Davis in the past, but that's about it. The only reason I get called a wild child is from the long line of hookups I've had that go as far back as sophomore year. Yeah, that long. But Rue was the last girl I was with.

"I hate to break it to you, but it's stopping me this time." I push past Rue and head towards the drivers side of my very old, dark gray, Toyota Corolla. Before I open the door, Rue taps me on the shoulder, urging me to turn around.

"You know, if you had started dating someone," she says. "You could have just said that."

I hold back an eye roll. "Would that have stopped you?"

"Possibly."

I'll take that as a yes. "Then yes, I have been seeing someone." I get the door open, enter the car, and close the door, making sure I lock it before starting the engine, hoping that it gives Rue even a slight hint that the conversation is over.

I drive off as fast as I can in the direction of my house.

Well...house isn't exactly what anyone else would describe it. But I've lived here since the fourth grade, so it's a house to me. When I was nine, I thought that it was a palace. When my grandpa—Dad's father—first got sick, Dad, Derek, and I moved over from Houston to help take care of him. And the house.

I'm still surprised how we've managed to keep it somewhat neat. Hardly any of us are home, especially with Dad's job keeping him out of the house more often than not.

After parking the car in the driveway and walking inside, I grab a protein bar from the pantry and head upstairs to Derek's room, opening the door without knocking.

"Hey," I say. "Did I miss it?"

Derek turns around in his chair, shaking his head. "I was just about to call her." "Do you think she's even awake?"

"Ian." He sighs, pinching his nose. "It is noon in Sydney. Of course she's awake."

I take a spot on Derek's bed as he starts the video call with our mom. We do this as often as we can. Despite mostly living with Dad, Derek and I have always loved our mother a little bit more. But because she's a pilot, working for one of the biggest airlines in the world, she's almost always traveling. This time, she's in Australia for another day or two before heading back to Texas.

After a few rings, she answers, and we can see her blond hair—the same color as my own—which is normally short and just at her shoulders pulled back into a ponytail.

"Hey, boys! Oh, how I've missed you both." Her smile is bright and her blue eyes that hide behind glasses are just as warm as I remember them.

"We missed you too, Mom," we both respond.

"How's Sydney?" Derek asks.

"Definitely cold. It's like living on another planet over there." She shivers. "But enough about me, how was the first month of school?"

"Good," I answer. "We won last week's game."

"I'm so proud of you, Ian."

We continue to catch up with her for a few more minutes. Even though we spent the month of June in Texas with her, our stepdad Paul, and our little half-sister, Arya, it feels as if time never passed and I can never run out of things to tell her.

"And that's only the starting team," Mom continues. "It's crazy how much love drama a soccer team can ensue. Anyway, what about your love lives?"

Derek always blushes whenever Mom asks about our love lives. And every time, he gives her the same answer. "Nothing new for me, Mom."

"Nothing? No pretty girl?"

He shakes his head. "But Ian got a love letter from someone today!"

I punch my brother in the shoulder as soon as those letters come out of his mouth.

"You're kidding." Mom's eyes find me, where I'm slowly but surely ducking myself out of view from the camera. "Ian Elliot Bale, get your ass over here!"

Oh great. It's never a good sign when your mother calls you by your full name. Elliot, pfft. What kind of inane, weirdo has that name?

Oh right. That's Dad's first name.

I pop my head into view. "I'm here."

"Tell me more about this letter," she prompts.

I hold back a sigh and shrug. "It fell out of my locker."

"Oooh! This is so exciting!" she claps her hands twice. "My baby bad boy has got a girlfriend."

"Woah," I say. Pumping the brakes on Mom's excitement there. "Who said anything about a girlfriend?"

"Well, clearly, that letter was a love confession."

"That's what I said!" Derek practically shouts. "There was a heart on the wax seal."

I give my brother a side-eye. "A heart can literally mean anything."

"Was it pink?" My mother asks.

I shake my head. "It was blue."

"Eh, color doesn't matter anyway. But was there glitter?"

I nod.

She throws her hands up. "Then it was a love letter. Jesus, boy did you even use your hands and open it?"

I raise a brow at the screen, earning myself an eye roll from Mom.

"You know what I mean," she says. Then mutters, under her breath, "dirty little worm." There's the Southern side to her that I miss. Blunt, honest, and quick-witted when it comes to insulting just about anyone. Even her own son.

"Probably," Derek answers for me. "But he knows who it's from."

Mom's eyes light up.

"Okay, I'm heading out." I stand up from my spot on the floor and start to head towards the door.

"Wait! Don't leave yet," Mom wails. "You didn't tell us the name of your lover."

This leaves Derek rolling on the floor, laughing.

"I'm not going to. And she's not my lover." I grab the doorknob.

"Come on, Ian." Mom's voice is softer—or as soft as it can get. She has a naturally loud voice. "Just sit back down."

I do as I am told.

Mom rubs the back of her neck. "I know you've been out and about these past couple of years—"

My eyes widen. How did she...

She laughs at the look on my face. "I'm your mother, Ian. I know you better than you think. What I don't know is why you won't hold onto a girl like that."

"You don't even know who she is," I point out. Attie didn't mean for me to even see that letter.

"I don't need to. Anyone who is willing to make the first move deserves to be held onto. She's got the gall to tell you how she feels and even if you don't feel the same way, you have to at least appreciate it."

I let those words sink in. Mom's right—I mean, she usually is. I've known Attie for years, and that princess isn't exactly known for speaking loud. She's not as social as her friend Amy, not as vibrant. In fact, she prefers to stay in the shadows. It's as if she feels... safe there.

But the letter? Probably the bravest thing she's ever done. Put herself out of the shadows and hold her heart out, even if I was the only person to see it, despite it being an accident.

"Thanks, Mom," I tell her.

"Of course." Her eyes move slightly to the top left corner and then widen. "Oh! I have to get going boys! I promised one of my coworkers I'd meet with her in half an hour."

"Talk to you later, Mom," Derek says.

"I love you boys. Remember that. Forever and always." She blows kisses at the screen before hanging up. I get back up from the floor and just about to head out when Derek says, "so, you and Attie?"

I raise a brow. "What about it?"

"I knew it." He smiles triumphantly. "I knew there was something going on with you two."

"What makes you think that?"

"You don't just call a girl princess for no reason." His facial expression basically says, duh, man. "You're not exactly a nickname guy. Well, except for me." He smirks. "But that's only because I'm your brother and I'm extremely awesome."

"I am totally a nickname person," I argue. "Besides, you're not that awesome."

And with that, I run out the room as fast as I can before the words can settle into Derek's brain and head into my room. My brother is stubborn so it's going to take a while to convince him that there's nothing going on with me and his best friend's sister.

But I'm too tired to try again tonight, so I'll try in the morning.

Chapter 7

I used to like Fridays. It always meant the weekend is nearby, I can stay up late, and Jason's usually on a date so I don't have to hear his shitty singing voice every time the Beatles or Panic! At the Disco plays in the background.

Now, however? I hate them.

And that's solely due to the quiz that me, Jason, and Amy have to endure in our physics class. At least we'll get to suffer together. Right?

The moment Amy hands me the stack of blank quizzes, I take one and pass the rest back to Jason, who has a neutral expression on his face, but I just know he's quietly tapping his left foot underneath the desk. It's a nervous tick he has. Without his ritalin, it wouldn't just be the tapping foot. It would be the tapping finger on his desk, grinding his teeth on his mechanical pencil, and clicking the bottom eraser over and over again until the teacher calls him out for it.

His ADHD has always been pretty bad when we were younger. But when he's nervous? It's so much worse. I don't understand why, though. My brother is honestly one of the smartest people I know. Could easily be at the top of the class if he wanted to. I'm not just saying that because we're related.

I'm looking over one question, then skipping to the other when I start to hear someone whispering. I turn my head to the right slightly to find a pair of unfamiliar eyes that I don't recognize staring back at me.

Bro. If you're trying to get answers off someone's quiz, then look behind you.

I tilt my head back to signal that they should be looking over Jason's shoulder instead of mine, but the person just keeps staring at me. I start to feel just a tiny bit uncomfortable and try to focus back on the test. I know that physics is only math on steroids, but I think I might be fucked.

Who in their right mind even invented the pop quiz? I genuinely hope they are burning in the pits of Tartarus right now.

I'm only halfway through the quiz when I see Jason place his quiz on Mr. Ali's desk. What the hell?? How did he finish so fast? And why did he get all the brains in the womb and leave none for me? That's unfair.

I narrow my eyes at Jason as he turns around and walks back to his desk. All he responds with is a mediocre shrug, as if to say, what can you do?

This asshole...

I finally reach the last question, which is multiple choice, and I silently cheer to myself. Most of the quiz was open ended, with the exception of two other questions. By the time I've turned in my quiz, there are still a few other seniors and a couple juniors taking the quiz. I understand why the class is mostly seniors now. I'm starting to regret taking this class.

Once I turn around, I find more than just a pair of eyes staring right back at me. Almost everyone except Jason and Amy are staring right at me, as if I'm a question on that physics quiz they are trying to solve. They seem to be mostly seniors, and I start feeling a little squeamish.

Nope. Attie, they are just eyes. If you look away, you won't see them.

I try my best to ignore the stares as I head back to my desk. Once I sit down, a piece of paper drops onto my desk. When I unfold it, it reads:

Y tf is everyone staring at u? - A

We're not allowed to use our phones in class. Disadvantages of having a really young teacher who could sniff out texting like a hellhound. At least he can't smell paper.

When I look up, I see Amy's hair pushed to the side, and her eyes are trained on me. Her brows are furrowed, as if she's just as confused as I feel. I shrug, and she turns back around. We're not doing anything the rest of the period, so I just take out my notebook and start sketching out ideas for the next project. If they don't get chosen for our first meeting of the year in a couple of weeks, then I can always add them to my portfolio.

Once the bell rings, signaling the beginning of lunch, I pack my stuff away and head out of the classroom towards the direction of my locker. The entire walk I'm met with thousands—okay, maybe not thousands—of pairs of eyes staring right at me. What the hell is going on?

I always kept my head down at this school. It's been my goal all along: try not to stir up any more drama if I want to make it to graduation in one piece. The most embarrassing thing that's happened so far has been accidentally placing that letter in Ian's locker.

But that was about a week ago. Surely if he was gonna break this promise then he would have done so when he could. But he promised me that he wouldn't say anything.

A hand grabs my arm and pulls me into an empty, dark, classroom. Okay, I'm starting to feel like I'm in a parallel universe. Shit like this shouldn't happen in Attie Ryder's life. It happens in books and movies and TV shows. And if the heroes in Greek Mythology went to Santa Barbara High, then this would happen to them too.

"You said you weren't dating him!" The high pitched voice shrieks. It's so loud and annoying that I have to rub my ears. Wait, a minute...

I trace my fingers on the wall until I find a light switch and flick it. As soon as the lights turn on, my eyes begin to adjust to the light and the blurry figure standing in front of me, in an olive green and gold cheer outfit, is Rue Barlow. And let me tell you—she does not look happy.

Not in the slightest.

I take a deep breath, count to three in my head, and let it out. Jason does this all the time when he's annoyed so I'm taking a page out of his book. "What are you talking about, Sue?"

She scowls. "It's Rue. You know who I am."

I obviously knew that. Again, taking a page out of my brother's book. Shrugging, I say, "I'm just not that good with names." Yet another lie.

"Whatever. The point is, you are one lying bitch."

I may be someone who keeps their head down and avoids conflict but. ..that's it. I'm just going to do what I always do: avoid conflict.

So I walk out of the classroom and into the hallway, towards the cafeteria. I can hear footsteps behind me. She must not be done ranting about Ian. Well, she can rant about him to those cheerleading bimbos for all I care.

"Are you listening to me?!"

I stay silent. I am so close to the cafeteria doors right now, I can smell the freedom. She doesn't strike me as someone who wants all the bad attention aimed towards her.

Before I can take one more step closer to the cafeteria, she grabs my shoulder and spins me around. If looks could kill, I would be as dead as Bambi's mother right now. I swear steam is coming out of her ears because she looks so angry.

"I don't understand why you're so angry," I say. "He is literally just a guy."

"Just a guy? Ian Bale is not just a guy. He is my guy."

I try to hold back a laugh. "Your guy? Since when?"

Rue opens her mouth. Then she closes it. Opens it again. Then closes. Open.

Close.

It feels like I'm watching a venus flytrap snatch its prey up, or when a cartoon character opens their mouth so wide to consume a ten-foot-tall PB and J sandwich. Rue Barlow—speechless. Never thought I would see the day.

Also what's with this whole "my guy" bullshit? Last I checked, Ian didn't even do relationships, never mind claiming a girl as his. And the day that happens, I will jump into a swimming pool. Or a lake—that's not as deadly for me. Specifically, one that is infested with piranhas or chlorine.

"What's going on?" A familiar voice asks. Speaking of...

"Ah, finally." Rue crosses her arms over her chest. "Someone to put this liar out of her misery."

I turn to my right and find Ian standing right by the row of lockers across from us. He's wearing his football jersey with the number eight in bright gold, sans tie. Since it's a game day, the entire varsity team has to wear their jersey and a tie to school. And he's without his glasses. A rare sight since I'm so used to his glasses.

Instead of facing Rue, Ian's eyes move to me and he raises a brow. He doesn't exactly know what's going on but the panic in my eyes must make it clear enough for him. I try to maintain eye contact but it's a little hard because he just caught me in the hall.

In yet another embarrassing situation.

"Ian, are you really dating her?" Rue asks.

My head turns to Rue so fast that I get a minor whiplash. Seriously? She straight up asks about it? No pause, no slow building—just dives right into it? She might just be as unhinged as Timmy Turner.

"Rue—" I begin before a strong arm sneaks around my waist.

I can feel Ian's lips near my ear before he whispers, "trust me, princess," and my breath hitches at those three words.

He then lifts his head up and answers, "Yes, Rue. I am. Why is that so hard to believe?"

Rue crosses her arms as her eyes bounce between me, Ian, and his arm around me.

"Well, a few seconds ago," I tell him, a playful yet deceiving smile on my face. "She did refer to you as her guy." I add air quotes around the last two words.

His eyebrows shoot up his forehead. "Well, really? She must have been referring to another guy, then."

I may look like I'm smiling on the outside but on the inside, the alarms in my head are ringing like in Spongebob Squarepants, where all the mini versions of him are freaking out about forgetting his name. I certainly can remember my full name at this moment but the tiny voice in my head is screaming at me. What the hell am I doing?

Wait, I know what I'm doing. Trying to get away from Rue. And then all of a sudden, Ian sweeps in—like the knight of shining armor he's been acting like lately—to save the day. Or at least, to save lunch.

"Well, it was nice talking to you, Rue," Ian says. "But Attie here promised to help me with a little project. So, I'm going to need to steal her for now."

And with that, he grabs my hand and pulls me in the opposite direction of the cafeteria. Damn, I could really use some food right about now but it will have to wait.

As soon as Rue is out of earshot, I pry my hand from Ian's and turn a full one-eighty to face him. "What the hell are you doing?!"

Chapter 8

Attie's question isn't exactly random and out of the blue, considering what had just happened only moments ago.

"Ian," she grinds out. "You better answer that question."

"I was trying to save you from Rue's clutches," I answer.

"I didn't need saving," she argues. "Or for you to do... whatever the fuck you had just done."

"Are you sure about that?" I cross my arms over my chest and raise a brow. "Because I saw the panicked look on your face and that was enough to tell me otherwise."

"I wasn't panicking." Lies. "I was just surprised you were watching." She places her hand on her forehead and leans on a locker, groaning. "I don't even know why she thought you and I were dating. I tried to tell her that wasn't true, and there you go—throwing away all that hard work."

"Hold on there, princess." I place one hand over her arm. "Calm down."

"Calm down?" She shoots a pointed glare in my direction. "This is not a time to calm down, Ian!"

"Then, come on." I look around and try to find the nearest classroom. Jackpot! I take her arm and bring her over there. I open the door and turn on the lights. At least it's empty. Would have been weird if a random student was asleep in the classroom. "Come in."

Attie cautiously steps into the classroom, and I follow suit. Once we sit down—me on the front desk and her at one of the actual student's desks—I notice her unconsciously cracking her knuckles.

Shaking her hands, Attie takes a deep breath before forming her words. "Let me get something straight: you told Rue we were dating? You." She points to me. "Lied to someone about your dating life?"

The words, or lack thereof, are not lost on me. She didn't say them out loud but I just know that she was thinking them. Unlike her twin brother, she knows better than to say that out loud.

"I told her that I was seeing someone," I clarify.

"That's not helping your case. You still dragged me into this."

"How was I supposed to know she would bring you into the equation? I didn't even think Rue knew who you were." Rue Barlow doesn't even care for people younger than her which, in my opinion, is bullshit.

I thought Attie would glare at me, but instead nods vehemently."I didn't, either. But she saw us talking one day and—"

"When was this?"

"Last week, when you..." Her face turns pink as she trails off. Right, the letter. I had kept it safe and hidden in a drawer of my nightstand for the past week and it hasn't seen the light of day since.

That same day, when Rue had asked me out for the last time and failed.

I groan and rub my hand against my forehead.

"What now?" She asks, her voice tinted with worry.

I recount the events of my conversation with Rue to Attie. Starting from the moment she had asked me about having a girlfriend to me saying I did just so she would get off my back. That Thursday was probably the most unhinged day I've had this school year, and it's only early-September. I'm honestly a little worried about how the rest of the year will go.

"So she didn't bother you for eight days," she repeats after having a minute to soak it all in. "And then chooses today to pull me into a classroom to confront me and call me a lying bitch?"

My brows furrow. "What?"

Attie waves her hand to dismiss it. "Never mind. The point is we are now in this situation because you couldn't tell Rue Barlow, of all people, to stop bothering her? To put it politely."

"Yeah, that's about it." And the worst part is that she's not the only one who thinks that.

"What did you just say?"

Oh, shit. Did I just say that out loud?

"Nothing you need to worry about," I tell her before standing up and trying to walk away. Unfortunately for me, Attie grabs onto my wrist a little too tight and pulls me closer to her.

"Hell no, Ian." Her face is bright red now. Not in embarrassment or nerves. But in anger. And according to Jason, you don't want to get Attie riled up. Last time he did, it ended with minty Oreos, or something like that. "Sit your ass down and tell me."

I'm not sure if I should tell her because it could get Attie more riled up than she already is.

She raises a brow at me. "I'm not letting you leave until you do."

"Goddamn," I mutter as I sit back down. "Alright, fine. Rue may or may not be the only person who thinks this."

Attie takes a while to process this. I can tell because her blue eyes tend to get a little unfocused for a moment before widening to epic proportions. "Who else?" Her voice is so low I almost don't hear her.

I hang my head. "Derek keeps on pestering me about it and—"

"Wait—Derek thinks we're dating?"

I look up to see her running a hand over the strands of her long, dark hair, and I nod.

"If Derek thinks so, then it's no reason to not believe that he told my brother about this."

Now it's my turn to freak out a little. No hate towards Jason—he's like a second brother to me—but he has a bit of trouble keeping a secret.

"I realize that," I say. How am I so calm about this? If there was a rumor going on about me dating Rue, I would have freaked out. Maybe because I can't help but feel a little responsible for this. I did lie to Rue just so I could get her nagging self off my back and breathe a little.

"I need to tell them the truth," she mutters. "Fuck, this is going to be embarrassing."

At that thought, I feel a lightbulb flicker on in my head.

"What if you didn't have to?" I ask.

"What do you mean?"

I adjust myself into a more comfortable sitting position—which is just leaning back and placing my legs on the desk. "What if you didn't tell them? Made them think you were dating me."

Her dark brows dip as she thinks. "You know, Ian. If you're trying to ask me out, all you had to do was ask."

I let out a sarcastic laugh. "Very funny, princess."

She shrugs. "But seriously, what are you talking about?"

"I mean," I begin. "There are probably more people who already think we're dating, right?"

"It could be why half of my physics class was giving me weird looks," she says.

"What?" I straighten up a little in my seat. "Because of that?"

"Yeah. It felt weird." She rubs her arm. "I thought there was a huge hole on the side of my overalls or something."

I take a moment to observe her clothes. She's wearing a bright blue tank top that matches her eyes over a pair of dark blue overalls with what looks to be spots of dry red paint—or blood—trailing up her right pant leg. Something you would expect a farmer or an extremely messy painter would wear.

"No holes, maybe a little paint," I assure her. "But think about it. We might as well let people continue to think that."

"So we lie to the entire school—our families included—about our relationship?"

"And no one would be the wiser."

"But you don't lie," she points out.

She's not wrong about that—I don't, at least to a lot of people. Sure, I hate lying as much as the next person but that doesn't mean I've never done it before. "There's a first for everything."

She's watching me like I'm about to mess up on a football play. For anything that could indicate bluffing. I'm not one for bluffing but I could understand why Attie would do this. It's in her nature. Not just as an artist but as someone who's always observing.

"What could be in it for you?"

I blow out a breath. "Rue."

"What?"

"Rue's been on my ass about going on a date with her." Among others, at least.

Attie raises a brow. "I figured as much but you don't exactly... date."

I point to her. "Right. Last week, when I tried rejecting her for the..." I try to count in my head the amount of times Rue has tried asking me out and failing and just shrug. "I may have lost count at around seven. I had lied to her about seeing someone. I didn't say who it was—I just left it at that so I could go home. It worked, for a while. At least until..."

"Today," she finishes for me. "So we get Rue to stop annoying you?"

"As well as other people. And you don't have to embarrass yourself in front of your friends. It's a win-win scenario."

Before Attie can answer, the bell rings, signaling the end of lunch. She lets out an exasperated sigh, wrapping both arms around her stomach. "Dammit, I'm still hungry."

I wince. "Sorry, princess. I completely forgot."

She waves a hand. "Don't worry about it. I'll just grab something from the vending machine to tide me over." Attie hauls her bag over her shoulder and starts walking over to the door.

"Wait," I say. "Do we have a deal?"

She stops before her hand can touch the door knob and swivels on her left foot to face me. "I don't know, Ian. I'll think about it. See you later."

My shoulders sag a little as she walks out. I'm not surprised she said that, if I'm being honest. We both probably know that I could have asked any other girl to do this. Yet the first person I asked was her. Why? I could just chalk it up to Attie being at the right place at the right time. Or just being one of the few girls I haven't been with.

But maybe there's more to it.

Chapter 9

I'm definitely saying no.

I spent the last two hours of school contemplating whether or not I should take it upon myself to say yes to what Ian had suggested. Not like what I had expected him to say. At all.

Can you even believe it?

One of the most honest people I have ever met... suggested lying to everyone.

I pinched myself at least once in the past two hours every time the thought crossed my mind.

I can't lie to that extent! Sure, I've lied in the past but they've only been tiny, white lies. Like telling Jason about his summer girlfriend, Lily Schwartz, and how I liked her. That was completely wrong and I thought it didn't matter because Jason usually does his own thing. Meaning they were no longer a thing by July.

"Attie?" Amy's ring-clad hand is waving up and down in front of my face. "You haven't sung along to a single Taylor Swift song this entire drive! Something is definitely up."

Damnit. Thanks to Ian and the whole fake relationship proposal thing, my mind is as scrambled and confused as an entire episode of Clone High. This is messing with my mind too much.

Amy and I are heading over to my house. Jason's staying late and heading to tonight's game with Derek and two more of their friends, so I have the

Jeep to myself. We haven't had a sleepover since before high school and I'm glad that her dad allowed us with the condition that we study for the PSATs coming up in late October while she's over.

"Come on, At-bat," my best friend says. "What's on your mind? Or who?" She wiggles her eyebrows.

When the light turns red, I turn up the volume of the car speakers. My phone is connected to the speakers so the only thing that's playing is Taylor Swift. If there's one person I can't keep a secret from, it's Amy. She knows me better than anyone except Jason, and I can keep a secret from him—I have. I've only managed to keep one secret from her in the past eleven years and I still hold onto that.

I allow myself to take a deep breath and let it out. "Ian."

Her eyes light up. "Oh my God! I was going to ask you about it! Jason kept pestering me in English class about you two and I didn't exactly know what he was talking about at the time."

"What did you tell my brother?"

"I told him to ask you," she answers while looking into the mirror to reapply her lip gloss. "Again, I was confused. I thought you were in love with Derek. And then he says you're dating Ian. What is going on, Attie?"

"Well—" A car horn is blasted from behind and I keep my focus back on the road. "I'll tell you everything when we get back to my place."

"Promise?"

I scoff. "Well, duh."

The rest of the drive home is mostly peaceful. Amy drops her stuff off at my room and we sit down on my bed as I change out of the tank top I wore all day to a more comfortable shirt that already has paint splattered onto it and tell her everything. And I mean everything. From the wrong letter accident of last week to Rue interrogating me like Phineas and Ferb looking for that little button-eyed doll, and even Ian suggesting that we pretend to date.

"I can't believe you kept this from me," Amy says once I've finished. We're laying on the bed, staring up at the ceiling where I've painted a shit ton of stars in the past two years. Mom and Dad gave me and Jason permission to fully personalize our new rooms the way we want to once he moved out of what is now my bedroom. While he has posters of his favorite classic rock bands and movies, I took it upon myself to fill every inch of this room with any reference to my favorite animated cartoon shows and other masterpieces.

I can't list them all but the ones that I'm staring at are the second star to the right and the Tinkerbell silhouette from Peter Pan that took me an entire weekend to work on. "I didn't know how I felt about it to begin with." In fact, I still don't know how to feel about it. Embarrassed, maybe. Shocked, possibly. Confused? Oh, hell yes.

"You should do it."

I sit up from the bed and look at my best friend with complete and utter shock. "I'm sorry, what?"

Amy sits up on the bed, leaning on the wall with my unfinished painting of the Mad Hatter's tophat—a crazy character but now, I think it's fitting for this situation because I'm staring at her like she's insane. "It sounds like fun."

"But it's a fake relationship," I remind her.

"So?" She shrugs. "Celebrities do it all the time. And it sounds fun."

"In your books," I tell her. "But this is real life, Ames. And high school. Why would anyone—especially Ian—pretend to have a relationship?" I just finished To All The Boys I've Loved Before yesterday and despite loving it, I thought that there are many other ways to tell a guy how you felt about him.

"I'm serious, though," Amy says. "No broken hearts, no real feelings. You can have all the fun of a relationship without any of the consequences."

"Except everybody else would think that I am in an actual relationship," I say. "How do people do this? Lying to this extent sounds stressful." And I'm trying to not have a stressful junior year. Which sounds like an impossible mission at this point.

"I won't say anything," Amy assures me. I know she won't. I don't need to make her promise under our oath—best friends first, sisters second—for an extra layer of security.

"Attie?" A familiar sounding voice calls from downstairs. Mom must have finished her class early. She's a classical studies professor at UC Santa Barbara, which is only about a fifteen or twenty minute drive from home, and I'm pretty sure loves geeking out about ancient Greece to a bunch of eighteen year-olds. However, she's technically still on summer break and doesn't start the new semester until next week. Doesn't stop her from driving over there for meetings.

I head downstairs to find my Mom placing her bag on the ground gently right by the door and I wrap my arms around her. We don't look that much alike, but we have the same long dark hair that could pass for black when not in direct sunlight. My arms are also longer on account of my height which means I give out the best hugs—I dare you to prove me wrong. "Hi, Mom. How was work?"

"It was fine, Owl," she says before hugging me back. "Thinking about making my students argue over who the best greek deity is on their first day"

"Oh, it's definitely Athena," I reply, smirking.

Mom scoffs. "Of course you think that." She looks over my shoulder to the staircase. "Is Amy here?"

"Hi, Mrs. Ryder," Amy calls as she heads out of my room and down the stairs. While her aunt Mary is like a big sister to her, my mom is the closest Amy has to a biological mother. In fact, my parents adore Amy so much that they've insisted on not letting Amy be so formal while addressing them. But it's ingrained in that girl's system.

Mom hugs Amy next and it's not long before we head into the kitchen. I grab a small bowl and pour some jalapeño chips into it. Amy grabs a glass of water from the fridge and Mom sits down at the dining table, a little tired after a long day.

"How was school, girls? Did you pass your physics quiz?"

I shrug. "I don't know about me, but Jason definitely did." That's what I get for spending too much time working on that vault puzzle Taylor Swift left on Google instead of studying.

"How does your brother do it?" Amy asks. "He could easily solve world hunger if he wanted."

"Don't look at me," Mom laughs. "I barely made it through basic algebra when I was your age. If it wasn't for your father, I'm not sure I would have even passed college." At the brief mention of Dad, Mom smiles and her eyes get a little distant. I just know she's thinking about her happiest memories. My parents met in college, fell in love, and are still that sappy couple you'd find holding hands at every chance they get. That's mainly why I want to wait until I'm older to fall in love. Because I'd rather risk it when I'm older and less naive—not young and vulnerable.

"Speaking of..." Mom's hazel-green eyes now focus on me. "Can you explain to me why Jason was the one to tell me about your dating life? And not you?"

My eyes bulge out of their sockets like every one of my favorite animated characters from childhood. Even Mom knows?? You've gotta be kidding me right now. This is not happening. I pinch my leg under the table in hopes I'm dreaming but Mom is still staring at me with a raised brow and that look. Everyone knows that look when a parent is trying to get something out of you. Sometimes, you have no choice but to give in. Other times...

It's a little hard to omit the truth.

"I don't know," I answer while trying to figure out a way to divert the question and switch to a new topic. "What exactly did he tell you?"

"Not much. Just brought up Ian."

"Which Ian? There is more than one Ian in this town." I'm bluffing right now. I might actually be right about that but I don't care at the moment. I'm just trying to delay the inevitable.

"I only know of one Ian Bale."

Amy looks so smug as she's sipping her water. I give her a pointed glare and she nearly spits it out back in the cup but manages to control herself.

"Honey, why didn't you say anything?" Mom places her hand on the table. "We would have understood. And I would have liked to hear about it from you. I would have preferred it with your father around but...when did this happen? How? And also finally!"

The last sentence catches me by surprise. "What? You're happy about this?"

"Yeah!" Mom laughs. "Once Jason started dating Kira—"

"Kelly," I correct her.

"Whatever, she's still blonde."

Mom's bluntness makes me and Amy laugh.

"Anyway," she continues. "I was basically praying for you to get a boyfriend. Your brother has dated more girls than you've painted cartoon characters on your walls. And Aphrodite finally answered my prayers! Thank goodness."

Mom's sense of humor has always been centered around Greek mythology for as long as I can remember. Along with that, the tone of her voice when she's serious is so similar to when she's joking around. So one can imagine how conflicted I could possibly feel knowing she indirectly insulted her two children in front of me yet not be sure of whether she's serious.

"I'm going to take a nap," she tells us. "I'll talk to you later, girls. And Attie?" She gives me a warm smile. "I know first relationships are hard so you can always talk to me about it if you need to."

Mom heads upstairs to her room and leaves me with a now empty bowl and Amy with her glass half-empty. I can't help but feel guilty. Mom always wishes for the best and Dad would definitely side with her.

I turn to Amy, who has a grin wider than the Cheshire Cat. "I have to do it, don't I?"

She nods, and I just know my best friend is holding back her urge to laugh. "This is going to be a fun year."

Groaning, I take my phone out of my pocket and scroll down to find Ian's contact before shooting him a text.

Me: I'll do it.

There. That doesn't sound so cryptic. He'll understand as soon as he looks at his phone. May act surprised at first since this is the first time I've ever actually texted him.

"We should watch something!" I suggest grabbing the remote from the couch and turning the TV on.

"As long as it isn't Phineas and Ferb," Amy says. "I'm down."

I place the remote down on the table as quickly as I picked it up. Amy can read me like one of her books.

Shaking her head, she grabs the remote and selects Prime Video. "Attie, you are so predictable sometimes. We've seen that show, like, a hundred times so far."

"You can never get tired of it."

"I got tired of it the fifth time we watched." She scrolls down until she reaches a show that I've never watched. "Let's do this one."

"Teen Wolf," I read before shaking my head. "I'm not really into teen dramas."

"You like Bridgerton."

"That's not a teen drama," I point out. "It's a historical piece."

"Of fiction," she adds. "You do know that some of the best things in life are fictional. Like the Percy Jackson series, fictional boyfriends, your romance with Ian." She wiggles her brows.

Before I can argue that, my phone vibrates on the table. Amy snatches it before I can and her eyebrows flying off her forehead can only mean one thing. "Speaking of..." She shows me the text he sent.

Ian: Glad you're up for it, princess.

"Oh my gosh," Amy squeals. "This is more exciting than watching a rom-com." Her eyes then light up. "You know what would be even better?"

I raise a brow, feeling a little suspicious. "What?"

"If we went to tonight's game, you know? Give them a little show."

"You lost me at the game, Ames," I mutter.

"Why not? It's, like, a written rule. If you're dating an athlete, you have to go to their games to support them. Unless you have other important things to do." Of course she would say that.

"It's a football game," I remind her. "After last year, I'm not going to another." I already didn't exactly like going to sports games in the first place. One of the only reasons I went to the vast majority of the home games last year was because Amy didn't want to go alone. On top of her—at the time—blooming relationship with Carter, she also had to take photos for the yearbook. She owed me so many chili cheese nachos. "And

I do have important things to do today. Like having a sleepover with my best friend."

"Aww," Amy gushes. "It's so sweet that you think you can get away with not going." She flings an arm over my shoulder and steers me in the direction of my room. "We can still do all of that and go to the game." When we reach my closet, she pushes the slide door open and observes all the clothes on the rack as if she's looking for the first time.

"I'm keeping the overalls on," I tell her.

"Okay, then that should make this easy." She pushes each hanger aside until she finds an olive green tube top that I haven't worn since I bought it. "Gotta stick to school spirit. You still have the gold eyeshadow I got you for your birthday?"

I nod. She had gotten me that and a new sketchbook. The latter is almost filled up with how much I've used it whereas my gold eyeshadow has barely seen the light of day since my makeup routine is mostly concealer, brow gel, mascara, and white eye liner—I don't consider tinted lip balm to be makeup.

"Perfect," Amy claps before handing me the hanger with my tube top. "I'll be outside, reading."

"What about you?" I ask.

She unzips her windbreaker to reveal an olive green tank top with the words, SBHS GO DONS, in glittering gold letters. "I've had it all day. Forgot to tell you that Taylor needs me on standby in case her camera gives out so she could use mine." She winks before walking outside of my room to no doubt read one of her e-books.

She didn't forget to tell me. Amy never forgets things like that.

I stare at the hanger and the tube top when it really hits me. Shit, I can't believe I'm doing this. I sigh before closing the door and changing tops. I take a look into the mirror, reminding myself that I'm still the same Attie

Ryder that I've always been, regardless of who I might be dating, whether it's real or not.

But it's time to head out there and face the music. Or in my case, the crowds of screaming highschool student and supportive parents.

Chapter 10

"That was a bloodbath!" I shout over all of the cheering. Our team had finally scored another touchdown and the scores were about tied by the time the second quarter was about over.

"Yeah, but at least we got some good photos!" Amy shouts back. Turns out that the head of the yearbook committee's camera had died and there was no charger available. A good thing Amy was on standby because when the first quarter was over, we were headed away from the bleachers and nearing the track.

There was no way in Tartarus that I was staying on those bleachers.

The marching band heads onto the field to start performing and I take that moment to head over to the concessions booth and grab some water. I ask Amy if she wants anything and I make my way over to the long-ass line for the snacks. I should have brought some jalapeño chips from home because this line moves slower than those snails from Turbo.

"Hi Attie!" A perky voice says from behind.

I turn around to find my brother with his arms around Kelly. Of course I would find Jason and Kelly here. My brother goes to every football game with Derek and has done so since before we were in middle school. I knew I would have to face him soon when I gave in to the thought of attending tonight's game.

At least Derek's not with them right now.

"It's nice to see you!" Kelly says. If one was searching the words "blonde beach girl" on Pinterest or just Google, you could easily find a photo of Jason's current flavor of the month, Kelly Sprague. It's not that I don't hate her—I've never had any problems with Kelly at all since I hardly know her—it's just that she of all people should know what she's gotten herself into. Every girl gets with my brother thinking that they could be the "one to change him" only to miserably fail.

"I didn't think I would see you here," she continues. Okay, maybe the fact that she talks a lot could possibly annoy a few people. Then again, I'm used to it. "Jason told me that you don't really come to these games."

"Well, that's not the case, now," Jason mutters with his eyes narrowed at me. I narrow my eyes back at him. Two can play this game, brother.

"Oh, right! You're here for Ian. It's great that someone finally trapped him in a relationship."

I move my eyes from Jason to Kelly. "What do you mean trapped him?"

Her face turns red. "I didn't mean it in a bad way. It's just that he's never seriously dated anyone." She winces. "I'll shut up now."

Jason kisses the side of her head. "It's alright, Kells. I thought the same thing, too."

I hold back an eye roll at my brother's statement. In his defense, I did say over and over again that I would never go to another football game again after what happened the last time I went.

"I'll be right back," Kelly tells Derek before pressing a kiss to his cheek and walking away from the line, leaving him with me.

I make a show of gagging at the display of affection, which only causes him to shove the finger in my face. "Like you haven't done that."

"Well, I haven't."

It's his turn to roll his eyes. "Fair point."

I take a step forward as the line finally begins to move up. Jason follows me and rubs his forehead. "I still can't believe it. Ian? Of all the guys you decided to date, it had to be him?"

His straightforwardness causes me to raise a brow. "I don't see why you're confused."

"I'm not confused, sis. A little worried, yeah. Not confused."

Worried? My brother—the care-free, energetic playboy—is worried? My face softens. "Why would you be worried?"

He sighs. "Because I don't want to see anything bad happen again after last year."

I'm not the most affectionate person on the planet but hearing those words come out of Jason's mouth makes me want to bring him into a hug. He had gotten the unfortunate front-row seat of the first attempt at trying to get over my crush on Derek and I didn't think it had as much of an impact on him as it did for me.

But instead of thinking back to that last football game I went to, I try my best to bring myself back into the present. "I can handle myself. Besides, Ian's different."

"I can take the next person in line!" The guy at the kiosk shouts. I turn around to find that I am currently at the front of the line. I make my way over to the window and order chili cheese nachos and a Sprite, while grabbing a bag of Skittles for Amy.

Jason follows up behind me. "I'll take a Dr. Pepper," he tells the guy in the booth before slapping a twenty on the counter. "I'll pay for both."

The guy rings up our order a few minutes later and before Jason and I part ways, he puts his hand on my shoulder. "Are you sure you'll be okay? I mean, after..." He stays silent. My brother knows better than to say his name out loud.

I nod. "It's sweet that you're being over-protective, man. But shouldn't the roles be reversed?"

He rolls his eyes. "Just because you're older, doesn't mean you can protect yourself." The glare I shoot his way only causes him to hold his hands up in surrender. "I know you can. Don't hurt me, please." He says that last sentence so fast it makes me laugh, because I manage to understand it.

"Just head over to your girlfriend." I gesture to the student section, where most of the popular people are decked out in school spirit and most probably on some sort of drug. "I'll be fine. I've got Amy. And if he breaks my heart, I'll send her after him."

This earns me a laugh from Jason. "Amy couldn't hurt a fly even if she tried. She is literally the size of one."

"I heard that, asshat!" Amy's voice shouts over the marching band and loud conversations.

Jason's head turns in Amy's direction. "I swear you can't keep anything from her," he mumbles before turning back to me. "At least something good came out of this relationship."

I raise a brow at him.

"Endless teasing about that huge crush he's had on you since elementary school."

"Elementary school?" I ask. This surprises me for multiple reasons, the biggest one being that Ian's never had a crush on me. Of any kind. I've always just been seen as either a friend or Jason's sister. Or, as of now, a fake girlfriend.

My brother laughs, running a hair through his hair that has become a lot darker over the years. The short locks of hair that used to be this light mahogany color have now become almost as dark as my hair, making us more alike than we ever were to begin with. Yet, even then, that's where our similarities end. "Duh. You can't just call a girl princess for no reason. Even

I'm not like that." He's got a point. Jason has a multitude of nicknames for Amy, none of which are out of the blue—all of them refer to her height. I would name a few of them but then I'd be standing here until after the game ended.

"Whatever, dude," I say. "Don't you have some disgusting PDA to inflict upon the rest of the student body?" I give Jason a two-finger salute before heading back over to where Amy and Taylor are standing. I don't know Taylor Wolfe that well. We've seen each other in passing but I highly doubt she remembers my name.

"Has the game finished yet?" I hand Amy the bag of Skittles and start munching down on my nachos.

She shakes her head. "No, but I still need photos of the marching band." She puts the camera away from her face and leans closer. "Did you tell Jason?"

I swallow. "No. Tell him what?"

"About..." she trails off, hoping that I figure out what she's trying to imply.

Oh, yeah. That. "Why would I tell him?" The whole point of the agreement with Ian is basically to pretend that we are actually a thing. With Amy being the one exception, NO ONE is allowed to find out that my romance with Ian is a ruse.

"Because he's your brother," Amy says. "I wouldn't be surprised if he found out almost immediately."

I shrug. Jason and Amy are the two people on this planet that know me best. Lately, whatever twin telepathy I used to have with Jason has become a little rusty. Regardless, he is the only person who knows about what happened with the unnamed last year so him being suspicious about this new "relationship" doesn't exactly surprise me. Even Amy has no clue.

The game immediately starts back up and I see the starting line-up get in position. I don't know much about what happens in the game of football—I mostly went last year for Amy but didn't pay much attention to the game—so I'm just watching cluelessly as I hear a familiar voice call out what must be football plays.

Ian's voice.

I couldn't point him out in the middle of the first half even if I wanted to but now, as I spot the bright number 8 from where I'm standing, he's the only presence I feel. The only voice I hear.

And when his eyes meet mine under his football helmet just before he shouts, "HIKE!" All I can see is him.

Chapter 11

I won't lie and say that tonight's game was easy.

Because it sure as hell was a bloodbath. The last two games were not so bad. In fact, they were easy wins in comparison to tonight. Yet, at the last quarter, we're barely ahead. This is the closest game in what might be years, at least according to Coach Wells in his halftime "inspiration speech." A lot of words could be used to describe our middle-aged football coach but motivational isn't always one of them.

Surprisingly, we managed to score one field goal and take that final win. As good as that had felt, I couldn't help but feel a little tense. I brush it away before changing out of my gear and into my shirt and jeans. Once the jacket's on, I walk out of the locker room, slapping hands and bumping fists with my teammates. Braiden meets me outside the locker room and we make our way out to the bleachers, where a lot of people still stand. I head over to the far right corner of the student section as soon as I spot my brother with Jason and an unfamiliar blonde. Must be Jason's girl of the month.

I can't help but notice Derek looking a bit more at ease. Usually, he's a little uncomfortable around PDA but I guess that's not the case anymore. His wandering eyes spot me and wave me over to him. It's not long before Jason notices me.

"Bro, why did you come see us first?" Jason laughs. His arms are wrapped around his girlfriend and his brows are raised. Must be surprised to actually see me there.

"Why wouldn't I?" I ask. It's a routine I've done for a while. Derek always makes sure to attend my games with Jason, while I force BJ to go with me to Derek's volleyball games.

"Honestly, I thought you'd be stopping to see your girlfriend," my brother teases.

My eyes move over to the track. I noticed Attie standing by the track with two other girls at halftime. Actually, I felt it. Her presence. Even when the second half of the game began and I saw her eyes connect with my own just before it began. She's still standing there and I make a mental note to myself to catch up to her before she leaves.

I tousle Derek's hair. "I couldn't leave without acknowledging my cheer squad at least once."

"Ha ha, very funny," he mumbles.

"I'd head back down there if I was you," Jason says. "You know, before Attie gets antsy."

I raise a brow. "I'm surprised you of all people are kicking me out of this little circle." I gesture to the four of us, especially his girlfriend, who has been quiet the entire time I've been around. Huh, she must be shy. "If anything, you're the antsy one here."

"Keep in mind, Bale. You're dating the female version of me." His girlfriend chuckles underneath him. "We're both antsy people. It's in our blood." He makes a fly swatting motion. "Shoo."

"Alright, I'm going," I say, giving Jason the finger. "I'll see you guys at Tyler's bonfire?"

They both nod. I make my way down to the bleachers, past the cheerleaders who are packing their things. I hear Rue call my name but I manage to ignore her and head towards Attie's direction. Her back is turned against me as she's talking to Amy so I try to sneak up behind her and wrap one arm around her waist, unintentionally getting hit with the smell of mangoes.

I hear her gasp just before I lean in to whisper, "it's just me, princess," into her right ear. Whatever tension she had in those two seconds leaves her body as fast as it arrived.

"You could have tapped me in the shoulder first," she whispers back.

"Noted," I mutter. From a distance, anyone else would think that I'm whispering sweet nothings in her ear. And by anyone else, I mean the two blondes in front of us, Amy and Taylor. I nod to them both. "Hey."

Amy waves back while Taylor—the other girl—isn't paying attention but texting on her phone.

"Nice to see that Jason wasn't spewing bullshit," Amy smirks.

Attie shrugs in my grasp. "Ian doesn't like lying about things."

Oh, the irony.

"Yeah, I bet he doesn't." Amy winks at her. I try not to read into it because girls are already complicated enough. "Anyway, are you ready to go?"

"You guys are headed to the bonfire?" I ask. "I can just give you a ride."

Attie shakes her head. When she turns around to face me, the one detail that is impossible not to notice is how slowly she moves. It never occurred to me how tired she could be. It's only 9:00, and usually most teenagers are just as awake as ever.

"I didn't know how tired you were," I tell her. I let her head rest on my chest. It's as if she's going to nod off right now at this moment.

"Sorry," she mumbles against my chest. "It's been a long day."

Yeah, I bet it's been a long day. In the span of less than twelve hours, Attie has dealt with the repercussions of Rue's words, and I can't help but think it's all because of me. I know that I'm somewhat at fault for this.

"Do you girls need a ride at least?" I ask. Aside from the field lights, it's basically dark out.

Amy shakes her head. "I'll drive her. We arrived together." She holds out her hand. "Come here, At-Bat." As soon as Amy grabs onto Attie's elbow, I manage to let go of one of her arms, only for Amy to nearly drop my fake girlfriend to the floor.

"Ames," Attie mumbles. "What's going on?" I've seen Attie extremely tired before. Even as a kid, it didn't matter how late it was, she could barely keep herself awake without a damn good distraction after the moon's out.

"Need help?" I raise a brow, and Amy's eyes are basically saying thank you.

"Finally! A decent person. She's not that heavy, I swear." I wrap one of Attie's thin arms over my shoulder while she does the same with the other. Amy and I manage to leave the stadium and begin our trek toward the parking lot. The familiar blue Jeep Wrangler sits isolated in the middle of the parking lot, and I can see my car, which isn't so far from it.

Amy manages to grab the keys from Attie's purse to unlock the car and after opening the passenger door, I lift Attie off her feet and place her inside, making sure not to hit her head anywhere. "Drive safe, okay?"

Amy nods before starting the engine. I move Attie's long braid over her shoulder and say, "goodnight, princess," before taking a step back and watching it drive off. I'm probably one of the only people still here, aside from Coach and a few others.

It really has been a long day. Especially because I haven't left school at all since arriving early this morning. Tonight was our first home game and if there's anything to say about how the rest of this final season will go, it's that it will be hell. It's my final year of playing football since I don't plan on playing after I graduate so I would definitely like to go out with a hell of a bang.

"Hi, Ian."

Oh, boy. Time to face the music, I guess.

I turn a full one-eighty and see Rue standing right in front of me. I take a step back because she's so close and I value at least some of my personal space. "Hey, Rue." Did I sound like I was about to head to my doom? Because I feel like I am.

"So," she says, twirling her brown ponytail. "I was wondering if you were heading to Tyler's for the bonfire."

The pandemic had banned bonfires on the beach back in freshman year and that has yet to be lifted. Luckily, a high school alumni named Tyler Kowalski and his family own a beach house on East Beach with its own firepit. He was last year's football captain and his family donates a lot of money to the school.

I almost always go. Yet, for some reason, I don't feel like attending tonight. It has nothing to do with Attie not attending—okay, maybe a little—or the meteor shower that's coming to a close next week. Okay, maybe both of those things are reasons as to why I don't want to attend. But there's still one more.

I don't want to be around Rue.

So I put the one year of drama class to use and stretch my arms out and fake a yawn. "Sorry, Rue. I'm gonna sit this one out."

"But it's only 9:30. You can't be that tired."

I shrug. "I woke up early." Which is true, but I had an energy drink before the game tonight so I don't feel the slightest bit tired. And I had a nap.

She pouts. "Oh, okay. So I guess you can't give me a ride?"

I shake my head.

"Fine. I'll see you later, Ian."

She waves and walks away, no doubt trying to give me a show. As soon as I turn around and head towards my car to start the engine. I may have gotten a B in drama, but at least those lackluster skills didn't fail me.

Knowing that I'm able to fool Rue Barlow while getting to hang out with someone as chill as Attie is a win-win scenario in my book.

Chapter 12

T he weekend with Amy was a blast, if you don't count all the homework we had to do and the times Amy texted Carter in the middle of the night. It got to the point where I had to put a boy ban on the rest of the weekend but it was so worth it.

Unfortunately, the boy ban gets lifted on Sunday, when Jason knocks on my door while Amy and I are still asleep. "Wake up, losers!"

I throw my pillow at him, only to miss his face by a huge margin. "Get lost!" I'm groggy, and it's Sunday. Which is always optimum for catching up on all the hours of sleeping that I missed out on during the school week. It's also the one day a week Jason wakes up early.

"I wish I could," Jason begins with a mischievous smile. "But I don't want to. It's noon, Attie. Besides, Mom made croquetas."

As soon as the word leaves Jason's mouth, I'm immediately awake. Because Mom hasn't made those in so long. Croquetas are these delicious fried treats that are similar to a hybrid of a mozzarella stick and a donut. You could add meat to the filling but my family and I prefer it with just cheese.

"Okay, I'm up." I tap Amy's head next to me. She's on the inflatable air mattress and her hair is such a mess it's kind of funny. Almost cartoonish.

"What?" Amy asks groggily. She rubs her eyes and it takes her a minute to be fully awake. She sees Jason standing in the doorway and narrows her eyes at him. "Do you have any sense of privacy?"

My brother shrugs. "You've seen worse of me. Now hurry up before we eat them all."

My body stiffens up. "Who's we?"

"Me, Dad, Mom, Derek, and Ian. I thought that was obvious enough." Jason's head pops out of the room and I force myself to get up and out of my bed. He's not wrong since I can never finish as much food as the rest of my friends and family.

Wait, did he just say that Derek's here? In the house? And with Ian? I mentally facepalm myself. It's one thing to be in the same room as your crush. But when he thinks you're dating his brother? That's a whole other set of complications. Especially because Derek isn't just Jason's best friend. We basically grew up with both Ian and Derek. Despite Ian being a year older, he and Jason are still close.

"This should be interesting," Amy says as she removes the bandana from her head, despite it having done nothing to protect her curls. "A shame I have to leave soon."

I'm a little sad too because without Amy, I don't know how I am going to handle brunch. Then again, she was only supposed to spend Friday night here and head back home Saturday. I have my amazing persuasion skills to thank. Or, just sheer luck that her dad was in a good mood.

"Do you want me to drop you off?" I ask while rummaging through my drawers for a pair of shorts and t-shirt. Score! My Nirvana t-shirt still resides in my closet, despite the multiple colors of dried paint that surround the smiley face.

"Mary said she'll pick me up. That way, you can have more time with your boyfriend." She says that last sentence in a teasing way. I'm starting to regret telling Amy about the fake relationship when I remember that she has more experience with relationships than I do. I can't ask my brother about this shit!

Amy and I get dressed and make our way downstairs to find the kitchen more packed than usual. Mom's reading on her tablet, Dad's drinking his cup of coffee while chatting with Ian—probably being grilled about me or talking about football. As for Derek? He's on the couch, hovering over Jason's shoulder. Both of their eyes are trained on Jason's phone.

All five of them are eating the delicious-looking croquetas.

Amy looks down at her phone. "Oh! Mary's waiting outside. I wish I could stay but I have to go." She waves at my parents with a smile. "Goodbye, Mr. and Mrs. Ryder. Thanks for having me!"

"Bye Amy," Mom and Dad say as my best friend heads towards the door, leaving me in the clutches of my parents. And my brother.

And my crush.

And my fake boyfriend.

Le sigh. I am in for a long Sunday, aren't I?

I can feel my stomach beg for food, so I sit myself down on the only available seat next to Ian and grab the last croqueta on the plate. Seriously? Only one left? Well, beggars can't be choosers, I guess.

"You want to try to not use your elbow so much," Dad is telling Ian. "You need to move your shoulder forward a little more. That way, it doesn't hurt as much." I can see Ian bobbing his head up and down, as if he's listening to what my dad is saying. He probably is because my dad has worked with a lot of football players over the years. It's the one sport that has the most injuries, and as a physical therapist, he knows a lot about what not to do.

I take my last bite just as Dad's eyes—the same color and shape as my own—find mine with a smile. He rounds the table and kisses the top of my head. "How did you sleep, Owl?"

I shrug before wrapping my arms around my father. "Pretty well."

"Any plans today? Homework to finish?"

I shake my head. Luckily, I was able to finish all my homework with Amy yesterday. Her dad is pretty strict about schoolwork, which is expected since he's our school principal. My only plans for today were to finish painting the bears I had begun working on and the Mad Hatter's tophat. Maybe I'll add more to the wall but that won't be for a while.

"Your mother and I are headed out," Dad tells me and Jason. "Try not to make a mess of things while we're gone." He has a pointed look at me.

"Why are you looking at me?" I ask. "I'm not that messy."

He gestures to my shirt. In my defense, paint is hard to remove from clothes once it dries up. Especially acrylic. And I may not be the cleanest person in the world but at least I try. Sometimes.

"Where are you going?" Jason asks, not even looking up from his phone.

"Shopping," Dad grumbles.

Mom laughs. "It's our anniversary this week, remember? And—as much as he loves me—your father wants to be there when I choose his gift so we won't be long." Mom's eyes then finally move to me. "By the way, Owl, your package is upstairs in my room."

My eyes widen. Shit, I completely forgot about that thing...

It is then Jason looks up from his phone. "On a Sunday?"

"It arrived yesterday. But since she was busy hanging out with Amy, we hid it in the closet. You know how your sister is."

I scoff. "I'm right here, you know." Although I can't argue that they're right. When I have my mind set on an art project, whether it's painting my walls or related to animation, I zone in on that. There's nothing wrong with focus but as soon as drawing is involved, people become out of sight and out of mind. Mom was right to hide it from me.

"We'll see you kids later!" Mom loops her arm around Dad's and they both exit the kitchen, heading in the direction of the front door.

"Make sure to keep your door open!" Dad calls out, eliciting a groan out of me. I don't blame him for wanting to keep the smell of acrylic paint out of the air vents.

I excuse myself from the kitchen and head upstairs to grab everything I need, but not before deflating the air mattress Amy had used this weekend. I grab all the materials I need from my closet and my parents—paintbrushes, paint colors, paper towel roll, to name a few—and lay them out on the floor. Taylor Swift's 1989 album blasts from my phone and I hum to my favorite song, New Romantics, while picking out the colors I need.

My cousin Andy has always wanted a new mirror after breaking her own a long time ago with a softball. After mindlessly scrolling on Tiktok last month, I came across a girl painting clouds on the bottom half of an oval-shaped mirror. It sparked my interest because I've never used a mirror as a canvas before. If it fails then at least it's the thought that counts.

However, the mirror I had ordered back in August had problems with shipping and it took more than a month to arrive, despite all the calls I had to make with USPS and the company I had ordered the mirror from. So I couldn't give it to Andy when my family and I were in Pioneer Valley for the Labor Day weekend. Luckily, my cousin doesn't mind. She's not the most punctual person I know.

At some point, my humming turns to me just dancing around my room and singing the lyrics out loud. I'm not a great singer by all means but at least I don't sound like a dying cat.

"It's a good thing your voice is better than Jason's."

I freeze at the sound of Ian's voice, which carries over the loud music. I turn to find him sitting on my bed. How the hell did he get there? And without me noticing?

"Uh," I begin to say. "How long have you been there?"

He shrugs. "Not that long. Think I lost track of time the second time you started tiptoeing around your art supplies."

I can feel my face burn hotter than the sun beating on me during the day. Yeah, he's been sitting there for a while, just watching me dance. Just as the song repeated itself.

Chapter 13

"Come on, princess. You weren't so bad." My eyes wander the walls of her room. Last time I walked into here, it used to belong to both her and Jason. A lot has changed in the past four years. The bunk beds that were covered in permanent marker and paint were replaced by a rather clean single, queen-sized bed with blue covers. Everything that was remotely Jason's is gone and in a new room.

This whole room screams Attie.

"That's new." I point to the drawing of three bears—I think they're bears—on top of each other.

She looks near the window. "Yeah, I still have to finish that."

"Is that what you're doing right now?"

She shakes her head. Pulling the closet door open, she grabs a thin, rectangular-shaped cardboard box, and lays it on the floor gently. "I forgot about my cousin's birthday gift so I'm trying to finish that real quick."

"A birthday?" I stare at her blankly. "You forgot about someone's birthday? That is not like you," I feign shock. She knows I'm messing with her, even if I might be just the slightest bit surprised because Attie hardly forgets about a person's birthday. When we were younger, the first thing we ever bonded over was how close our birthdays were, mine being the day after hers and Jason's.

"I didn't forget, per say," she argues, placing her hands on her hips. "I just...had a lot of things on my mind."

I raise a brow. "Were any of those things about a certain guy? You know: tall, sexy blond hair, on the football team."

She shakes her head and her lips turn upward and I get a glimpse of little dimples that I never knew she had. Were they always there? I guess but they were never so noticeable before.

Maybe I need a new prescription for my glasses or something.

"Nope. Doesn't ring a bell." She taps her chin with her index, laughing. "I am seeing this guy whose head is a little too big for his glasses, though. Does that count?"

I scoff. "Fair game, Ryder. Tell you what: I'll help you with your gift."

Her dark brows fly over her head. "Really?" Then, her smile is flipped slightly upside down and her eyes show a hint of confusion. "Are you sure about that, Ian?"

I nod. "It's not that hard to wrap a mirror, right? Just don't break it or we'll both get seven years of bad luck."

"That's not—" she begins to say before I hop off the bed and sit myself on the floor, next to the mirror, trying my absolute hardest to not squish any of the bottles of paint or step on the brushes that are on the floor. She has a lot of stuff for someone who only paints as a hobby.

"Okay, I guess there's no changing your mind," she mumbles before reaching for her phone and stopping the music. "Yeah, I'm not wrapping the mirror just yet."

"But it's just a mirror," I point out. No shit, Sherlock. "What else are you going to do with it?"

She smiles mischievously as she opens the box. "Do you know how to draw?"

"How does that sound?" Attie finally asks.

She had just told me her plans for the mirror, after getting off-topic one too many times whenever Jason entered the room for something or whenever something reminded her of her favorite Taylor Swift song.

Which is a lot. That girl really likes Taylor Swift and Jason must leave a lot of his stuff in this room. Either that or he was playing the big brother role and having way too much fun with it.

"I won't lie to you, princess," I begin to respond. "I hate painting but you have fun with it." I'll just sit back and watch the artist at work.

Her jaw drops like I just told her that her dog died. Last I checked, the Ryders never had any pets. "That's not possible."

I don't know what to tell her. Other than that I do not have any good memories associated with painting so I would strongly not prefer to visit those.

"I didn't think such a thing existed," she mutters. "That's just wrong."

"How is not liking something wrong?" I ask.

"Painting isn't just something," Attie says, pushing herself up off the ground. "At least...to me it isn't. Sure, some people find it boring but how would you feel if someone insulted football or video games?"

Attie has me there. I wouldn't feel offended on the outside but this girl wears her emotions on her sleeve. I just wouldn't exactly say that football is my number one favorite thing on the planet. Or playing video games. Sure, I like them both but there's one thing I like more.

Is it the girl in front of me, trying to persuade me into thinking that painting is the best thing on the planet? Well... let me get back to that.

"Personally, I've just never heard of someone actually disliking paint." She shakes her head in dismay. "Not even in elementary school?"

I shake my head. "I'd rather jump off a cliff." That sounded harsh, I know that. But I have jumped off a cliff before and that was easier than rehashing old memories from painting.

She whistles. "Damn. I guess I got my work cut out for me."

"What work?"

Attie grabs a paintbrush from the floor and holds it out to me. "I'm gonna try to change that little mind of yours."

I look at the thin paintbrush in her hand and back at her. "Are you sure about that?" I'm usually set in my ways when it comes to certain things.

She nods with an assured smile. She's so confident that she can change my mind about painting but I have my reasons. "Without a doubt."

I hesitantly take the paintbrush from her hands, pretending that I don't feel the brief contact our hands made. "Better make good on that promise then, princess."

Taking a white crayon in hand, she places the bottom half of the mirror onto her lap. "Don't worry, four-eyes, I will."

I cringe. "Four-eyes?"

She groans. "You call me princess for some unknown reason, so I might as well try to give you a nickname."

"Could it be a good one next time?" I tease.

"I'm working on it!"

Attie starts drawing petals on the mirror. The concept she had in mind was to draw sunflowers—which is apparently her cousin's favorite—at the bottom of the mirror, and stars on the top. I'm not the best at drawing flowers of any kind but she's letting me do the stars, so I'm just patiently watching her draw intricate designs.

This girl...she has this whole aura around her when she draws. I've seen her at lunch, her head down as she draws in her sketchbook and it's peaceful. I can almost never see her face since her dark hair—which fades into a lighter shade of brown at the end—but now, her hair is pulled back and I get a clear view of her side profile.

Attie eventually looks up from the mirror and turns her head in my direction. "What are you staring at?"

I blink out of whatever stupor I was in. "You." I won't lie to her about anything. Even now, I'm the most truthful around her. "It's not like I can stare at the wall." I make a point of staring at the light switch in front of me. "See? It's not exactly—wait, is that Snoopy?"

Her eyes move to the light switch and chuckles at Snoopy, asleep on top of the light switch. A small smile appears on her lips. "Oh yeah. I forgot that it was there."

I can imagine. I swear these walls have every cartoon character or memento to exist.

When Attie's done drawing the sunflowers, she hands me the white crayon and instructs me as to where I should draw the stars. I won't lie to you or be humble about this: I'm damn good at drawing stars. Everyone has their niche thing: some people, it's knowing the lyrics of every song by a certain artist. For me, it's drawing stars. So I try to draw them of all sizes and shapes on the mirror.

"Wow," Attie says when I finish. "You're pretty good at this. If I need a professional at star drawing, then I know who to call."

I wink at her in response. "Glad to be of help in the future." In your future.

Shaking that random thought out of my mind, I wait for Attie to pick out the colors of paint. She hands me a bottle of white paint before grabbing a second one for herself. Then, she finally instructs me to paint the stars. I do so as she picks up a white piece of plastic that looks like what Bob Ross owned and starts mixing colors.

"It's for the center of the sunflower," she tells me, her head not moving as she mixes the yellow and brown.

Music is playing as we work on the mirror, which is flat on the floor as we're both on different sides of it, painting. I won't lie—this isn't as bad as I remember.

In fact, I'm so engrossed in painting the stars that I don't notice any of my surroundings until something cold touches my face.

I move my free hand to my left cheek and feel something cold. Wait a minute, that's paint. Some of the yellowish-brown color has transferred to my fingers and I look in front of me and see Attie holding back a smile.

"Princess?" I ask, the tone of my voice is so calm it's almost creepy. "What's on my face?"

She shrugs, trying to focus her attention on the mirror. "I don't know. It's your face. You tell me."

And I thought my fake girlfriend would be the observant one.

I eye her for a couple more seconds before resuming. She doesn't own up to it but I know she's responsible.

Once I finish painting the last star, I place my paintbrush down and watch Attie at work. It's hard to watch people in their element and in the eight years I've known Attie Ryder, I've never seen her paint anything. Sure, she has her sketchbook on hand. But painting and sketching are still pretty different. Personally, I think it's harder to paint.

Not for this little princess here. She makes the damn thing look so easy.

In fact, she's in her zone. Probably won't notice if something got in her hair...

I take what's left of the white paint, drop some onto the brush, and quietly make my way over to the other side of the mirror. Carefully, I hover the brush over the top of her dark hair and wait until one drop of white paint falls off the brush and lands on her head.

It takes a while and I watch the brush while also simultaneously trying not to get distracted by the scent of mangoes that surrounds Attie. I swear

I never told her that I loved mangoes yet every time I'm around her, I smell it. Everyone has that one thing they find so attractive it's hard to look away. Or even take one step back.

I think I just found mine.

"Oh my—" Attie touches the top of her head and squishes the dollop of white paint. When her ice blue eyes meet mine they narrow and she says in a playful voice, "bring it on, Bale. Bring. It. On."

Taking her paintbrush, she lightly smacks it across my left cheek, and spreads it over my nose, barely missing my glasses. Maybe I should have taken them off but I'm enjoying them too much to care.

I'm already having too much fun. And I'm nothing, if not competitive. With my paintbrush in hand, I smear some white acrylic onto Attie's face, going from one cheek to the other.

And the next thing I know, green paint touches my shirt. Specifically, Attie's handprint.

"Oh, this is war, princess" I chuckle, grabbing the first bottle I see, squirting it onto my hand, and smearing it on her forehead. The light blue paint goes over her eyebrow and she closes her eyes fast enough so the rest of the paint only touches her eyelid.

And in the next thirty seconds, we're a mess. Literally. A bright, colorful, mess.

Yet I've never felt so alive.

"Okay, you were right," I give in, placing a bottle of purple paint on the ground as my white flag. "You were right. Painting's not so bad."

Attie smiles in triumph. The dry blue paint that covers most of her forehead and cheeks crinkles as her dimples come springing back. Her eyes, normally the icy blue that I've come to know all these years, light up as if the sun was buried in them all along.

"I told you so," she singsongs, the smile on her face only becoming even brighter. Forget the sun—I can see the entire galaxy in her, stars and all.

Chapter 14

That was probably the most invigorating thirty seconds of my day.

Scratch that—my entire life.

I was only teasing him when I said that I could easily change his mind about painting. What I didn't expect was for about ten percent of my paint to go to waste on an all-out, kid-like, painting frenzy, where my entire room became a mess.

Okay, not my entire room—that's being a little dramatic—but Ian and I are definitely covered in paint.

Head-to-toe, covered in acrylics.

In fact, his once all-white shirt now looks like a rainbow got plastered, ate one too many edibles, and then projectile vomited all over him. I don't even think I look that bad.

"Oh shit, you're shirt," I say. "The paint probably transferred through."

Ian blinks himself out of his stupor and looks down at his shirt. "I'll be fine. Why don't you worry about yourself?"

I shake my head. "No way, Ian. I have plenty of experience with paint splatters." I gesture to my shirt. There was already dried paint all over it from last week so it doesn't look so bad. Most of the acrylic paint got on my bare arms, legs, and face, with a little on my hair. Thankfully, it's easy to remove. "On skin, it's not so harsh but most of the paint is on your shirt."

"Thanks for that astute observation," he mumbles.

"At least get a shirt from Jason," I suggest. "He won't mind." Jason wears tight-fitting shirts and hoodies anyway. I doubt he cares about most of the loose shirts he's bought from the family vacations we've had.

"Princess, it's alright."

"Ian, it's my fault. Please let me help." He offered to paint Andy's mirror with me so the least I can do is help him get changed.

Ian's face softens and he finally agrees to let me help. That doesn't take me by surprise. However, I do not expect him to do exactly this: to remove his paint-splattered shirt from his body—with one hand, mind you—and give me a full-on IMAX screening of his abs. And he does exactly that.

Oh, sweet Apollo of the flaming chariot.

Of course, I know he has abs and is objectively attractive—maybe not a full Adonis but still toned to the nines. I had just never seen them before. It's similar to a relative you've never met. You know they exist but you can't put a visual to them. That is what this guy's abs were to me.

And the script on his abdomen. Wait a minute—

"Did either of us use black paint?"

Ian shakes his head. "No, why?"

I tilt my head to the right. "No reason." My eyes can barely trace the black writing because—just as I predicted, some of the paint on his shirt transferred onto his bare chest and torso. But if we didn't use black paint for the mirror and the events that followed, then the writing on his body can only mean one thing.

Ian Bale—teenage all-American quarterback, Captain America reincarnate—has a tattoo. And not just those bold temporary tattoos you can find on Amazon. I mean the real deal.

"That's a new sight."

A confused expression appears on his face but then fades away when he looks down and finds what I'm staring at. "Never had someone read my body like a book before."

"That sounds like a lie..." My voice trails off as I try to read the letters on his body. Is that a vowel? Maybe it's a T...

"Princess, you can just ask me about it," Ian laughs as he balls up his shirt.

"Hang on, I'm tryna figure out what it says."

A soft chuckle escapes his lips. If Taylor Swift's Lover album wasn't blasting on my phone right now, I would have called it music to my ears. Ian doesn't laugh a whole lot, so being the reason he does is just like winning a prize at a carnival from one of those rigged game booths.

My eyes eventually move back to Ian's ocean blues, and I sigh in defeat. "What does it say?"

"Wait, you couldn't figure it out?"

"Would you be able to read it from where I'm standing?" It's small and written in cursive. Who the hell invented cursive writing?

I can just barely hear the words "okay, smart-ass," mumble as he tries to wipe the paint off his abdomen. It mostly flakes off, considering that acrylics dry pretty damn fast and some of the skin underneath is red—not just because of the paint.

I take a step closer to read it better. I can now read it just fine and—I shit you not—it's only four words: Don't Stop Me Now written in this cute cursive font, in between two clusters of tiny black stars that remind me of Peter Pan's second star to the right.

"Queen?" I ask.

He nods. "Something wrong with that, princess?"

I shake my head. No way. I love that band. Granted, it's a favorite in the Ryder family. I don't think I've met anyone that dislikes Don't Stop Me Now.

"Hang on," I say. "You still have some paint on that star."

He tries to rub it off, but it doesn't move.

"Here. Let me help." I take a step forward and remove it myself. Thanks to long nails, it comes off pretty quickly. But I notice the detail and my index finger doesn't move from where it touches. Actually, my nail traces the design. Why am I even so interested in this? Both of my parents have tattoos and I wanted to be a tattoo artist up until I was in the seventh grade. This shouldn't faze me, yet it does.

On anyone else, I wouldn't have cared. Guess I'm learning not to assume how people would react to tattoos because until this moment, Ian was the last person I would have expected to get inked at any age, nevermind seventeen. However, it's pretty damn...sexy.

Wait, snap the hell out of it, Attie!

"When did you get that?"

"Last year, when I turned sixteen."

And his dad was just okay with it? I don't really know his dad all that well but he doesn't exactly strike me as someone who is laid back, like my uncle Damon. Or my dad, for that matter.

"There's nothing wrong with it," he says.

I shake my head and finally remove my gaze from his abs and meet his ocean eyes. "I didn't say that."

Someone knocks on my door. "Hey, Ian, I was just gonna—"

We both turn our heads to my painted door and find Derek, brown eyes wide and bouncing between me and his brother. It's then that I realize how close Ian and I are standing. Sure, I knew but the thought never fully submerged into my brain until Derek walked in.

What surprises me even more is that I completely forgot that Derek was still here.

Ian lets out a puff of breath before pinching the bridge of his nose. "Did you want anything, D?"

He shakes his head, pressing his lips together. "Nope." The next sound that comes out of his mouth—actually escapes might be a better word for it—is a choking sound.

Wait... is he trying not to laugh right now?

"Yo, Derek! What's taking so long—" Jason stops at my door, next to his best friend and his hazel-green eyes widen to epic proportions. However, he does nothing to hold back his laughter. Unlike most people, my brother has no qualms against laughing at people—especially right in front of them. "Bro, what happened? Wait, don't answer that question. I don't want to know." Jason then reaches into the right pocket of his shorts, holds out his phone, and I hear a clicking sound.

My jaw drops as I take a step back from Ian and glare at the guys at my door. "Did you just take a photo of this?"

His laughter eventually dies down enough to answer me. "I took a video first, then a photo." He doesn't say duh, but it's definitely implied. Like I would know that to be common sense.

"Just get out, please," I tell Jason. "Oh, and can Ian borrow a shirt?"

His eyes move to Ian. "Did my sister rip your shirt off attempting to do some kinky shit?"

"No! God!" I feel my face turn as red as the paint on Ian's bare chest. Jason, can you please shut up? Or better yet—where's the duct tape? "Get your head out of the gutter."

"You're a gutter," my brother mutters under his breath but since he's a naturally loud guy, I hear it.

Deer looks between all three of us before clearing his throat, only proving how awkward this must be for him. In a world of crazy scenarios and quirky characters in cartoon shows, he's merely an audience member. "Ian, can I borrow your car?"

Nodding, he says, "the keys are downstairs," as if just being shirtless and covered in paint is the most normal of circumstances.

Derek backs away from the door and heads off, probably to grab his brother's keys off the petri dish that rests by the front door. It's where all the keys go whenever we aren't using them and guests are expected to follow that rule.

Jason holds out his hand. "Come on, dude. You need a frickin shower. You look exactly like that peanut butter kid that was on Vine but with paint."

Ian looks at me with laughter in his eyes, slightly shaking his head. "That was a little rude."

"The truth is never rude," I respond, laughing. Anyone can laugh at Jason's lack of filter. I would call my brother dramatic if he wasn't right. I gesture over to my brother, indicating to Ian that he should go if he doesn't want the paint to permanently stain his skin. He follows Jason out of my room and I'm left all alone.

With a bunch of paint to clean up and a whole lot of thinking.

Chapter 15

"Hey, can we pick up Amy from her place?" I ask Jason as I grab the last piece of bacon from his plate. Granted, it's a little dry because he air-fried leftovers but it's still good.

Jason glares at me for taking his food. "Why are you still here? I thought you left a while ago."

I shake his head. "And leave you all alone? Never."

"Booo." He holds out his fist, which showcases a thumbs down.

I smile in triumph.

"What happened to your boyfriend?" He grumbles. "Couldn't he drive you?"

"Nope." Ian had texted me last night about that same thing. Like all the other sports our school has to offer, the varsity football team has practice both before and after school. "My boyfriend didn't want to have to force me to wake up at the ass-crack of dawn just so he could give me a ride." Which was honestly nice of him.

"I'd rather he did. I almost never get the car to myself."

"That's too bad." I fill up a glass of water for myself and take a seat across the table from my brother. "Do you think we'll have time to stop by Groovy Smoothie?"

He shakes his head. "If we're going to pick up Amy, then no. It's in the opposite direction from school."

Drat. Amy lives closer to school so unless we want to be late, then we can't. "After school?" I take a sip from the cup.

He nods. "Deal."

Groovy Smoothie is this seventies-themed chain smoothie stop that can easily rival Jamba Juice. The smoothies are healthier, taste better, and the place is bigger inside than out. There's tables and since we live close to a pretty big university, a lot of college kids would go there just to sit down and study. It's been our favorite place since the first one opened up not far from the beach when Jason and I were ten.

Jason stands up with his empty plate. "Let's go."

It doesn't take long for either of us to head out to the driveway, where our beautiful Jeep sits in the bright sun of 7:45 AM. I enter the passenger's seat while Jason makes himself comfortable in the driver's seat. With the Beatles playing in the background, we head off in the direction of Amy's house and school.

"Are we not picking up Kelly?" I ask. With the exception of me and Ian, it seems normal to pick up your significant other and take them to school. Then again, I've never been in a serious relationship myself.

He shakes his head. "Her parents don't know about me."

I turn to him in surprise. "What?"

He shrugs. "She's technically not allowed to date."

But he's doing it anyway. Either he really likes this girl or Kelly's not as innocent as she appears.

"Hypocrite," I mutter, pinching his right shoulder. "And you criticized me for not hitching a ride with Ian."

"Sorry." He rolls his eyes, gripping the steering wheel a little tighter. "But at least he's not under the bleachers, getting high off his ass." Then, his eyes widen.

He wasn't supposed to say that out loud. I figured, because I knew what—or rather, who—he's referring to, so I keep my mouth shut. I can't argue with him. I've never seen Ian drink or do any other drugs but I can't say the same for myself. But I don't want to think about it. I was a sophomore who didn't know better. At least I'm trying.

If pretending to date Derek's brother means trying, then I'll take it.

I just want to wait for Amy to get out of her house. I know she's a hardcore morning person so there's no way in hell she's not awake. In fact, her text she sent me this morning woke me up five minutes before my alarm. Jason parks the Jeep in the Pierce driveway and after two minutes, Amy walks out her front door, holding what could look like a cup of hot coffee to the average person. I happen to know it's her iced chai latte with brown sugar oat milk creamer that she makes every morning, without fail. Amy doesn't drink coffee. Like Jason, she can't stand that stuff.

Amateurs, am I right?

Amy enters the backseat, a little surprised to see me. "At-Bat? What are you doing here?"

Right. That text from this morning? It was for me to pass to Jason since he never answers his texts.

"Not that I'm happy you're sitting here," she says after entering the car and buckling herself in. "I just don't get why Jason's driving. Should I hold onto something? I should call Dad and tell him I won't make it today."

Jason glares at Amy from the rearview mirror. "Nice to know you have faith in my driving skills, you yapping Yorkshire."

"Lack thereof seems more accurate."

I snicker. I'm kind of glad Ian couldn't drive me to school because it gives me some good road entertainment.

"Nice alliteration," I say, holding my hand up for a high five. Jason smacks it.

"Seriously, Athena? Not taking my side?" Amy gasps for dramatic flair.

I shrug with a smirk. "He's my brother, Amy."

We eventually make it to the student parking lot with twenty minutes to spare. Usually, it gets hard to find parking at this time but when your twin brother's driving skills consist of cutting people off and making other drivers angry, then it's not so bad. I sometimes pray that I wasn't so nice when driving but I can't help it—anxiety gets the best of me.

Which is a bad thing when you live in California with a driver's license.

Jason, Amy, and I part ways, since all of us are headed somewhere different. Jason's probably going to meet his girlfriend at her locker, Amy's headed to her dad's office and I'm going to my locker to empty out my backpack.

Except when I get to my locker, Ian is standing right next to it. He's looking down at his phone, not noticing that I made it.

"Sleep well, princess?"

I guess he did notice.

"Yeah," I answer while entering the combination. A little tired, sure, but I slept better than most days. I think it had something to do with knowing that I finished Andy's birthday gift and can mail it. Albeit, two weeks late.

Once I open the door, I'm greeted with a black blob with eight legs, hanging on a string, and my heart jumps in fear. "Shit!" I gasp, jumping back from my locker. But a second glance is enough to tell me that the spider hanging inside my locker is fake.

That can only mean one thing. "Oh. My. God."

Chapter 16

I nearly drop my phone when Attie basically screams the moment she opens her locker.

"Woah there, what happened?" I ask, but she doesn't respond.

Instead, she peers into the locker again and mutters the words, "oh. My. God," before reaching into her locker and pulling out a plastic spider. "Son of a bitch."

I raise a brow. "It's a spider." A fake spider.

She nods. "I noticed. I'm just wondering how Jason got it in here."

I shrug as I observe the fake tarantula. "Maybe he got here early."

"Impossible. He drove us here. I saw him." Then, realization dawns on her face. "He had your brother do it. Ugh, they're both gonna get it."

I shake my head. I remember Derek telling me about a prank war between Attie and Jason a while back. The details were a little fuzzy to me but apparently my brother got caught in the crossfires of Attie's last prank. Man, I wish I was there to see it unravel. "You know, it makes sense why he asked to borrow my car today. I had to ask BJ for a ride to practice."

"I'm keeping this on me for the near future." She places the spider back in her locker. "Gives me a good idea for Halloween."

"Like?" I'm becoming very invested in this prank war now.

Attie moves her fingers across her rosy lips in a zipping motion before winking. "I'll never tell."

"You can't tell your boyfriend?"

"Nope. I can't deal with snitches." She playfully smacks my chest. "You know what happens to them."

"Oh, yeah," I respond, a hint of high laughter in my normally deep voice before slinging my arm over her shoulder. The motion catches her by surprise.

"What are you doing?" She laughs.

"I'm wrapping my arm around you," I answer. It seems obvious enough. "Am I not allowed to do that?"

"Oh, right. I forgot for a moment." Yeah, she forgot that we're supposed to be dating. I'll be honest, it felt natural to do that. I'm a physical person—comes with the territory of playing a contact sport—so handshakes, hugs, kisses, anything beyond that doesn't make me feel uncomfortable.

A few people wave at me before noticing the brunette under my bicep and waving at her, too. Attie stares at the group that passes by before waving back with a smile. "Is this normal for you?"

I shrug before we start walking down the hall. "I hardly notice it sometimes. I'm guessing this doesn't happen to you a lot?"

She lets out a laugh. "An understatement. Aside from you, Derek, Amy, and a few others, nobody knows my name. They either don't think I exist or I'm just 'Jason's sister' to them."

"Well, in the next two hours," I say. "Everyone will know who you are, princess. Don't you worry."

"Eh. I don't really care about that."

I turn to face her. "You're not like most teenagers?" Struggling to find popularity amongst their peers by doing anything and anyone? A shocker. Not to say that she couldn't be popular if she wanted to. Attie is easily one of the prettiest girls that I know and that alone could do wonders.

"I wouldn't say that," she corrects. "I'm mainstream in the little things. Like my taste in music. Most of my Spotify consists of Taylor Swift songs and the occasional Gracie Abrams and Harry Styles. I dress like a normal girl, I wear makeup but I'm not a crazy wild child, like you."

"Okay," I say, interrupting her. "I'm not that wild."

She raises a dark brow at me. "You don't jump off cliffs every once in a while or play pranks on teachers?"

I sigh. "Okay, maybe the cliff jumping is true but that's about it." The rest of my teammates are the ones who play pranks on people. I have better things to do with my time than leave a whoopee cushion on Mr. Bradshaw's chair. "Besides, that happened one time."

But I can't argue what Attie had said earlier. She isn't crazy in the sense that she'll rebel at every chance she gets. She's also not shy. Attie's merely...cautious. That's the best way to describe her. Coincidentally, it's also the least extreme description, according to her brother.

Since I don't need to grab anything from my locker, Attie and I have been walking over to her first class. Which, come to think of...

"Where's your first class?" I ask her. We've just been walking down the hallway for no apparent reason.

"Oh, we walked past it a minute ago."

After turn back around and actually stopping at our destination, I remove my arm from her—which is beginning to feel abnormal at this point—and wait for her to enter the class. I notice a redhead sit down next to her and shake Attie's arm, animatedly gossiping about something. I can't make out what the girl is saying but it might not be worth the brain workout to dissect. My first class of the day is math so I need to save my brain for the inevitable drainage of energy that is Mr. Gardener's equations.

The day goes by and since Attie and I don't share any classes, on account of being in different grades, I don't get to see her until lunch. Since I have a free period before lunch, I take my car and head out to the beach. I hardly ever leave campus during my free period, or even at lunch. Today, I'm making an exception since I haven't been in a while, which is only since July.

I don't walk on the sand but find an empty bench and look out. Since it's late September and only ten in the morning, there aren't that many people and the weather's starting to cool down. No burning benches or crowds. I don't see many surfers here, either. All I see is an old couple, holding hands as they walk along the shore.

It's just quiet. And I like it a lot. I take a deep breath through my nose and smell the ocean air and breath out through my mouth. I'm not one for meditation but it's going to be a stressful year so I might as well get started. Anything to keep me from going insane.

Unfortunately, I'm not at the beach for long so I walk back to my car and drive to Groovy Smoothie. The one necessity to a half hour at the beach: smoothies. Don't argue about this with me because I know I'll prove you wrong.

I grab two smoothies—one mango smoothie for me, and blueberry for Attie (she likes blue, so she's getting blueberries)—and head back to school five minutes before the bell rings. Luckily, she shares a class with Jason so I know exactly where to go. Especially because I have this same teacher for class after lunch.

I wait outside until the bell rings, signaling the end of class and the beginning of the lunch period before a bunch of seniors exit the room like a monster is chasing them. Eventually, Jason walks out of the room, spots me, and smiles. "Hey, man! Did you get one for me?" He tries to reach for the purple smoothie but I hold it out of his reach. He's only slightly shorter than me but my arms are longer.

"Sorry man," I tell him. "If you wanted a smoothie, then you should have texted me. And then paid me."

"Wait, then why do you have another smoothie in your hand?" He argues.

Just then, Attie exits the classroom with her best friend. Jason looks between the two girls, realization crossing his face for a moment. "Never mind. I'll see you later."

Jason heads towards the cafeteria. Meanwhile, my fake girlfriend doesn't see me until Amy walks off in the opposite direction. "Ooh, is that for me?" She points to the smoothie. I hand it to her and she takes it and immediately starts drinking out of the straw. "How did you know my favorite flavor?"

We start walking towards the cafeteria. "I remember everything about you, princess."

She scoffs. "Not everything."

"You'd be surprised." I'm good at remembering the things I want to remember. Sometimes I'm good at remembering the things I don't want to remember. "But I saw you drinking this smoothie one day when I went over to your house to pick up Derek."

"Oh, yeah," she says. "I forgot about that day. Man, I was in a mood."

We make it to the cafeteria doors, watching everyone who's there clustered into little groups and the occasional sprinter. I usually sit in the very back of the cafeteria, where most of the varsity team congregates as well as a few cheerleaders. I'm not sure if Attie wants to join us but part of the reason we started this whole thing is to get Rue off my back.

"Into the colosseum we go," Attie mutters before downing the last of her smoothie and throwing the empty cup in the trash. How she managed to drink it that fast is beyond me—my cup is only three-quarters empty.

"Colosseum?" I ask.

"An inside joke," she tells me.

"Should I be worried?"

Attie shakes her head, her two braids moving along with her. "Not really. First day of high school, Jason and I walked into the cafeteria and nearly got trampled before grabbing a tray. When we told our Mom, she claimed that it was similar to those tournaments they had in ancient Rome."

"Should I be worried?" I ask as we get in line for food.

"Nope. I made it out alive. Can't say the same for those warriors, though."

That totally assures me. I grab two trays for the both of us and hand her one. "You're telling me more about that later." We pay for our food and head to the back of the table. I had assured Attie that most of the guys and cheerleaders are not so bad but she has yet to believe me, since her only interaction with a cheerleader has been with Rue and...well, you can imagine how that went.

"There you are!" BJ calls out. Sophia's right under his arm and if it wasn't for the bandana wrapped around her hair then I don't think I would have noticed her. When she sees that I'm not alone, her eyes bulge out their sockets and a wide smile splits her face in half.

Everyone else is staring at Attie and I can tell by the stiffness in her shoulders that she's not used to this. I put my tray down on the table and wrap one arm over her shoulders. "Guys, this is Attie. My girlfriend."

The reactions are all mixed across the board. My teammates couldn't care less but BJ slaps me on the back and mutters, "finally" under his breath. Sophia is clearly happy for me, while her best friend stands with her arms crossed over her chest, and pointed eyes at the girl standing next to me, who is clearly burning red.

I pull out a chair for Attie and gesture towards it. She gives me a small smile and sits down. "Nice to meet you guys." Again, she isn't shy so Attie must really feel uncomfortable.

"How did you get your hair so long?" Sophia asks. "I've been trying to grow it out for years but it always stops here." She places her hand right below the ends of her curly dark hair. "It's really pretty."

Attie cracks a smile, this one not looking as forced as the last one. "Thanks. I don't really do much with it, so I can't really help you with that."

"Don't worry about it. We have different hair textures anyway," Sophia points out as she takes a sip of her water. "Isn't her hair so pretty, Rue?"

The tall brunette standing next to Sophia doesn't say a word. Rue doesn't even smile—nope, she stands still like a statue. "Yeah, whatever." She flips her hair back and sits down. "So, Addison—"

That causes Attie's head—which has been lowered slightly due to her constantly stabbing the salad in front of her with a fork—to snap up faster than the speed of light. "It's Attie."

"Yeah, that's what I said. Isn't Addie short for Addison? I'm not wrong."

Attie shakes her head. "I guarantee you that you're definitely wrong." Oh, this should be fun.

"Then what is it?" BJ asks me.

I hold my hands up in surrender. "Don't look at me. It's not my name." I'm not saying that I don't know her full name, because I do. First, middle, and last. And the reason she was named that.

Attie puts her fork down on the tray. "My name's not Addison." Her gaze is aimed directly at Rue. "It's Athena."

"Ooh, that's pretty," another cheerleader named Lacy says. "Why do you go by Attie, then?"

Once again, Attie's cheeks turn redder than the cherry tomatoes in her salad. "I don't know."

"What do you mean, 'you don't know?'" Sophia wonders.

Attie's eyes move away from the crowd and focus solely on me. As interested as I am, I also know when to not push boundaries such as this.

But I try to show my support by patting her jean-clad leg. "It can't be that embarrassing," I say, trying to lighten the mood.

She shakes her head, blue eyes wide. "It's not." Then, in a hushed tone, she admits: "I genuinely don't know. I'm just used to it."

"That's a little stupid." Rue scoffs earning a punch in the shoulder from Sophia. Thank you, Castro.

"Rue!" Sophia scolds. "That wasn't nice."

"It's just funny," Rue laughs. "How is it hard to say your name?"

"Nicknames are just random." Attie rolls her eyes. "Of course, you wouldn't know, Sue—your name is only three letters."

Rue sneers, clearly annoyed. "My name is Rue. Get it right."

"Yeah, that's what I said." Attie's tone screams innocence and I have to stop chewing the slice of veggie pizza I had been eating in order to avoid a choking hazard from laughing. Since I'm trying so hard not to laugh at Attie throwing Rue's words back at her face.

Once I swallow the slice, I wrap both arms around Attie. "That's my princess," I whisper. Instead of stiff shoulders, she wraps both of her arms around my torso and rests her head on my right pec. This lunch period just got better and better.

But it doesn't last long because I then get roped into another conversation with Ethan Haynes about how brutal this morning's practice had been and the next thing I know, the bell rings and lunch is over.

"You have to show me that soon!" Sophia exclaims. "I would love to see it."

"When it's done," Attie promises.

Sophie walks off, giving me a wink as she grabs BJ's hand and he helplessly follows her. Man, he is whipped.

Then again, so am I. Supposedly.

"You ready?" I ask Attie, grabbing both of our trays in hand.

She nods, slinging her bag over one shoulder and eyeing the trays stacked on top of each other. "You don't have to do that. I can carry my own tray."

I shrug. "I know. But what kind of boyfriend would I be if I didn't?"

"Fair point."

After exiting the cafeteria and walking Attie to her math class, I walk over to my AP Physics class. I usually don't mind this class but this happens to be the one I share with Rue. And since Mr. Ali is the Type-A, OCD kind of teacher, our seating arrangements are in alphabetical order.

Therefore, I have the utmost pleasure of having Rue Barlow sit right behind me. Why, oh why couldn't my last name start with a Z, like Mom's did?

Once Mr. Ali starts the class, I feel a tap on my shoulder and the next thing I know, a piece of paper is resting on my right shoulder. Phones aren't allowed in the class because our twenty-something year old teacher can sniff out texting like a blood-hound—I would know since I got caught checking a text from my Dad on the first week of school—so everyone has resulted in passing notes, in good-old fashioned ways.

I unfold the note to find Rue's handwriting.

Really, Ian? Of all the girls you picked, it had to be her? You couldn't have picked a real one?

I roll my eyes. This girl, I swear, is going to give me a heart attack just from her incessant flirting. I don't even bother to respond to it and focus my eyes back to the board. It's supposed to be easy, avoiding people you don't like.

Chapter 17

Throwing those words back at Rue yesterday was so satisfying you have no idea.

Today, however, was very much the same. I sat with the football team, ate lunch, and other somewhat normal things. The only difference between today and yesterday is having to stay after school for the first official animation club meetings with the newcomers. Sierra and I had talked about today's meeting countless times during math because we didn't exactly have a full-on plan. Last year's president and vice president graduated and moved away, so that means we're basically starting off from scratch.

"But did you see Leslie's face when we told her about the semester project?" Sierra cackles as we walk out of the classroom.

"It was funny," I agree. I've never seen someone both so excited and terrified for a project.

We pass the hall of fame and open the doors to the other parking lot. This school has at least three exits, and one of them leads directly to the football field. Since Sierra's brother is also on the football team, I agreed to walk with her to the bleachers so she could stay until practice lets out. It's a bonus since Jason stays after school to use the weight room and I need to look like a good "girlfriend" by watching Ian practice.

"I still can't believe you didn't tell me about your relationship with Ian," she whines. "If I had known that you were dating the hottest boy at school, I would have died." She's kidding. I think.

Pulling my sketchbook out of my bag, I say, "that's kind of why I didn't tell you." Sierra is a bit boy-crazy. I know this because she's the first girl my brother ever dated. At least nothing bad happened between them—their relationship lasted one month of the seventh grade—so I had been able to stay friends with her. "Whatever happened to Caleb, anyway?" I inquire. She's been crushing on this guy from Suze's—the best diner in Southern California if you ask anyone with working brain cells—and I've heard every minute detail she could give me.

She sighs, loudly. "I don't know what's going on. I mean, I think he likes me but it's hard to tell." She rests her head on my left shoulder. "How did you know Ian liked you?"

I freeze. Legit, my pencil stops moving over the tree trunk I began drawing. I hadn't discussed this with Ian. Shocking that we never came up with a backstory about how we got together. Should I have known better after reading an entire trilogy about this very thing I got myself into?

"Well," I begin, tucking a piece of ombre hair behind my ear. I tried dyeing my hair sophomore year but the bleach job didn't go so well so I'm stuck with this madness until I can either cut it or dye back to my natural hair. "He told me."

"He told you?" Sierra asks, a puzzled look on his face. "That doesn't sound like a lot of guys."

"Ian isn't exactly like a lot of guys." I move my eyes back to the sketchbook, adding some branches to the tree. "He's never lied to me in the past so I had no reason to not believe him." The irony is strong with this situation I'm in. Look at us—lying to everyone we know about our feelings for each other.

"So should I've believed you when you had told me—not two weeks ago, might I add—that there was nothing going on between you and the Captain America reincarnate standing on that field right now?"

I don't say anything for about five seconds before finding my voice again. "I didn't think there was before he told me." I should really talk to Ian about this. Coming up with a backstory is going to make this whole fake dating thing so much easier.

"Aww, look at that," Sierra giggles. "Looks like he is softer than I thought."

"Are you done with twenty questions now?" I laugh.

She shakes her red mane. "No, I have one more and then I'm satisfied."

"Shoot."

"Is Ian as good of a kisser as they say?"

The question catches me off-guard. Not because I don't know how to answer the question but because of how straightforward it is. But that's Sierra for you. "Um..." I try to think of a good response to say when Rue catches my eye. She, along with the rest of the cheer squad, is out on the track field, practicing. The others are focusing on those pyramids. Rue is at the bottom but her eyes are not focused on her teammates at all. Instead, those brown eyes have been shooting metaphorical lasers at me.

Sierra and I are not that far up on the bleachers which means there's a chance she might hear us. If I raise my voice loud enough for her to hear, then I could kill two birds with one stone.

"Actually," I begin to say to Sierra. "He's even better."

My friend's green eyes light up and she squeals. "Oh my goodness, I'm so jealous and happy for you at the same time! Oh, you lucky, lucky bitch!" She squeezes me tighter, making me laugh before peering over my shoulder to glance at the tree I'm drawing. "The apples shouldn't be that round."

Oh, goodie.

We spend a good chunk talking about the placement of the branches and the apples in the sketch. I'm glad I have friends like her and Amy in my life. Amy Pierce will always be my ride or die no matter what—that is definitely a promise I can make—but I enjoy talking about cartoons and animation software with Sierra. Amy sketches fashion designs pretty often but she's been spending more time texting and video chatting with Carter lately and I've missed her.

The sun begins to set and practice lets out almost an hour later. I stopped paying attention to my phone because Sierra and I got into an argument about the best bear in a cartoon show we love to watch called We Bare Bears. I say it's Ice Bear because he's just funny and relatable. Sierra claims that Panda is adorable (which is true) and therefore, he is the best.

"Cuteness doesn't always mean iconic," I argue.

"I don't know," a deep voice inputs. "You'd need some damning evidence to back up that claim."

Sierra and I look up to find Ian with Ethan Haynes sitting on the bleachers in front of us. Both blond boys must have been standing right by longer than I had assumed because Ian has his hands holding his chin like a little kid and Ethan doesn't look bored out of his mind.

Sierra rolls her eyes at Ethan and breaks the atmosphere of silence the clouds us. "Finally! Can we go home now?"

"Nice to see you too," he mutters. "Let's go, squirt."

Sierra and Ethan say their goodbyes and head off the bleachers, leaving me and Ian alone. Jason left a while ago with Derek and Amy's with her Dad at their house so I don't exactly have a ride home unless I want to call my brother. Or...

"Can you give me a ride?" I ask Ian, bringing out the innocent doe eyes. It works every time. "Please?"

He chuckles softly. "Sure thing, princess."

Standing up from the bleachers, he holds his hand out and I take it, following him down the steps to his designated parking spot. It has a black background and I can't see what's underneath it. I glance at the parking spot next to it. Bright green, with a crudely drawn... is that supposed to be a paw print? A pom-pom? I don't even know.

"What's that supposed to be?" I point to the black silhouette.

Ian looks in my direction and tilts his head. "Honestly? I'm not sure."

"Who's parking spot is that?"

"BJ and Sophie's," Ian answers, pressing the button on his key fob to unlock his car. "I think it's supposed to be a cat's face."

I wrinkle my nose. "That is not a cat's face." Maybe if Grumpy Cat was their inspiration then it would have worked. Who am I kidding—the five-year-old kid I babysat for last year drew a better cat than that.

"And I assume you would have done better?" Ian opens the car door and hops into the driver's side. I hop into the passenger's side and place my seatbelt on.

"Oh, Ian," I sigh. "You know I would have done better."

He shake his head. I don't want to be so cocky but Ian knows that I'm right about that. I would have definitely done a better job at drawing Grumpy Cat's face.

The car starts moving, with Ian and I sitting there in silence. I don't know what he's thinking right now and part of me is so interested as to what it could be. Whereas I am trying to think of how to phrase my current thoughts out loud. Just say it, right?

"We need to set some rules down," I finally say.

He doesn't say anything until we reach a red light. Only then do his eyebrows practically fly off his head. I'm guessing the words didn't register in his mind until right now. "I'm sorry, what did you say?"

Or maybe he didn't hear me at all.

"I think we should set some rules," I repeat. "For this whole..." How should I phrase this? "Arrangement."

Ian's blue eyes are even wider without his glasses. Honestly, I think I might prefer him with his glasses on. "Rules? For dating?"

"Basically."

"I didn't think we needed rules, princess."

"Might as well." I shrug. "I've been asked so many questions about how we happened—" air quotes around that last word—"so I wanted to be sure we're on the same page."

"The same page," he repeats. "Exactly what are you talking about?"

"I'm talking about us being on the same page when it comes to certain things, such as how we first got together, how long this arrangement will last, personal boundaries—now that one is especially important—"

"I'll stop you right there," Ian interrupts before I can continue. "Firstly, who would be stupid enough to cross boundaries?"

I shrug. I can think of one person who would do it intentionally but I don't say anything about it.

"Secondly, I thought it was just about putting on a show so that you wouldn't have to embarrass yourself in front of your crush. Who, by the way, I don't know about." For all the words he said in that one breath, you would think he was a little pissed. If I didn't know any better, I'd think he was. But based on the furrowed brows and the lack of harshness in his voice, it's safe to assume that Ian's merely confused.

And I'm not telling him about that. There's no way in hell that I'm going to let Ian find out that the letter was supposed to be for his brother and not some random guy.

"But if it's that important to you, then fine," he surrenders. "What have you said so far?"

I think back to Sierra's questions from not that long ago and tell him what I told her. I was pretty vague about my responses. I give myself a mental pat on the back for it.

"Okay, what do you think?" I finally implore after minutes of silence. The car starts moving again and Ian doesn't say much. He must be like Dad in that sense—doesn't speak when he's driving because he could lose his focus entirely. I don't exactly feel the most comfortable in silence. At least, complete silence, that is.

Ian glances quickly in my direction and he must notice. "Did you want to play music?" His eyes move to his phone, which rests in the cup holder between us. It's connected to a charger, so that means the USB port is connected to the speakers.

Which also means...

"You're about to regret asking me this, Ian," I laugh as I take the phone out of the cup holder. When we reach a stop sign, I hold the screen up to his face to unlock it and go straight to Spotify. Once I find my account, I press follow and then select the Taylor Swift playlist I made called Attie's Guide to Taylor Swift. Immediately, Foolish One starts up—Spotify has a cruel sense of humor—and I begin to sing along to Taylor's beautiful voice.

I'm not a good singer by any means. It's apparent when my voice cracks from time to time and I'm unable to hit the high notes. Even Ian notices because he keeps stealing glances at me throughout the rest of the drive. I know this because I may or may not be doing the same thing—stealing glances at him, that is.

We eventually reach my house just as the song ends and he turns off the engine. "That's alright. The background."

I turn to him with a hopeful look on my face. "Really? Because there's more."

"Shoot."

I thought he was going to stop me right there. Guess he's actually interested. "How long do you want this to go on for?"

"We're setting a timeframe?"

I nod.

"Seriously?"

I nod again, the lack of yeses leaving my mouth has Ian shaking his head.

"Homecoming, then? That's a month away, right? If we went together for homecoming and then break-up afterwards, then people would believe that we just parted ways, right?"

Wow. That's a really good answer. I didn't have a timeframe in mind but for someone who's just thinking on the spot, Ian knows what he's talking about.

I guess how surprised I am is reflected onto my face because Ian follows that up with, "I've done research."

And this guy never fails to surprise me. "You know people who have faked relationships?"

"No, but all of Jason's dating stints lasted a month so that has to count as research, right?" He gives me a wry smile that makes me place both hands over my face as I burst into giggles.

Ian's hands find mine and basically pry them off my face. My eyes are still closed so I find myself opening them to see Ian's huge hands holding my very nimble and thin fingers. "What'd you do that for?"

He shrugs. "No one should have to hide their face like that when they're happy."

And cue the butterflies.

And the ringing phone. Specifically, my phone. I answer without looking at the caller ID. "What now Jason?" I know it's him because Jason hates texting people. Even if it's something miniscule, he'll call. He calls me more than anyone else in my life.

"Yo, can you stop making out with your boyfriend and help me with this thing?"

I groan out loud. "We're not even doing anything right now."

"We can see you from the window!" Another voice calls out from the phone.

Ian mouths, "Derek?" with wide eyes. Yep. Definitely Derek. "Pervs," he says.

"I'm definitely rooting for you guys," Derek continues. "But I don't want to leave my dinner sitting on Jason's bedroom floor."

"Hurry up—" Jason tries to say before I hang up.

"Well, that was...something," I declare, slowly backing up from Ian's grasp. My hands slowly leave his warm grasp and begin to feel cold immediately. "I should actually head inside, though."

Before I open the door, Ian's hand grasps my shoulder. "I do have one more thing."

"Yeah?"

"You gotta leave letters in my locker."

I turn back around because he can't be serious, right?

"Letters," I repeat. "In your locker?"

He nods.

"Why?"

"Isn't it how this all started in the first place?" The smile that appears is comparable to the grinch in its mischief. "You write a letter, leave it in my locker, and I'll feel like a princess until homecoming."

"Every day?"

"Nah, not every day. That seems a little excessive." Oh thank goodness. I could get a cramp if I had to write this much on a daily basis. "Maybe once a week. Or more, up to you." He winks.

Choosing not to question his thought process, I only nod. "Deal. Every Friday for the month." I don't know if I should regret this or not. Maybe I will.

But what's done is done and it's only the beginning.

A beginning that almost terrifies me.

Chapter 18

On Friday morning, after what seemed to be the longest meeting I ever had to endure, I open my locker to find a little letter, floating gracefully onto my sneakers for what seems to be the second time this month. Geez, if I knew a fake relationship would mean I could get love letters then I would have done something sooner.

I know that letters were a part of the agreement that Attie and I had made back on Tuesday but if I'm being honest? I just wanted to see what she would have written in a letter for me. I lift the wax seal—now green instead of blue—and open the letter to see what it would say.

Dear Ian,

Okay, this letter is a bit rushed since it's midnight and I have a history paper to start, so please just laugh like I'd just written something funny.

That first sentence causes me to laugh a little too loudly and a few heads turn in my direction. I quickly search the small crowds around me only to not find Attie. Okay, she's not watching so I can at least read my letter in peace. None of my friends are there either, which is honestly a little better. I don't hate my friends at all. Due to this stupid social ladder that exists, I'm basically on a rung that can reach the top layer of the Earth's atmosphere.

I need to finish reading this letter so I move my eyes away from the halls and focus on the paper in my hands.

What am I supposed to say? Ugh, I'm reading that sentence over again and realizing how lame that sounds. I'm starting to sound like Jason. But what would you want to read? Please tell me next time you see me. It's a good thing you probably might not see this until after class or something.

She was wrong. This is one of the first things I've seen all day.

But whenever you read this, I just want you to know that I wish you and the team the best for tonight's game. Obviously, I'm going to be there. What kind of girlfriend would I be if I didn't, right? Lol. Anyway, this whole letter is a jumbling mess so I'm just going to stop it right here. I know it's short but I promise to write more next week. I'll see you later and you can tell me how much you loved reading it. Like, right in front of my face.

Attie.

A permanent grin is etched across my face as I close the letter and place it carefully in my locker. Specifically, between the pages of the big history textbook that I know I won't touch today. I actually don't think I've touched that book since I first grabbed it.

"Bale! What's up, man?" A finger jabs my shoulder. "Another away game!! Let's GOOO!"

All that shouting and excitement can only come from one person. And it's not my brother. I swivel around so that the palm of my hand makes contact with BJ's fist before he can hit my shoulder. "Woah there, BJ."

"Bro, did you just turkey me?" His face is filled with laughter and for the first time in a while, he's here alone. No teammates, no siblings, and no Sophia.

"What happened to Sophie?" I ask.

"Won't be here until lunch. Had a family thing."

I frown. "I hope she's doing alright." I knew Sophie before she and BJ became a thing and I know her home life isn't exactly sunshine and rainbows. At least BJ is trying his best to bring light into her life. My best friend really loves his girlfriend. It's obvious to anyone with eyes.

"It's weird not seeing one without the other," I tease.

He furrows his brows. "But there's practice."

"She's still on the field for cheer," I point out, much to his dismay. I got him there.

"Every day I hang out with you, I get mercilessly teased and taunted about my relationship. Now, guess what? You can't do that anymore." BJ's smile is so smug. "I don't know how we are the only guys on the team with relationships but..."

"Here we are," I finish for him. He's right about one thing: I don't even know how the rest of the team is still single. Last year, Chase Hardwick, our old running back from last year, was seeing some girl in secret and no matter how much we pestered him—and by we I really mean me, Ethan, and BJ—Hardwick wouldn't budge. Aside from that, I don't know about a single relationship on the team. Then again, we don't talk about relationships in the locker room. Or on bus rides.

"Taken like pieces of bacon," BJ says, causing me to burst into laughter.

"What kind of saying is that?" I ask in between breaths before laughing again.

"I tried to think of something that rhymes with the word taken. It's hard, okay? This is why I stick to football."

"Noted."

The bell rings and BJ and I head over to our first class period of the day, English. The only class we have with each other.

"Hey, Ian! Can you hang on for a second?" Oh shit.

The good thing about the dating deal Attie and I had made is that it basically kept Rue away from me, one goal the ruse is supposed to accomplish. She hasn't tried asking me out again but I do hear the snide remarks she makes when Attie is nearby or the looks she gives her. Luckily, Attie knows how to hold her own. I've had to step in only once because

Attie Ryder is nothing if not calm. Actually, she acts so calm when talking back that it almost scares me.

I turn around to find Rue in her cheer outfit, head bent as she stares at her phone. "Can it wait until after class, rue?"

She shakes her head. "No, because I need it today."

"Need what?"

"Confirmation. For the dunk tank." Oh, right. One of the requirements for the senior prank is fundraising and to do that, a good chunk of the football team signed up for a dunk tank. A basic but very popular game that the school does every year. Since Sophia—the senior class president—isn't here, I'm guessing that leaves Rue to take charge of a few things.

"Yeah, whatever. Can I go now?"

"Eager to see your girl or something?"

Is she insinuating something? If so, then what?

"I just don't want to be—" I begin to say before the second bell cuts me off.

"Ian, are you going to be joining us today?" Mr. Howard calls from inside the classroom.

Late, is what I was about to say. Because the school doesn't give a shit if you're an athlete. Tardiness can't be tolerated.

I find half of the class with their eyes on me. BJ has a raised brow and all I can do is just walk right into class, without another word to Rue and take a seat at the only vacant desk next to BJ. I just want to get to lunch.

Thankfully, the time passes by really fast. I don't get to see Attie until lunch begins, which is kind of annoying since I was hoping to know how she felt about writing the letter, since it's the first of many letters to come. I'm going to have a hell of a time reading them all. And then probably reread them, which says a lot because I'm not much of a reader, if at all.

Before class, a voice calls out my name as I'm walking to Attie's class. I turn around to find a dark-haired dude I haven't talked to outside of football in about two years.

"Hardwick! What's up, man?" I stop in my tracks and give him a fist bump. "Are you high right now?"

He shushes me but his red-rimmed dark eyes are the sole indicator. See, Chase Hardwick is not just a former running back—he's also the guy you'd go to for weed. Every school has at least one stoner. I don't know all of them, just Hardwick.

"Yeah, you're definitely high," I mutter.

He rolls his eyes. "I need something to make these classes bearable. I can't stay sober in Laughlin's classroom, man. And it's just one edible. Not like she'll notice or anything."

"You're not wrong," I agree.

"I came to ask if you were doing the dunking booth," he says, running a hand through his messy hair.

I nod. "The guys got dragged into it, too."

Chase exhales, and I get a small whiff of what he definitely smoked. There's no doubt about it. "Thank God. I won't have to suffer alone."

"Glad we saved your sorry ass from boredom and not the ten milligram gummies that sit in your bag all day," I chuckle, turning my head in the direction I was headed. "I gotta go, but I'll see you around?"

"Totally." Hardwick heads back in the direction he came from and I finally arrive at Attie's physics class. The door's closed, which is a surprise to me because Mr. Ali usually doesn't keep students after the bell. Maybe it's different with this class.

About a couple seconds later, the door opens and Jason heads out. I grab his arm, preventing him from walking any further.

"Hey, what the fu—" his demeanor changes when he sees the person who just grabbed him out of nowhere. "Oh, never mind."

"How are you the only one leaving?" I ask him.

"A test," he responds. "Specifically, one that's killing the entire class."

"You came out unscathed though," I point out.

Jason shrugs. "Physics is easy for me but the questions on that test were hard." He puffs out a breath. "I can only imagine what Attie and Amy are thinking. I was the first one done and everyone still had their heads down. You're going to be here for a while if you're waiting fro you're girlfriend, man."

"It can't be that bad," I say.

Jason snorts. "Have you taken physics before?"

"I'm in his advanced class after lunch."

His eyes widen to the size of UFOs. You would think that people would assume I'm smart because of my glasses—ones I'm not wearing in favor of contacts for tonight's game—but because I play football, most people let the whole "smart guy with glasses" stereotype fly over their heads.

"I'd get lunch now and wait," he advises me. "My sister probably won't be out until after lunch ends." He turns around and walks away from the classroom.

I look down at the watch that wraps around my wrist. Lunch began five minutes ago. I know that physics is an objectively difficult subject so I might be standing there for a while. I text BJ that I might be late and slide myself down to the floor. Good luck, princess.

Chapter 19

I slam my complete test on Mr. Ali's desk and grab my stuff from my desk as fast as I can.

"Wow, you must seem proud," he mutters to himself while nibbling on a date.

Amy, who had finished her test minutes before I had, decided to be a good friend and wait for me to finish up. Bad idea because I just happened to be the last person in the class to finish the chapter test and lunch is almost over. If we even wanted to grab lunch, then we'd have five minutes to run over to the cafeteria to wait in line, grab food and eat at the speed of rabbits eating carrots before the next class.

Amy opens the door for me since I'm still trying to gather my stuff all in one big pile before the cold air hits me, causing me to shiver. I shouldn't have worn such a thin sweater, especially in the late hours of September.

My arms start to feel tired and I let Amy get a head start to the cafeteria.

"You sure?" She asks me. "I don't mind waiting."

"Your dad probably wants to talk to you anyway so I'll just meet you there," I insist. Her dad always asks to meet with her for a moment before lunch. I don't understand why but I'm not about to question his parenting.

"Okay." She peers over my shoulder and tilts her head. "Though, I can guarantee that you won't be alone." She nods at whatever's behind me before walking off, leaving me to ponder what it could be.

Curiosity gets the best of me and I leave my bag and books on the floor before catching a glimpse at Ian. He's not really doing anything but resting his head on the back of his lockers. His eyes are closed and headphones are in so I don't think he notices that I'm right nearby.

Is he asleep? I think so...

But who would fall asleep in the hallways? Apparently my fake boyfriend.

Neglecting my items, I take a seat next to him on the ground and wait. For what exactly? For the bell to ring since that will wake him up, no doubt. As soon as I make myself comfortable on the cold floor, I hear him stirring and his eyes slowly open. A grin begins to appear on his face the moment his eyes meet mine. "How long have you been sitting here?"

"Watching you sleep?" I raise a brow. "Not long."

"I wasn't sleeping."

"Sure you weren't," I tease. "It's not like your eyes weren't closed."

"That's all I did. I swear, princess. I closed my eyes for one second and you suddenly just appeared out of nowhere."

I'm just messing with him but the slightly petrified look on his face, matching perfectly with tinted cheeks—is just priceless. Like resting your head on the lockers is a crime punishable by death.

I bite my lip, holding back any laughter that dares to escape. "Okay."

"I just—" Ian glances at my face, which is probably beet red—I can feel how warm it's getting—and the color on his face is back to normal, narrowed eyes and a sigh replacing it. "You were messing with me."

Okay, so maybe some of that laughter I'd been holding back escapes. "It's so easy to mess with you."

"You and Jason are way too similar, sometimes," he mutters, shaking his head.

I lean my head back onto the cool metal of the lockers, shivering slightly. It's not even that cold outside but in the building? It's like Jack Frost has been sleeping in the air vents.

Ian must have seen me shivering because he takes off the dark blue hoodie he's adorned and hands it to me. "Here. Put this on."

"I'm not that cold," I try to argue through chattering teeth. Lying right out of my cold dead mouth right now since I get cold so easily.

He raises a brow. "Come on, princess. You're freezing."

"The cold never bothered me anyway," I retort.

"You did not just quote Frozen to me."

I shrug. He walked right into that.

"Please take the damn hoodie." If he didn't say please, I would have thrown out another Frozen quote. That film may be overrated but it's so easy to reference. Instead, I take the damn hoodie from his grasp and reluctantly put it over my head. The thing is so big that it practically swallows me whole but at least it's warm.

"I look like a gooey, blue marshmallow," I giggle.

"Hey, you're my marshmallow," he jokes.

"That was way too cheesy."

"Am I not allowed to be cheesy? I'm technically your boyfriend. That gives me the right to say shit that would let even mozzarella run for the hills."

Before I can answer that, the bell rings and I'm pulled out of this little bubble that I didn't even realize we were in. Those five minutes went by a little too fast. Couldn't they give us more time?

The thought that passed my mind surprised me. What? No, I'm totally not thinking about this. This is Ian. We're not really a thing. It won't last that long. He's just a friend. I'm crushing on his brother.

I'm supposed to be getting over my crush on his brother.

This must be what it's like for Jason. To have all these thoughts scrambled and running through your brain all at once.

"Where's your next class?" I ask. "Shouldn't it be my turn to walk you to it?"

He looks nothing if not amused by this but instead stands up and points to the door that rests behind all of my belongings. "I wish you could, princess, but that's my next class."

I turn to the door then back to Ian. "How?" I exclaim. Mr. Ali has his AP Physics class right after lunch. I know this because of the weekly agenda thing he's got going for all of the classes he teaches.

"Is that such a surprise for me to be in AP Physics?"

I nod. My thinking is completely logical because I barely survived the quiz I had just finished taking only a few minutes ago. "How are you surviving it? Teach me your ways, please. I beg of you."

Shock crosses his face so quickly I almost don't catch it. "Is it that hard?" He chuckles. "I thought physics was easy."

"Easy for you and Jason," I retort. "I'm normally good at math but this class is kicking my ass."

"Oh, you poor princess." He ruffles the top of my head as a playful gesture. "Struggling in a class."

"My complaints are valid," I pout, crossing my arms over the sweatshirt like a little kid. Despite my height, I probably do look like one.

"Of course they are." Ian holds his hand out for me to grab. I make sure to take my bag and hoist it onto my shoulder before grabbing onto Ian's hand. He pulls me up without ease, like I'm a stray feather being plucked off a pillow.

"Well, let me walk you the rest of the way." I make my way over to the rim of the doorway and gesture inside. "There's your class."

Ian burst out laughing. "You are something special, princess." I watch him enter the classroom and it's not long until he leaves my line of vision. I resist myself from looking back into the classroom and step away from the door, letting more students inside. I give myself five more seconds before I start walking towards my class...

And just as much time to run smack dab into Rue's shoulder.

"Ugh, can't you see where you're going—" Rue's words come to an abrupt stop when she realizes who bumped into her and when her brown eyes run down my figure—currently swaddled in Ian's hoodie—frown lines appear. She doesn't say another word before brushing past me.

Okay, that was a little weird.

Even for her. Usually, she'd make some snide remark in front of my face.

Whatever. I keep my head held high and survive the rest of the day. I only say survive because I had two more chapter tests, back to back, and my brain is seriously about to malfunction. I can spend the rest of my life without another quiz and die happy. Unfortunately, that's not going to be the case for the next five or six years.

I'm walking to my locker with Amy at the end of the day, who immediately notices my new article of clothing. "Nice hoodie," she remarks, a smirk appearing on her face.

I feel my cheeks get a little warm. "Thanks. It's new."

"I can see that." She laughs. "You're not gonna give that back when it ends, are you?"

I shake my head. Fake relationship or not, this thing is so damn comfortable! How Ian hogged this all to himself for years is beyond me. I get it, though—I wouldn't have shared a hoodie like this. I nearly fell asleep once or twice with it on in the past couple of hours because of how cozy I feel.

We finally arrive at my locker. "Seems like this ruse is going well," Amy points out. "Derek doesn't suspect a thing, does he?"

I freeze with my hand touching the lock. How did I forget about Derek? That's insane. I can't tell Amy that I had forgotten about why I started this fake dating thing in the first place. Or Mary, because Amy doesn't keep secrets from her aunt. So, of course, she knows too.

"Uh..." I try to come up with an answer that won't fool Amy. "Nope. Ian says that Derek's rooting for us." Okay, not a bad save.

I couldn't even get the words Ian had said to me after lunch.

You are something special, princess.

Those stayed with me for the past two hours and I couldn't fully dissect it. Was he saying that because there were people around? Did he mean it? Ugh! This is driving me through the roof and I can't help but wonder how I feel about it.

And maybe I've been questioning this for the past week: was I really in love with Derek? All this time?

No one's said stuff like that to me before. Not even—

Woah. I'm stopping myself right there. I refuse to think about him.

"At-Bat?" Amy waves a hand in front of my face.

I blink out of my stupor and turn to Amy. "Did you say something?"

"I asked about tonight's game," she repeats. "Are you okay, going solo?"

I raise a brow. "Why?"

A wide smile stretches across her face and her violet-blue eyes light up. "Carter's visiting this weekend!"

I gasp. "Aw! I'm so excited for you." Sort of. "Of course I don't mind!" Maybe a little.

She giggles, just in the way she does when Carter crosses her mind. "He has a morning class on Fridays and is on a train down here at the moment. I'm going to pick him up from the station in an hour and he's planning to take me out to dinner."

"That sounds nice!" As much as I want to voice my concerns about Carter to my bestie, I can't. This is Amy's first relationship and I'm not one for confrontation. I'm only able to give my support, no matter how high Carter is on my ick list. "Wait, how are you going to get away with this?" Her dad is nothing if not strict. I could chalk it up to being a high school principal but I've known him since I was five and he's always been like that.

"We're gonna go straight to dinner," she answers as I move my eyes to my locker. Once I enter the combination and fling the door open, a small piece of paper floats down. I managed to snatch it before it could touch the ground. What's this? I twirl it between my index and middle finger carefully.

"Maybe you should open it and see who it's from," Amy suggests, her tone conveying a hint of sarcasm. I was definitely about to do that.

"Not that it isn't obvious," she mutters to herself.

She's got a good point. I unfold the paper and the words on there make my heart flutter just a little.

Did I mention you look good in blue? I mean, it's obvious to anyone with eyes but I think it's time I let you know.

Okay, my heart is literally flapping its wings right now. Even in the bold, chicken scratch that is called handwriting, I just know who left that note inside my locker.

"If I didn't know better," Amy says. "I'd think you were falling for him."

I sputter. "What? That's not possible. It's only been a week." It would take longer than that, right?

"Love has no time frame, At-Bat. You also just had the giddiest of smiles on your face." She raises a brow at me and gestures to my face, the smile I didn't realize was plastered on my face already deflating. "You only look like that whenever you listen to your favorite Taylor Swift song. Not even Derek has got you looking like that."

And I've liked him for years. Surely, I've gotten all giddy over something Derek had done in the past. I just need to think about when.

Nope. I can't think of a single thing. Maybe because I had to keep my feelings in check most of the time I was around him, on account of Jason or Ian being in close proximity, and my inability to flirt.

"And he's definitely falling for you," Amy adds.

I shake my head. "Again, not possible." I pocket the letter in my jeans so I'm able to gather the rest of my books before slamming my locker shut. "He's doing this to get Rue Barlow off his back." Even so, he could have asked any other single, straight girl in this school. Or even in his grade. Hell, he could even get into an actual relationship with them. I don't know why he chose a high school junior, never mind me.

Amy stares at me with a dumbfounded look. "Oh my God, you're actually serious."

I lead her out of the building. As we push the doors open, I ask, "why wouldn't I be serious?"

Amy snorts. "Because fake relationships always lead to real feelings, At-tie. It's the principle of the thing. Even if neither of you are looking to date each other, you'd still end up catching feelings."

"Of respect?"

"No," she chastises. "Of LURVE!" At that, Amy burst out laughing as we walk to her aunt's car. Before opening the door, she sobers up. "I'm serious, At-Bat. We both know it won't last."

"Obviously," I say.

"And the last thing I want to see is Ian breaking your heart when it's over." Her violet eyes soften. "I'm only watching out for you."

"I'll be fine," I assure her. It's not going to be my first rodeo if it ever comes to that. If she only had a front row seat to the shitshow that was my love life, then she wouldn't be as worried about me. I get that I'm not exactly the most experienced when it comes to dating, romance, or really anything—my knowledge of love is mostly derived from Taylor Swift songs and my parents' PDA—but I've never minded.

Teenagers were never expected to know everything about romance. Take Jason for example: he's gone through more girlfriends than Phineas and Ferb have built obscure contraptions and he still can't figure out how to keep them. We're only sixteen! The last thing we should be worrying about is how to stay in a relationship. Shit like that is only meant for the adults.

I sigh. "I know, Ames. And I really do appreciate it but I promise you that nothing bad will happen."

Amy takes a moment to let that settle in before opening the driver's side. I hop into the passenger's seat with ease.

"Okay, I believe you," she finally answers. "But promise me that no matter what happens, that you will come to me. Jason be damned."

I smile softly. "I promise."

She holds out her pinky first. "Best friends first?"

I lock my pinky finger with hers. "Sisters second."

Chapter 20

I t's nights like these that make life worth living.

Specifically, nights spent by a bonfire roasting s'mores, and chatting with the rest of my teammates about the game that we demolished only two hours ago.

Attie and Spohie are sitting right next to me, chatting their ears off about Taylor Swift and I'm holding a marshmallow over the firepit, watching it slowly burn as I try to listen in on the conversation.

"Ian," Sophie says. "That thing is gonna burn."

I shake my head. "I like them burnt." A bit of a lie. I don't really like them completely burnt.

Just then, I move the mini pitchfork away from the fire and the marshmallow is now a little ball of fire hanging onto the stick. Attie quickly holds out her paper plate and, as if planned, the marshmallow falls onto it. "You look a little tired, Ian."

"Of course he is," Sophia chuckles. "The team just kicked Barin High's ass. Granted Barin sucked..."

"Well at least they tried." BJ interrupts as he hugs Sophia from behind. "How many s'mores has Ian burned so far?"

"Hey," I complain.

"My money's on twelve." He pats me on the back. "You are literally the only person who likes completely burnt marshmallows. That should be illegal."

"They're not completely burnt," I try to argue while reaching into the bag of marshmallows for the third time. The first one fell into the fire and the second on Attie's plate. Third time's the charm.

Attie takes the stick and stabs the marshmallow. "I'll roast this one. Braiden's right—that seems wrong."

"I like her," BJ tells me. "She has common sense."

"And I don't?"

He shakes his head and Sophia bursts out laughing at the shocked expression on my face. "No, yeah. There's a blurred line."

Attie, who sits in between me and Sophia, is covering her mouth with her free hand. The hand that is swallowed up by the sleeve of her hoodie. My hoodie. It's doing something to my brain and I can't figure out what.

But I like it. Maybe a little too much.

"WOOOOO!" An unfamiliar guy around my age, maybe older, stumbles around with a bottle of whiskey towards the firepit and proceeds to dump the whole thing into the fire. Attie pulls the marshmallow away from the fire before it can get splashed.

"Where did we even get whiskey?" BJ wonders, turning to me.

"I didn't see any in the shopping cart," I tell him, just as confused. We had to stop at a gas station on our way to the bonfire and since I'm currently the only one on the team with a fake ID, I had no choice but to accompany them. I don't even drink, for God's sake! And BJ has a fake too, but he lost it a couple months ago.

"Don't worry," the drunk guy slurs. "I accompanied it. Can't have a party without good liquor." His eyes meet Attie before letting out a low whistle. "And good women too. Hey, beautiful." He moves over and scooches between Sophia and Attie, his eyes staying on Attie's the whole time. More specifically, her body.

Oh.

Hell.

No.

"The bed of my truck is empty," he shouts. I think he's trying to whisper, based on how close he is to Attie's face but utterly failing to do so. "Enough room for the two of us." He traces one finger along Attie's arm and up to her neck. She turns away and I can see visible discomfort in her eyes.

"Hey, leave her alone," Sophia demands. "She's not available."

The drunk dude scoffs at Sophia's words. "I don't see a boyfriend around. So prove it, bitch." He puts heavy emphasis on that last word.

His entire body had shifted to face Sophia, who I know can handle her own. And BJ looks ready to enter a boxing match just to KO the drunk dude. I've heard that drunk words are sober thoughts and I can't help but wonder what guy in their right mind would call a girl a bitch? Even Chase knows his limits when he's baked.

But this guy, who reeks of whiskey, is definitely not in his right mind.

I pull Attie towards my chest and only hope that she knows what I'm trying to do. Thankfully, she rests her head on my pec and makes herself comfortable.

"Turn around."

To my surprise, the drunk dude moves his focus and his dilated pupils find me.

"Now you see him," I declare.

He gives me a once-over before rolling his eyes. "I don't really see much." His eyes focus on the girl in my arms. "You could do so much better than a lanky band geek."

Attie shivers beneath my arms and my grip on her tightens. I guess people like him are why she never really attends parties. But Sophia had convinced her to come to tonight's bonfire and you can't say no to Sophia Castro.

"Just leave me alone," she quivers.

"You heard her," I warn. "I'm not about to repeat it."

He scowls at me. "Whatever. Have fun with your little prude over here."

You can insult me all you want and I wouldn't dare bat an eye. But I'm drawing the line at Attie. Fake girlfriend or not, I will make that son of a bitch wish he didn't stumble upon our little bonfire.

I slowly remove my arms from Attie and stand up. "Come here," I gesture to the skinny young version of Jack Torrance.

"Oh shit," BJ mumbles.

"He's dead," Sophia agrees. They aren't being that secretive but that's probably because they're not even trying.

Ignoring BJ and Sophia's not-so-secretive commentary, he walks up and attempts to straighten his back and look so intimidating. He's only shorter than me—and maybe even Attie—so his presence doesn't scare me. I'm not easily terrified, anyway.

"Just a little closer," I nudge. He takes one step closer, and nearly trips over his own feet doing it. If I wasn't about to do what I intended, I would laugh. I place both hands on his shoulder, steadying him. This guy isn't going to know what hit him.

Literally.

Because in the next second, my knee makes contact with his manhood and he goes tumbling down faster than a game of Jenga.

"KO!" BJ laughs out loud.

"I was right," is all that comes out of Sophia's mouth a moment earlier, accompanying bouts of laughter.

I crouch down to his level and scowl. "You better watch your mouth or next time, there won't be one. You got that?"

Nodding, he pushes himself off the ground and hobbles back inside the beach house. The four of us watch until he disappears into the crowd. Attie takes a deep breath and lets it out. "Thank gods it's over."

"Are you okay?" I ask.

She nods, although her eyes almost say otherwise. "Yeah, I'm fine."

"Honestly, I was about to do that, too," Sophia says. "That guy made me uncomfortable."

"Uncomfortable enough to hurt him like that?" Attie's eyes widen in shock.

I laugh. "You'd be surprised." My stomach still hurts from the surprise party BJ and I threw her back in January. She can pack a mean punch with those tiny hands.

Attie nibbles on the marshmallow in her hands. With everything going on, I completely forgot about the marshmallows. But those were the last things on my mind.

"I wouldn't even wish that on my worst enemy," BJ says.

"Getting kneed?" Attie asks.

"No." Hazel eyes wide as he turns to me. "Getting Bale mad. It's a whole sight to see."

"That whole Southern 'gentleman' persona is wiped clean when he's mad," Sophie adds, with air quotes around the word gentleman. "Although, you didn't have to punch him like that."

I raise a brow. "What else could I have done?" I ask.

"Easy. You could've just kissed your girl."

At the mention of kissing, Attie nearly chokes on the last bite of her marshmallow. I rub her back in circles until the coughing stops. Did that shock her? I didn't think she had anything against kissing.

"That wouldn't have worked," I point out. "That dude was dense."

"Sometimes a little PDA can prove a point."

I look at Attie, who doesn't seem to be as comfortable. But it's only on the outside. When she brought up those rules—I still think having a time limit on a relationship is stupid, by the way—there was one little yet crucial element that we had forgotten: kissing. I'm not opposed to it but if Attie feels uncomfortable about the idea, then I won't force it on her. It wouldn't be my first rodeo but I'm not so sure about her.

"I don't believe it," Attie finally says after staying quiet for the vast majority of the conversation. Her eyes aren't on us but on her fingers as she rubs circles on the palm of her hand. She does this a lot when she's nervous, I've noticed. I hope that interaction with the drunk guy didn't shake her up too bad. Because then I'd be going back for another round.

"I really don't want to sound like a bitch right now," Sophia begins to say, a small Cheshire cat-like smile forms on her face. "But I dare you to prove me wrong."

"Soph," I warn. "We don't need to prove anything." I may have a competitive spirit but this isn't competition—it's pressure. No matter how much I would want to kiss Attie, I wouldn't do it if she wasn't down. Again, consent is important. I wouldn't be alive in this decade if it wasn't.

"Ian—"

"It's fine," Attie interrupts. "It's alright, Sophia. I'll prove it to you."

Sophia's eyes are wide at Attie's response. I don't know who's more shocked: me, Soph, or Attie.

All the while, BJ stands up from his spot and says, "this looks too intimate so I'm just gonna head inside and grab some drinks." He walks off. Well, that's one less pair of eyes on us.

My eyes drift to Attie's blue ones. The glow coming from the dimming fire isn't doing them justice at all, instead making the baby blues darker, almost like steel. "Are you okay with this?" I whisper, bringing my finger to her chin so I can see her face clearly. My eyes dart down to her rosy lips and back to her lashes. "You can back out at any time, princess."

She takes a deep breath and lets it out before inching her face closer to mine. "I'm alright, Ian. If anything, I should be warning you."

I chuckle softly. "Why?"

"Because I'm not that good at kissing."

Choosing not to retort with some sort of witty comeback or a cheesy sentence, I just go with what feels natural. I dive right in and press my lips to hers. Right then and there, everything I knew about kissing flies out the window and into the ocean breeze.

Holy shit.

It only takes her two seconds before she begins kissing me back and I'm officially done for. I begin to think on instinct and my hand makes its way to the back of her neck so I can pull her closer and deepen the kiss. It elicits a gasp out of her and I find myself smiling against her sweet lips. Of course, I knew kissing could be fun but has it always been this intoxicating?

I guess I've just been kissing the wrong girls.

She breaks the kiss after God knows how long. I open my eyes and find Attie's wide eyes and beet red face staring up at me. Her lips are a little swollen but that's normal. But her eyes... they're flooded with so many emotions that I can't keep them all straight.

What is she thinking?

"You alright, princess?" I tuck some strands of dark hair behind her ear. She nods but no sound leaves her mouth.

"Wow, even I'm blushing from that." Sophia's voice pulls me out of my stupor and Attie and I turn our heads towards Sophia.

"You asked for it," I remind her.

"I did and I kind of regret it now. No wonder you two don't do the whole 'PDA' thing." Her attention moves to Attie, who's face just turned more red than it was a second ago. A little alarming if you ask me. "Attie, are you okay?"

She nods. "Yeah, I'm fine. Just need to grab a drink of water." Attie stands up from her seat. "I-I won't be long." She basically high-tails it back inside the house, which isn't tiny but not big enough to hold as many people as it does. I'd follow her to it but my feet are rooted in the sand, unable to move.

Sophia must see whatever expression that's on my face because she stands up from her spot. "I'll go check on her. Don't worry, Bale." I'm now left alone by the fire pit, which has died sometime while I was kissing Attie. The only light coming from the back lights of the house.

My fingers merely hover over my lips for a moment before touching ever-so gently. I'd never felt this way about a kiss before in my life. Sure I've kissed girls and liked doing it—so sue me—but that rush of adrenaline that I had always searched for never came. Until now.

And the crash that follows is like the aftermath of a meteor shower. Except I'm a lonely meteor. And if things play out the way they currently are, then I might just be the only one falling. Which sucks, when given this context:

She doesn't like me that way. Attie's heart belongs to another guy, and a lucky one at that.

I know I'll just be that fake boyfriend she had in high school and if that doesn't keep me grounded then I don't know what else will.

Chapter 21

The first thing I do once I rush into the crowded beach house is head straight for the kitchen for a bottle of water. I may not be driving but that doesn't mean I'm going to drink. I'm not touching that keg with a ten-foot pole.

I wasn't completely lying when I told Ian I was thirsty but it's not why I left him by the bonfire. Flustered is just not a good look on me and I don't want to be like one of those weird, awkward girls you'd see on teen Netflix shows. And yes, maybe running like that was probably not the most ideal way to handle everything.

Neither is faking a relationship yet, here I am. At a party I would have never attended if it wasn't for his friends, kissing a guy I shouldn't be kissing. What's even stranger is that I'm enjoying almost every damn second of it. At least, the moments that transpired before my mini panic attack in this tiny kitchen.

How did Jason deal with his attacks again? It's been a long time since I last had one. Maybe it was just breathing. I hold tight onto the edge of the marble counter in front of me and close my eyes.

In, and out.

In.

And out.

Once my heart stops racing and I'm no longer in danger of reaching DEFCON Attie, I take a look around the kitchen, my eyes wandering a little too slow as it's not exactly state-of-the-art or ginormous.

I'm also not alone here. In fact, there's unfamiliar faces drinking soda and alcohol, a couple making out on the counter, and even a random guy smoking weed. The desire to not trigger my gag reflex has me out of the kitchen the moment the skunk-like scent hits my nostrils and I make my way to the couch in the living room to only bump into a tall body and basically fly into another. A pair of arms grab both my shoulders to keep me from falling to the ground. I'm about to thank the person when he speaks first.

"Whoa, there. Don't go crashing down on me right now, Ryder."

Those instincts of fear and shock are starting to kick in. Chills run down my spine at the sound of the coarse voice. Because even through the loud music, I'd recognize the voice anywhere.

Before my brain can tell me otherwise, my head tilts up and my eyes meet the dark brown orbs that belong to none other than my first attempt at getting over my crush on Derek. The tall, dark, and unfortunately handsome pothead known as Chase Hardwick.

I quickly untangle myself from him which isn't a hard task seeing as only his hands made contact with me.

"Come on, what's the rush?" He chuckles. Okay, that answers the ever-looming question: is he high? Yes, yes he is.

I can't remember a day where he isn't. For good reason, too. When he injured his foot last year, it's what he turned to. The substances, the numbness. He mostly just stuck to Mary J because it's easier to find in this part of the United States but that's not all he carries.

I would know.

Speaking of, he reaches into his front pocket and pulls out a lighter and a rolled up joint. I've had enough of him at this point and it's only been a few seconds. "I'll catch you later, Chase." No I won't.

"Come on, Athena," he drawls, placing the joint between his lips and lighting it. "Stay with me for a bit. Let's catch up, it's been a while since we last talked."

"We don't need to chat," I tell him. And for good fucking reason. I've avoided him for nearly a year now and though that streak has broken tonight, I'll continue to avoid him at every chance I have.

He pulls the joint and exhales, small puffs of light gray smoke leaving his lips. "Of course we do. You and I both know that it's bound to happen."

His last name fits him. Chase is definitely a hard ass, but I don't want to give in, like I always do. It's become a part of me and I hate that I'm almost tempted to talk.

Before I can say anything, another voice comes between us. "Hey, Hardwick! Go bother someone else your own size!"

Really, that snarky voice came from behind me. I turn around to find Sophia with her arms crossed over her cheer uniform and a hard glare pinned at Chase.

Since Chase is about as high as a kite now, he's unable to give a shit about her demands. "Come one, Castro. Stop being so uptight for once."

"Ugh!" She steps closer to me and wraps her arm around mine. "I'm not being uptight, Hard-ass. I'm being a decent person. So if you could stop acting like a stone-hard dickwad for once and leave Attie alone, that would be appreciated."

"Stone hard, maybe," he agrees, taking another drag. "But I'm not being a dick. Besides, Athena and I go way back."

Sophia raises her brows at me. I don't think she believes him but my history with Chase is probably the last thing on her mind right about now.

"She doesn't want to catch up with you, right now. Or ever. So leave her alone." Her attention then turns to me. "We can't keep our boyfriends waiting now, can we?" She winks before whisking me away from the couch. Away from my plastic water bottle—I lost track of that thing the moment it flew out of my hand. Away from Chase and though I'm a little annoyed with Sophia for what happened a couple minutes ago, I can't be more thankful that she swooped in at the right time.

Instead of leading us outside, however, she takes me up the staircase and into a significantly less crowded hallway. "Okay, I know it's none of my business but I just want to warn you really quick: stay the fuck away from Chase. I heard he drugged a girl at Ethan Haynes's party last year and though I'm not sure if that's true, I don't want anything like that to happen to you here."

My eyes widen at the warning. Not because such a thing has happened—this is high school, where it's unfortunately common no matter how fucked up—but because I, of all people, know that to be completely true.

"And secondly," she continues. "I just wanted to apologize for forcing you and Ian."

I raise a brow at her. "Why do you need to apologize?"

"I was going to finish my sentence before you jumped in and said 'I'll do it.'" She shrugs. "I'm never serious about dares."

"Well, then, why did you say it in the first place?" I ask. I would expect the whole "snarky mean girl" stereotype to come from Rue but not Sophia.

"I wasn't thinking. And clearly, you guys didn't need to kiss in order to prove a point."

"Clearly?"

Sophia nods, her dark curls bouncing as she does so. "It's obvious enough in the way Ian looks at you. Especially that kiss?" She fans herself with a perfectly manicured hand dramatically. "Damn."

"Wait, what do you mean, damn?" I ask. "The way he looks at me?"

"Yeah! It kind of reminds me of how Bray looks at me." At the mention of her boyfriend, the corners of her mouth turn up and form a giddy smile. It's only been a few days since I've met them but it's obvious that they really love each other. I've always thought that love wasn't meant for teenagers—who am I kidding, I still believe that—but Sophia and BJ might just be the one exception. It's a good thing for her.

But it's not meant for me. Sophia doesn't need to know that the relationship with Ian isn't really...well, real, for one. And another thing? It won't last forever. I've got until the end of next month (also known as the anniversary of 1989 Taylor's Version) to pull off this relationship pact and then Ian and I can go back to our normal ways.

That kiss, however? Didn't exactly feel fake to me. I never thought of myself as a good kisser but that's due to my past experiences with kissing not being so great. Why did I ever think kissing sucked? Past me definitely thought wrong.

Shit, did he think I was bad? Oh gods, I hope I wasn't. Then it'd be awkward for us both.

So many thoughts are running through my brain but I can't figure out how to regulate them. "That's some high praise," I comment.

"I'm happy for you two." Her smile turns from one of giddiness to comfort. "I'm glad he found someone like you."

Looks like I've got Sophia Castro's wax seal of approval. I wonder if that's how Hades felt when Persephone chose to stay with him. Okay, that's a bad comparison but I can't think of any other ancient Greek couple with a happy ending.

Can you? I don't frickin think so.

Okay, maybe Perseus and Andromeda—now that I think about it but that's it.

She hooks her arm with mine and leads me downstairs. "But seriously, we should probably head back outside."

"Guess you really want to get back to BJ?" I joke.

She laughs. "If anything, he's the clingy one. I wasn't here for half the school day and he wouldn't stop texting to check up on me."

Awww, that's really cute. See? That's love. Not wanting to spend a moment apart from the person you love. Meanwhile, I can handle being away from just about everyone in this beach house.

Okay, not everyone.

Sophia's becoming more of a person I would see myself talking to on a regular basis. BJ's hilarious and those two make a great pair. I know I can't stop gushing about them but that's because they're that couple who would still hold hands even when old and gray.

And then there's Ian.

I've known Ian since I was eight and he was nine. I always thought he was reckless. During games of freeze tag with our brothers, a good chunk of middle school.

Now.

But there's a side to Ian that isn't reckless but more playful. A side I got to see when we hung out on Sunday and started a mini paint battle. Even if nothing comes of this next month—and I know for a fact that nothing will change—I'll enjoy getting to know Ian a little better.

We make it outside, where BJ is sitting and drinking out of a red solo cup. Sophia lets go of my arm and sits down next to her boyfriend, resting her head on his broad shoulder.

Again, adorable.

I sit back down, grab another marshmallow and basically inhale it in one go.

"What happened to getting water?" Ian asks, eying me wearily.

I shrug before swallowing. "It literally flew away from me."

He laughs. "Since when did water bottles sprout wings?"

"Didn't you know? GMO is a thing. If grapes can taste like cotton candy, then water bottles can sprout wings and fly." I appreciate Ian trying to relieve my anxiety but it's not going to go away. Usually, I have to sleep it off before I begin to feel like my normal self again. Right now?

Call it what you want: adrenaline, butterflies, hormones. It doesn't matter.

Because it will all go away within the next morning, I'm sure of it. That's what I chant to myself in my head as I sit and watch three seniors interact with each other over a bunch of toasted marshmallows under the night sky.

In fact, that kiss plays on a continuous loop in my mind for the next NINE DAYS.

Nine days! How is that even possible? The longest any thought has been on the forefront of my mind has been six. Not even my first kiss had that much of an effect on me. And my favorite albums or quotes from TV shows have stuck in my head for that long. Either I've been severely deprived of any sexual interaction for too long, or Ian's a damn good actor.

My only other hope was to sleep it off. Again. October rolls around and though it still is hot as hellfire, all I want to do is just lay under the deep blue covers of my bed and sleep. Unfortunately, fate has other plans.

And by fate, I mean my family.

"Owl, wake up," Dad says, shaking me.

"No, I don't want to," I groan, hiding my face underneath my pillow.

"It's that time now."

"It literally just ended."

"Not that time of the month," Jason laughs.

Once every month, I am subjected to working out with my family. This includes my parents and Jason. I wouldn't be fully opposed to it if they didn't choose to wake up at the ass crack of dawn to do so. On a Sunday. Now, we may not be religious but isn't Sunday supposed to be God's day off?

"Wake me up on Monday." Sadly, I can feel my sleepiness just fly away like a bunch of cartoon birds. In case it isn't apparent, I do not like mornings.

I guess you could say I'm... a night Owl. That's a lie—I can barely stay awake at night without caffeine.

"No can do, loser." That's definitely Jason talking.

"Jason!"

"What? It's not like you never called aunt Carly a loser before, Dad."

I lift the pillow away from my face and sit up. "If I get out of bed, would you guys leave me alone? Por favor?"

Jason and Dad both nod before exiting my room. Thank the gods. I thought they would never leave. Chances are, they're probably going to wake Mom up since she, too, doesn't like waking up so early.

I grab my phone off my nightstand and shoot a text to Amy.

Me: Send help. I'm being imprisoned by my own family.

I turn my phone on the Do Not Disturb mode before grabbing whatever pair of sweatpants and t-shirt that I can find. A few minutes later, we start jogging. Yes, we're that kind of family. Because our schedules are so busy with school, work, and other activities, we hardly even have time to sit down and eat dinner. Dad's biggest fear is having us all drift away when Jason and I get older, so one Sunday a month, we are forced to get up and drag our asses all over our little neighborhood.

If we lived near the beach, the jogs would have been much more enjoyable. But the beach is a twenty minute drive and California traffic is complete shit.

I'm falling pretty behind since it's hard to catch up with Mom and Jason, who run like some minotaur is chasing them. Dad stays behind for my sake and even though we're far behind he still jogs at a steady pace next to me. I see Dad's lips move but due to Gracie Abrams singing Where Do We Go Now? in my ear, I can't hear what he says. I take one headphone out of my left ear. "Can you repeat that?"

"How's life?"

I shrug. "Decent. I think I'm learning too much about my physics teacher." I hate the subject but Mr. Ali's pretty cool. A decent guy.

"Anything else?"

I rummage through the past week. "I gave you the money back, right? For the movie on Saturday?"

"Yeah. Is that all?"

"I know you're wanting to ask about Ian," I give in. "He's fine, Dad. The game on Friday wasn't the greatest."

"Are you happy with him?" His eyes, which are so similar to my own that it's no doubt that we're related, are slightly cautious. What does he have to be so worried about? Oh right, he believes the whole ruse. It's in his right to be protective of his only daughter when she starts dating for the first time.

To his knowledge, at least.

"I just don't want you to get hurt," he says.

"I'll be fine, Dad," I assure him. Why does everyone think I'm going to hurt? Even Amy, who knows the truth, is worried for me when she shouldn't be. I won't be heartbroken or anything because I know what to expect. As soon as Halloween rolls around, everything's gonna go back to normal and I'll have some "experience" under my belt for the college dating scene. There isn't that much of a difference anyway.

"But it's your first boyfriend," he points out. "I remember when I first started dating—"

"Mom?" I interrupt. She was Dad's first for everything.

He nods. "I wasn't in the right headspace when we first met, you know." He stops jogging and we take a moment to breathe. "It's important that you know what you're going into. From what your brother's told me..." he trails off before he can finish that sentence. A pointed look and a raised brow in my direction are enough indication as to what he's trying to convey.

I hold back an eye roll. It hasn't happened much but the first thing that has come to mind when people talk about my quote-on-quote relationship with Ian is his reputation. Yes, I get it—he's made out with a lot of girls. I'm almost as pure as a daisy with only two-ish guys under my belt. You don't exactly need to rub it in my face.

"I'm in the right headspace, Dad," I say. "Although, if you keep asking these questions..."

He holds up both of his hands to surrender. "Alright," he laughs. "I'll stop now. But if that son of a bitch breaks your heart, I will break all two hundred and six of his bones. Without even breaking a sweat."

My eyes widen. "Dad!" He's joking, right?

My dad laughs again. "Only, kidding, owl." He pulls me in for a quick hug before letting go. "Mostly." We both stare at the trail in front of us for a moment before turning to each other. "Do you think we can catch up to them?"

I shake my head. "Not likely."

"Well, we can try."

So we do. Dad and I start running again and even though we tire our-selves out so we could catch up to Mom and Jason—who don't even look like they're breaking a sweat when we finally reach them—I still pat myself on the back for trying.

My legs are about to give out by the time we get back home. I flop onto the bed, not giving a damn about how sweaty I am and unlock my phone to see a message notification. I check to see who it's from and my eyes bulge out of my sockets when I find the sender.

Ian: Need rescuing, princess?

What? Huh? I scroll up to previous messages and—oh, shit! I acciden-tally sent that text to Ian. Why did my sleep-deprived little ass do that?

Me: Sorry! That text was meant for Amy.

Ian: You sure? Because I'm getting my climbing tools ready. I'm not sure how high that tower is.

If I had a nickel for every time Ian's said something cheesy to me, I'd have enough for a Starbucks drink. This dude is layering on the cheese. Well, bring it on—two can play that game.

Me: Put them away, Ian. Can you even see the top of the tower?

Ian: Low blow, princess. Low. Blow.

Ian: Enough said. Are you doing alright?

Me: Yeah, just dying over here, no big deal

Ian: ???

Me: Went on a run.

Ian: Willingly?

Me: NO

Ian: Thought so.

I almost take offense to that before realizing how right he is. I hate working out in public. I celebrated not having to take gym class anymore because California high schools only require you to do four semesters. I've complained more about the pacer test than about the difference between sine and cosine.

Me: I'm going to pretend that wasn't rude.

Ian: Was I wrong?

Me: No.

Ian: Then the truth is never rude.

Me: Who told u that?

Ian: u did, princess.

Me: Huh. Guess I taught you well.

I plug my phone back in after waiting a minute for a response. The bubbles seem to appear, and then disappear. As if he's trying to follow that up with something else. I can't explain it in its entirety but I'm starting to feel the awkward tension that's been looming over us since that party begin to dissipate.

After the messaging bubble disappears for the third time, I hop into the shower and get changed. The rest of the morning isn't so bad, thankfully. Waking up early usually means Mom's cooking breakfast—a rarity, indeed—and after all that, the four of us part ways. Well, not really part ways since none of us leave the house.

I'm in the middle of painting when I hear the sound of knocking on my bedroom door. No one in this family knows how to knock, so I wonder who it could be. I place my paintbrush away and hop off the stool I've been standing on and head towards the door. I turn the knob and open it just a crack to see Amy holding a huge tote bag.

"Ames." I raise a brow. I don't remember making any plans to hang out today. "What are you doing?"

Amy opens the rest of the way and walks inside. "You don't remember?" She sits herself down on the floor and empties the contents of her tote bag.

"We planned to make friendship bracelets for the concert-movie...thing you're renting."

"That was today?" I facepalm myself. "I thought we were doing it tomorrow."

"Nope. I vividly remember you saying we'd do it on Sunday. Last I checked, that was today."

I sit myself down across from Amy, shaking my head.

"Hey, it's alright," Amy assures. "We've all gotten our days mixed up. Nothing to get so upset about."

"I feel bad," I groan. "I completely forgot about all of this."

"At least you didn't have to pay for all the supplies." Amy starts unraveling the string. She reaches a desired length before taking a pair of scissors and cutting it off. She then hands it to me, and I barely fiddle with the ends of it before standing back up. I need coffee and chips to power through. "How long do you think this will take?"

She shrugs. "Not too long, right? I mean they're only bracelets."

"Good point."

Chapter 22

Oh how fucking wrong we were.

I was smart to get myself a cup of coffee and a bag of jalapeño chips before starting on the first bracelet. Because in the span of two hours, Amy and I have made a total of two bracelets.

"Stupid thin string," I mutter as it snaps for the sixth time. "Why can't you just stay together?"

"Maybe cut a longer piece of string?" Amy suggests. "Or tie it more than twice?"

"I tried that but it isn't helping."

She then hands me another strand. "Maybe use twice as much string?"

So I do. I remove all the beads and move them to the new string. After tying it—double knot, of course—I cheer out loud, over the music blasting from Amy's phone. "Amy, you are a genius!"

"I know. Duh." She flips her curls over her shoulder and goes back to her bracelet.

I laugh. "What kind of store sells such weak packs of string?"

Amy ties off her second bracelet. She managed to create cherries by tying some strings together or some other tedious process that I could not be bothered to do myself. "Michaels. They were having a two for one deal when I bought the beads."

"But was there a better string than this?" I laugh, picking up the roll off the floor and holding it up.

Amy only shrugs before grabbing her tote bag and pulling out her light pink polaroid. She's had that camera since we were ten, given to her as a birthday gift from Mary, and it's still in pretty good condition. Even now, she always wants to take polaroids of us on days like this, when we're just hanging out. "This is actually a pretty good pose," she laughs. "Smile!"

I laugh at the exact moment the flash goes off. She takes another. "Ames—" I begin to ask.

"Don't worry, I'll give you one of the pictures when they're done developing," she responds while watching the picture come out the top. The world of digital imaging is so popular and much more convenient these days and Amy still uses it but always prefers her polaroid. "I should also point out that you're stretching the string to the breaking point. Literally."

I place the tiny beads down on the paper plate next to me. We've been working on the carpet floor of my bedroom and since the beads are so tiny, it made sense to use plates to keep track. It was Amy's idea—type A and all that—so I didn't even bother to question it.

"Attie, did you happen to see my—" Jason's voice comes to an abrupt stop when he sees what and who's laying on my bedroom floor. "What is going on?"

"Go away Jason," I say, waving him off. "We're debriefing right now."

That doesn't actually brush him off. Instead, he walks into the room and jumps onto my bed, resting his head on my pillow. "Well make sure to include me. It's been a while since we've done a debrief."

"You want to be a part of girl debriefing?" Amy raises a brow at him. I get it, since it's been a while since Jason's done one with us. They end up turning into something similar to class lectures because we end up teaching Jason what to do and what not to do with his girlfriends. Yet, they've never lasted for more than a month.

Then again, he's also the one who always ends it.

"I need something to help me ask Kelly to homecoming," he retorts, which catches me by surprise since he said it so casually. "So, what should I do?"

"Couldn't you ask her friends?" I ask.

"I tried but none of them really like me." He runs one hand over his face. Wow, he must really like her then. "And it's her first homecoming so I want to make it special."

"A poster could work," Amy suggests. "But Kelly doesn't strike me as someone who loves grand gestures."

"Don't girls love little gestures that are catered to them specifically?"

"He's right," I tell Amy. "I know I'm a sucker for that." Like when someone remembers my favorite smoothie, or my favorite color. Kind of similar to what Ian's done. Maybe he should follow Ian's blueprint. Because even for a fake boyfriend, he's doing a spectacular job at making me think about him nonstop.

I snap another string in half and beads go flying everywhere. "Shit," I mutter.

"Woah there, sis." Jason removes the two halves of the string from my grasp and places them into his pockets. "Are you okay?"

I nod. "Yeah, I'm fine."

He stares at the scattered beads and broken strings on my carpet. "And the inventor of the friendship bracelet rests happily in her grave."

"Jason, could you leave us be?" Amy begs him. "We still need to finish our debriefing session."

"I thought we were still working on it," he wonders, all confused.

"No, we paused our debriefing session so we can start a debriefing session with you. Now that's over, your sister and I can finish our debriefing session. You got all that?"

Jason blinks once. Twice. Finally, he just hops off my bed and walks away in silence, muttering to himself, "I'll never understand that shit," which causes Amy to burst into laughter.

"Oh, that always works," Amy chuckles before wiping a tear from her eye. It wasn't that funny to me but that sentence basically went in one ear and out the other for my brother.

She sobers up and puts on a straight face, which is almost similar to her smile. "Okay, what's going on with you? You've been in a funk for days."

I don't answer.

"Is it Ian?"

I look down at my hands and fiddle with whatever tiny invisible bead is stuck to the palm, acting like I didn't hear exactly what she said. Which, in her mind, only answers the question. Amy gets up from her spot on the floor to close the door behind me before sitting back down. "What happened? You're telling me everything."

I hesitate. Should I really do it?

Fuck it.

"So," I begin. "Remember that party you didn't go to because Carter was visiting?"

She nods.

"Well..." I lay everything out on the table. Almost everything, since I leave out my mini interaction with Chase. I don't plan on telling her about it in the near future—or ever. It's one thing to make out with your fake boyfriend for show but another to run into your sort-of ex right after.

An ex that your best friend had no idea even existed in the first place.

"You WHAT?" Amy basically screams. "Oh my gosh, it happened! A week after it started, too." she laughs to herself. "That usually happens towards the end."

"I know, I know," I groan, leaning my back against the door. "But things are so awkward now."

"How?" She raises a blond brow. "Was the kiss really bad?"

"Far from it!" I wail. "I literally ran away from him just after it happened." Too embarrassing to recall but the awkwardness had to start somewhere.

"It was a panic attack, At-Bat. Those things happen."

"You've never had one before," I point out. I've seen Amy cry watching movies and over things. She's been really nervous about a few things but I've never seen her in the midst of a panic attack. Meanwhile, I nearly had one when I wrote that letter to Derek and slipped it into Ian's locker.

And again when Ian kissed me.

"Yes, I have," she tells me. "I used to get them all the time before I met you."

"Really?"

She nods. "That time before we met in kindergarten was probably the worst few months of my life."

"I'm sorry," I say. "Do you want to talk about it?"

Amy shakes her head. "This is about you, not me. Attie, anxiety from your first kiss isn't uncommon." If only she knew that it wasn't my first kiss. That happened a year ago.

"I remember my first kiss with Carter," she continues. "I was so nervous at the party when we got picked for seven minutes in heaven but he made sure I was okay with it. He didn't force me to do something I didn't want to but... you know what happened." I do, since that was all she had talked about for an entire night because Carter had asked her out immediately after.

I wasn't the one who initiated the kiss—Ian was. And I went along with it for reasons I don't fully understand. I've heard about soul-shattering kisses in the books that Amy talks about but I've always believed that the author was overreacting or some shit.

"So the point is..."

"Right." Amy clears her throat. "Maybe you should just talk to him. That could work?"

"How?" I throw my hands in the air. "That hasn't worked in the past nine days."

"It could work as long as you don't go into DEFCON Attie." Of course she would bring that up.

"I did not go into DEFCON Attie," I argue. Jason came up with that back in middle school and now he and Amy tease me about it mercilessly.

I'm met with a raised brow.

"Maybe a little," I resign. DEFCON Five maybe.

"He probably didn't notice, anyway. Ian doesn't strike me as someone who's super confrontational about things, so it's not like he's just going to storm his way up the stairs in full-on book boyfriend mode, demanding that he needs to talk to you."

Just as the words leave Amy's mouth, a knock sounds at the door.

"Not now Jason!" I yell.

"He's not here, princess."

Ian's voice coming from the other side of the door halts my breathing for a moment. I feel my eyes widen and I notice Amy's eyes go wide as well. Except, I'm shocked while my best friend looks way too excited for me. Whatever deity that's watching over us definitely has a sense of humor for listening to Amy's words and summoning him.

"Do you still need rescuing?" His voice calls.

Amy raises a brow in confusion and I just wave it off. "No, I'm fine!" When really, I'm practically paralyzed from the waist below in embarrassment and surprise.

"Can you open the door then?"

I count to three in my head before standing up to grab something from the drawers of my nightstand. I place it in the pocket of my overalls before turning my attention to the door. Here goes nothing. I turn the knob and open it to see Ian, dressed all casually in a pair of gray pleated shorts and a plain red shirt. On anyone else, I would have brushed it off but I guess my senses are heightened because I can't help but notice how different it is to what he normally wears.

Without climbing gear, no less.

But the next words that come out of his mouth bring me back to reality. "Can we talk?"

That's never good.

Chapter 23

"R ight now?"

I glance behind her shoulder to see her friend Amy watching the interaction. She's sitting on the floor but she might as well be on the edge of her seat if this was a movie.

"Yep," I answer Attie. "But alone." Can't risk her friend finding out about us.

She nods to Amy before stepping out of her room and closing the door. Attie then looks down the hallway, even though it's pretty empty. Jason had left almost after I arrived so I don't understand who she could be watching out for.

She's silent the entire time. Even the sounds of her breathing are quiet. Finally, she opens the door to Jason's room and motions for me to enter. "We can talk here."

We make our way inside and I close the door behind us. Since Jason's chaotic as all hell, it's an odd surprise to find his room clean and unsettlingly neat. It doesn't bother Attie though, not as she reaches into her pocket and pulls out a fake spider before hiding it under the covers.

The same fake spider I remember seeing in her locker only a couple of weeks ago.

"Is this seriously why we came here?" I ask.

She shrugs. "I needed to get rid of that thing somehow." Attie covers it up and neatens the bed as if it had been never touched before sitting down. I stay standing. Attie takes a deep breath and exhales before asking, "so what did you come over to talk about?"

I place both hands in the pocket of my shorts, and Attie's eyes follow the movement, resting on my leg. Her pale blue eyes dart from my face, back to my leg, and then back to me. She must have noticed the phases of the moon on my leg. In the past year and a half, I've noticed that Attie's the only one who's ever really paid any attention to both my tattoos.

I can ask her about that later. I've got more important things in mind. "Are you okay, princess?"

My question catches Attie off-guard. Her eyes are wider than normal and her face turns a bright shade of pink. This only answers my question and Attie hadn't even said a word.

"Why would you ask that?" Her voice went up a notch. Yeah, something is definitely up.

"You've been acting pretty weird for the last few days." Very standoffish. Not to be critical but she hardly even talked to me until this morning when she sent that accidental text. It was the first thing I woke up to and I even found it a little odd. Even then, I just knew something had to be wrong. But couldn't she have just talked to me about it? I wouldn't want anyone, especially her, to avoid it. She still wrote me the letter she had promised—once a week, on Fridays—but aside from that, she's been a little avoidant.

"What do you mean weird?"

"Weird since the bonfire." I know I've reached the tipping point because as soon as those words leave my mouth, Attie's face turns even brighter, something I didn't think was possible. It confirms my main suspicion.

I sit down on Jason's bed, placing my hand on Attie's shoulder and rubbing it in circles. "You know that I won't judge you, right? I promise," I tell her in a soft voice.

Attie closes her eyes. "Okay, fine."

"You'll tell me?"

"You're right," she answers. "But it has nothing to do with you."

"You sure?" It sort of feels like she's taking it out on me. I was a little worried because it reminded me of my parents. I was only eight when they divorced but I still vividly remember when the house would stay eerily quiet for days at a time. Like a burning match or until a star dies. The arguments burned brighter until they exploded and left nothing but destruction in its wake.

"It's not you, Ian," she assures me. "It's all me."

"Careful, princess," I warn playfully. "That sounds like a breakup. Wait, were you—"

She shakes her head. "No. I want to see this whole thing through."

I breathe a sigh of relief. I don't know why I'm relieved that she's not going to end this whole charade. "Then is it the..." I trail off because she would definitely know what I'm talking about whether I finished that sentence or not.

"A little," she mutters. I think back to the words she had said mere seconds before I kissed her.

If anything, I should be warning you.

Because I'm not that good at kissing.

And it all clicks.

She really wasn't annoyed with me or anything. It really is her. She probably believed that I thought the kiss had sucked when it was really the opposite. I tuck a piece of dark hair behind her ear as my mind thinks about how I could prove her wrong without making anything more awkward.

I can't claim to understand how her mind functions. Or even understand why she's acting like this. I only have what's in front of me and what she can show. "Attie, it's alright."

Her head turns to me with a hint of surprise on her face. I never use her first name—haven't done so for years. I won't lie, it even felt weird for me.

"Pay attention to what I'm going to say next, alright?" I wait for a nod of confirmation before I begin. "You have absolutely nothing to worry about. Do you hear me? Nothing."

"But it was so weird," she complains, burying her face in her hands.

I pry them off her face. "I didn't think it was weird."

"Really?"

"Yeah." I lift her chin up with my index finger to get a better view of her face. She's not crying, which is a good sign. "And if it helps, you are not a bad kisser."

She laughs lightly. "You remember that?"

I nod. "Honestly, it was better than most of the girls I've kissed."

"Ian!" She scolds but that beautiful bright smile of hers comes out and I already feel a little more light. "That was a little rude."

I shrug. "It's the truth. And you know I'm a man of my word, princess."

"That you are," she agrees. After fiddling with her fingers for a moment, she asks, "why aren't you so worried about it?"

I shrug. "Because it's already happened." I won't tell her that I've still thought about that kiss, even nine days after it happened. Or the fact that she tasted like mangoes. "We can't change the past, princess. So what's the point in fretting about it?"

Attie lets that settle in her mind for a bit. "I guess you're right."

"You guess?" I feign shock. "Of course I'm right! I always am."

She pats my shoulder. "Keep telling yourself that, four-eyes."

I shake my head. She really needs to think of a new nickname. For this fake relationship, that's why. No other reason. "Are we good, then? No stressing out about it?"

She sighs. "Fine. I won't go into DEFCON Attie."

I tilt my head slightly. "What?"

"Not important." She waves a hand to dismiss it. "I promise I won't overthink it."

I ruffle the top of her head. "There's my princess." I get up off the bed and open the door slightly. I look to find just about nothing. Honestly, I would have expected Amy to rest her ear by the door so she could hear the entire conversation. Or even Jason.

Speaking of...

I turn to Attie. "Why the spider? Didn't he prank you with that already?" It seems a little redundant.

She shrugs. "You reap what you sow, dude. Jason is terrified of spiders, so imagine how he'll react to finding one in his bed."

I laugh, because she's right about one thing: Jason will scream his lungs out of his body.

The two of us walk out of his room and back into Attie's, where Amy seems to be in the middle of a phone call.

"It's alright, Carter," she is saying. "You can still go next year. And to prom."

There's a moment of silence before Carter's voice is heard. "I know. I gotta go, Ames. Talk later?"

"Okay, bye." She hangs up and lightly tosses her phone onto the bed, which bounces off the mattress and hits the floor with a light thud. Her shoulders are slumped and she looks a little defeated.

"Ames, what's wrong?" Attie asks her friend.

She looks up to find us standing by the door. "Cater just told me he couldn't make it to homecoming this year after all."

As she sits herself down on the floor next to Amy, Attie wraps one arm over her friend's shoulder. "I'm sorry, Amy. Hey, at least you'll have fun with us this year."

"I know," Amy says. "But I was really excited for this one."

Attie's eyes bounce to me, signaling for help. I don't know exactly what to say, since I've always gone stag at dances and never really been on a date. I also was never fond of Amy's boyfriend. His head was basically outside the exosphere and a lot of the newbies were intimidated by him.

Amy's head swivels in my direction and I'm one placed in the spotlight, so all I can do is shrug. "There's always prom?"

I think that was the right thing to say—I'm not an expert on the opposite sex, I'll admit—because Amy lets out a chuckle. "That's true." She picks up a bead and some string from the plastic plate in front of her. "Anyway, you guys were out for a while."

"Yeah." I place my hands in the pockets of my shorts. "She wanted to plant a fake spider in Jason's room."

"Seriously?" She faces Attie. "You know he's gonna freak, right?"

"Then he shouldn't have had Derek put it in my locker." Attie shrugs before reaching for the box of beads in front of her.

I sit myself down on the floor. "What are you girls doing?"

"Making friendship bracelets," Amy answers while poking a red bead through the hole in the middle with the string. I knew they were close, but aren't those for kids or something?

"It's for this movie we're gonna watch on Saturday," she fills in.

"You need to make them for a movie?" I'm extremely confused. "Are you selling them?"

"No, we're trading them." Attie explains to me the whole Taylor Swift movie that I've been seeing on Instagram. I knew Attie loved her music but I didn't know the extent of it until now.

"Oh, I thought it was a little cult-ish," I begin to say.

Attie's jaw drops. "It's not—"

I hold a hand out, gesturing for her to let me finish. "But," I continue. "It's kind of adorable." Just like her.

Attie smiles at that and if I could bottle it up just for myself, I would. She seriously has the prettiest smile.

Amy hands me some string and I just stare at it in my hand. "What am I supposed to do with this?"

"I don't know, make a bracelet? You're still here, so might as well make yourself useful."

I look at Attie, who is focused on stringing some very small beads together and as confused as I am, I just try to follow what she's doing. Halfway through, the string snaps into two and I'm a little frustrated.

I hear giggles. "Look at that. Your boyfriend's first broken string."

"Yeah, yeah, take a photo Amy. Maybe it'll last longer."

"I know you're joking but I'm really tempted."

I take one half of the broken string and try again but the beads keep on falling out the other end. "How do people do this?"

Attie shakes her head but I can see her covering her mouth with her free hand, holding back any laughter. "Oh you poor thing." Yeah, poor thing. Totally.

I come to get some peace of mind and stay to be insulted by my fake girlfriend and her best friend. Again, how my life has become.

"Here, let me help." She makes her way next to me and grabs both pieces of string and sets them off to the side before grabbing a huge roll of string and some leather. "You need a longer piece of string so you can tie off the ends."

I watch Attie at work, grabbing a bunch of tiny beads from the plastic container filled with them. Next to the box are a few bracelets that had possibly been made before I had arrived. All of them have references that

I'm not familiar with. What really catches my eye however is a red and black bracelet.

I pick it up and observe it. Half black, half red, and in between the colors is gorgeous, in black, bold letters.

"Did you make this for me, princess?" I slip the bracelet over my wrist. It's a little snug but I don't mind it.

She looks over from her string. When she notices the bracelet I slipped on, her blue eyes widen. "Ian..."

"I'm keeping this on," I tell her.

"That thing looks like it's about to snap," she points out. "Your wrists are too big."

"No such thing," I huff as I play with one of the red beads. "It fits fine."

"What about games? Don't you need to take them off?"

I shrug. "Coach doesn't really pay attention. If this bracelet wins us Friday's game, then I'm never taking it off. It'll be my good luck charm." Friday night's game was literal hell. I've had worse games in the past few years but I was really hoping for an undefeated season.

"I don't think you need a good luck charm, Ian." she smiles shyly before bringing her focus back onto the bracelet. Meanwhile, I'm pretty sure I can feel my cheeks heat up. Was that a compliment? I think it was. Flirting? I don't think Attie flirts.

But then why do I feel a little giddy? I've been complimented before but I've never felt like this.

"And that's how you do it." She holds up the bracelet, made of a multitude of colors. It's so bright that it's almost hurting my eyes as she slips it on her wrist. "Now you try."

She hands me the string and immediately I know what to make. "Hold out your wrist for me, princess."

Chapter 24

I did not have "making friendship bracelets with my fake boyfriend" on my Sunday bingo card.

I also did not have "Ian stealing my favorite bracelet" on that same imaginary card—especially the first one that had not snapped on me. But today is filled with a load of surprises.

Like this one: me holding out my left wrist for Ian to measure out how much string he needs to use.

Is he making me a bracelet?

That seems about right.

He doesn't ask me anything else but as soon as he catches me staring, he stops. "Close your eyes."

I raise a brow. "Why would I need to do that?"

"It's a surprise. Trust me."

I don't close my eyes but I lay down and pay attention to the stars on the ceiling. Even though the painting is technically done, I always go back and add more little stars. You can never have too many, right? One of these days, I will have filled it completely before moving off to college. I can only hope.

I don't remember how long it's been before I feel a hand grab my wrist and slip a beaded bracelet on. "You can look now, princess."

I don't get up from the floor so I hold out my wrist in front of me and gasp. It alternates with blue and white—my two favorite colors—and eight letters that spell out princess. I've been using Taylor Swift songs for all of my bracelets but I somehow prefer the one on my wrist to all the others Amy and I have made.

I guess I have a new favorite.

And a whole other set of butterflies bussing around in my stomach.

"Now you have your own good luck charm," he says in a humorous tone, lying down next to me. "Wow."

"Yeah, I know. It's a lot."

He nods. "Was this here the last time I came over?"

"Uh huh. I spent a good chunk of summer working on it."

"I can see that." He doesn't say anything else, only continues to look up. I notice his eyes bounce from one little star to the other and since I know he's not an art critic, I can't help but wonder what he could possibly be looking for.

"Did I forget something?" I ask out of panic.

"Just wondering why there aren't any constellations."

Wait, what?

"Constellations?"

He turns onto his side to face me. "Yeah, constellations."

"Like what?"

"Well, Ursa major is definitely important. Can't be a night sky without it." I barely recognize the name of any constellation. And I think my confusion definitely shows because his face turns a little red as he mutters, "the big dipper."

Oh.

Wait, how does he know this? I mean, I know Ian's smart—anyone who even understands the concepts of physics is automatically a genius in my book—but I'm starting to realize that Ian Bale knows a lot more than he lets on. From the tattoo on his leg to the names of random constellations that even I never thought existed, I can't help but wonder:

What else does he know?

"Oh he is totally in love with you," Amy laughs just as he leaves the room. We're still resting on the carpet of my bedroom floor and I have yet to get up.

"No he isn't." Deny, deny, deny. It's not denying if it's the truth. He isn't in love with me—he's just pretending to be since he thinks that Amy believes the whole ruse. I didn't tell him otherwise because Amy made me swear to secrecy.

"At-Bat, it's so obvious." She starts holding up fingers for each reason. "He asked you to do this fake dating ruse." That's one. "He has a nickname for you." Two. "And let's not forget that he just sat with us for a whole hour just to make bracelets." Three.

"That could mean anything," I point out. "We're only friends, Ames."

"Friends do not tell you that you're a good kisser."

My eyes widen at that declaration.

She rolls her eyes. "I was listening to you guys talk until Carter called." Why does that not surprise me?

"It's not like your first kiss was bad."

Amy lets out a belly laugh, as if that's the dumbest thing I've ever said. "Oh no, it was terrible."

"I thought you liked kissing Carter."

"Oh I do," she tells me as her laugh dies down. "But he wasn't my first."

"I'm trying to find a point to this," I say.

"Right." Amy clears her throat. "Like or love, he definitely has some sort of feelings for you."

"And that feeling is friendship." I start picking at the tufts of my carpet, specifically one with dried blue paint.

"Not in the way he looks at you."

I look up at the serious expression glued to Amy's face. "No."

But she nods vehemently. "I've read about this before. Personally, I think it's a kind of placebo effect. The more you pretend that something exists, the more likely it is to come true."

"That sounds a lot like manifestation."

"That's different."

"Regardless, this isn't a romance novel, Amy. I can go through the next three weeks and be just fine," I assure her.

"You say that as you play with the bracelet he made you." I look down at my hands and realize that she's right. I am fiddling with the blue bead. I drop the bracelet from my grasp though it still hangs onto my wrist. "I did say I was worried about this. Either one of you falling in love."

I raise a brow.

"One of you is going to end up heartbroken. I just hope you know what you're doing, Attie because those pieces you'll be picking up are." She places one hand over my wrist.

"I promise, I know what I'm doing. I think you might be drinking too many chai lattes if you're starting to doubt me."

She shakes her head in defiance. "No such thing."

I laugh as I look back down at my wrist and play with my bracelet. Do I know what I'm doing? I think that answers the question if I'm starting to doubt myself two weeks in.

Maybe I'm not developing feelings of love but an interest in who Ian really is. I'm no detective but I wouldn't consider myself someone who goes for the surface. If I want to get to know someone, then I want to know all of them. Flaws and all.

Chapter 25

"Hey, Bale!" Ethan catches up to me as I'm walking out the locker room. "The rest of the team's heading out to Suze's tonight. Wanna join?"

"Why there?" Most of the guys don't really go there to hang out after practice on account of how crowded it usually gets.

"I don't know about the rest of the guys but I'm going to embarrass Sierra while she's working." He chuckles. "You down to join me?"

I'll admit: it does sound entertaining. I would totally be up for something like that if I was even in the mood.

"Sorry, dude," I tell him. "Maybe next time."

My eyes unwillingly move to the bleachers. Ethan's head swivels in that direction. "Ohhh, I get it. Guess our quarterback is too good for some shenanigans now that he has a girlfriend. I swear you're turning into BJ."

I shake my head. "Never."

Ethan shakes his head and starts walking backwards. "Keep telling yourself that in a few months." He then turns around and starts his trek to the parking lot.

The stadium's parking lot isn't that big, so it's easy to find Ethan and a bunch of other guys hopping into their cars and driving off. I know I should probably hang out with them, it being the one year I have to make the most of, but I know there's always the next time.

I head over to the bleachers where I find Attie, sitting all by her lonesome. I noticed her during practice, when she's usually accompanied by one of her friends while waiting for me but I guess today's not one of those days. I sit down in front of her and she doesn't bat an eye. Probably because she's too focused on her arm.

She makes some strokes with a marker on her forearm before placing the lid on top. Attie doesn't notice me until she places the marker back in her bag. "How long were you sitting there?"

"Not that long." My eyes move to her arm, where she's drawn a pretty damn intricate, star-shaped flower with a few large leaves. I want to say that it's a rose because that's the only flower I know but I might be wrong. "No sketchbook today?"

She shakes her head. "I ran out of blank pages last night."

"That hasn't stopped you." I point to her left arm, which also still has the bracelet I made her earlier this week. "You're still wearing it."

She nods to my wrist, her cheeks turning pink. "I could say the same thing about you."

"Princess, I did tell you that I'm not taking this off." And I didn't. I hardly take it off my wrist these days. I only bluffed about it being a good luck charm but it's actually working for me because so far, nothing has turned to shit this week. I've been killing it at practice, I finished half of my college applications, and—the best part—nobody's been on my ass about anything else.

"I know," she giggles. "I didn't think you were serious."

"Oh, I am always serious." I raise a brow Dwayne Johnson-style, which has her laughing and nearly falling off her seat. And because Attie's laughter is too contagious, I can't help but join her.

Eventually, our laughter dies down. "But seriously, how is running out of paper possible? Are your drawings too big?"

She shrugs. "I just used it a lot. I thought I could go a whole day without drawing but..."

"Impossible task, I presume?"

She nods. "You presume correctly."

It doesn't surprise me that she can't go an entire day without drawing. At least, not completely. Even looking at the flower, I can correctly assume she wasn't just born with the ability to draw. Talent like hers takes time to develop.

So I roll up the sleeves of my shirt and hold out my arm for her. "Here."

Attie stares at my arm blankly. "What do you want me to do with it?"

"If you need a blank canvas to practice your art, then I'll gladly let you practice on me."

Her eyes light up. "Really?"

I shrug. "Why not? I'm perfect for it." I wink. Plus, it could give me ideas for the next tattoo I plan to get. Yes, I already have a couple but they're addicting. Sue me.

She fishes the marker back out from her bag and uncaps it. "Okay, but stay still. I don't want to ruin it."

At this point in our lives, Attie should know that I'm not picky about my style choices so I give her free range. She grabs onto my hand and chills run up my arm and down my spine, though I try not to show it. Who would have thought that I would be spending my Thursday evening getting temporarily inked?

Not me.

I watch the sunset as Attie's marker moves across my arm. After a few minutes have passed, I take a quick glance at her progress and—

Whoa.

That looks fucking sick! Attie chose to draw a dragon, wrapped around my forearm. A very detailed dragon outlined in black. I can feel my jaw drop as I watch each tiny detail being added and I have to force myself to look away. Okay, I knew she was talented but damn.

"Maybe I should have you design my next tattoo," I mutter.

She chuckles. "Maybe not. I can't be trusted to do that."

"Sure you can. In another world, I could totally see you as a tattoo artist."

"Me?" She laughs. "I specialize in child-like cartoons, not detailed designs. Besides, those are permanent."

"Nothing I've never done before." I can already imagine getting that dragon on my arm one day. Maybe not while I'm in high school but in the far future. "So, what got you into drawing in the first place?"

She shrugs. "Boredom, really. Jason and I were five and anytime he went to the pool, I couldn't join him and had to stay home with my dad."

"Neglectful parents?" I ask.

Attie shakes her head and pushes a strand of dark hair away from her face before resuming. "The exact opposite, really. I couldn't go to the pool because I'm, like, severely allergic to chlorine and nearly died the last time I stepped inside of one." Her eyes bounce to mine and back to my arm. "It's a little embarrassing."

"Nah, allergies aren't embarrassing." Granted, I'm not allergic to anything. "Derek's allergic to blueberries."

A soft chuckle escapes her lips. "That sucks. I love blueberries."

"Me too."

"Anyway, I couldn't stand still for the life of me one day, so Dad gave me his stash of coloring pens, a huge stack of paper and told me to go crazy." Her smile softens as she recounts the memory. "I wasn't great at first but I kept on trying and... well, the rest is history."

A few minutes later and she's done. I take the time to admire the dragon on my arm. "This looks bad-ass, princess."

She blushes. "I'm glad you like it."

I love it. That's what I really want to tell her, what I really mean but I can't get the words out because my phone starts to ring. And not just any ringtone—the one Derek set for himself.

The Star Wars theme song.

I hold back a groan and press the green button, placing the phone screen to my ear. I don't even get in a hello before.

"Where the hell are you?" My brother basically yells. So loud that I have to cover my left ear.

"Why? I've still got time. I'm with—"

"Yeah, I know who you're with but hurry up! I'm about to start the call."

The call? I check the time on the screen and—shit, I'm late! I guess I lost track of time with Attie.

"Shit! How long can you stall for?" I ask. Well, really beg.

"Five minutes, but you better hurry up, nuisance."

"I'll try my best." I hang up the phone and let out a breath. I am so going to be late but for the first time in, well, ever, I don't really care.

"That sounded urgent," she comments before grabbing her bag and standing up from the bleachers.

"Wait, you're going now?" I didn't think she had a ride back and was planning to offer her.

"I was just going to text Jason." She shrugs. "No big deal."

"Here, let me drive you." I grab her bag from her shoulder.

"Ian..."

"Let me point out that I'm already here, with a car available," I remind her as we walk towards the parking lot. "And that I'm offering to be your knight in shining armor for a few minutes and drive you home."

"Knight in shining armor?"

"Chivalry never dies, princess." I unlock my car and open the door for her.

She gets in the car and before I can close the door, she answers, "I guess it's still alive."

I make my way to the driver's side and right as I start the engine, she announces, "to your house we go."

"I still need to drop you off."

"I don't mind if we have to stop at your house on the way." She smiles.

I shake my head. I know that she's trying to be a good samaritan but... "My house is in the opposite direction."

Almost instantly, her smile drops. "Oh. I still think we should stop at yours."

Since I don't want to argue with her, I give in and start driving towards my house, with Attie's music in the background. I don't really care about what music I listen to—if I'm driving alone, then I don't play any—but the amount of Taylor Swift I've heard on the fifteen minute drive to my house is starting to grow on me.

I think I get the hype.

We get to the house and the first thing I notice is Attie's jaw basically falling to the floor. "You live here??"

I chuckle. "I sleep here, if that's what you mean. How did you not know this?"

"Because you and Derek prefer coming to my house all the time." Jason's been over here a few times in the past, but that's only to go swimming, since we have a pool that doesn't get used as often. "If I'd known that my fake boyfriend was rich, I would have agreed to this deal months ago."

"Wow."

She turns to me, blue eyes wide. "I didn't offend you, did I?"

I shake my head. "I was kidding."

She exhales and places a hand over her heart. "Thank gods, because I was joking, too." I know she was.

We grab our stuff and head inside the house. Attie spends the next minute marveling at the entire first floor before footsteps are heard coming down the stairs. Derek makes his way towards us.

"Fucking finally, dude!" He exclaims. "I need a barrier here." He finds Attie. "Hey, Attie. I'm guessing I have you to blame for making my brother late?

She blushes. "A little. Late for what?"

"Video call." He smirks, and it's not a friendly kind of smile. Oh, no—he's got something planned. "With someone who really wants to meet you."

He takes my arm and drags me upstairs with Attie following us. I can hear her mutter, "who would want to meet me?" as we inch closer and closer to Derek's room.

I can only think of one person who would want to meet Attie. Well, anyone with half a brain would love this girl after the first interaction but that's just common sense thinking.

When we finally do reach Derek's room, he sits me on his chair, right in front of his desk, which rests his laptop.

"Hi, Mom." I wave at the screen in front of me. It's dark out for her, so she must be in the same hemisphere or something.

Mom beams at me. "About time you made it. Young man, where have you been?"

"Football practice."

"That ended a half hour ago," she points out. "Now answer that question again. With the truth."

"Mom, that wasn't a lie," I say. It wasn't. Technically, I was at practice, but I stayed a little longer.

"He was with his girlfriend," Derek shouts. If only the glare I shoot him could burn a hole into his brain right now.

Mom doesn't say anything for a few seconds. In fact, when I face the computer again, the expression on Mom's face is almost priceless. She's not one who can easily be surprised but seeing her jaw on the floor so imagining what could be running through her mind when those words leave my brother's mouth. "You were late because of a girl?"

I lower my head slightly and mutter, "yeah."

"Well then where is she? Must be someone special."

"She's right here, Mom." Derek quickly exits the room and pulls Attie inside. Mom doesn't see her right away—either due to my tall frame covering up a good chunk of the screen or Attie attempting to hide from behind me, I'm not sure—until Derek pulls her into view.

From the screen, you can see a glimpse of Attie's long dark hair, which fades to a medium brown at the end. That's definitely not enough because Mom basically shouts, "come closer, sweets!" With how loud she was, I'm surprised the screen didn't crack.

Attie is hesitant at first before inching closer to the chair and resting a hand on my shoulder, probably to calm my nerves. I didn't even realize how tense I was until I feel myself relax and my shoulders drop just slightly. Especially when my mom's face lights up at the sight of my girlfriend.

"Well aren't you a doll?" Mom's born and raised deep in the south, so when she gets all riled up—in situations such as meeting her son's girlfriend for the first time—her drawl comes out stronger than a harsh tackle from a linebacker who benches three-fifty. "What's your name?" Her eyes quickly bounce to me. "And don't answer that question for her."

Next to me, Attie's at a loss for words. "Uh..."

I rest my hand on top of hers. "She doesn't bite, princess," I whisper.

"You try meeting the parents for the first time," she whispers back, side-eyeing me. I chuckle softly not just because she's cute when nervous—she's got a point. If I hadn't known Attie's family for years, then

I would've been quaking in my sneakers just to shake her father's hand because he kind of terrifies me. I'm taller than Mr. Ryder and yet he's intimidating as all hell.

"Y'all gonna keep me waiting?"

"It's Attie, ma'am," she finally answers.

Mom waves a hand. "Darling, you don't have to use any formalities. I know how old I am. But I must say, that is a beautiful name. Is it short for Addison?"

My mother, ladies and gentlemen.

"Thanks, and it's not Addison." Attie must get asked that question a lot because her response is almost immediate as she explains her name to my mother, who listens intently. It's then I notice Attie's shoulders drop slightly as it progresses.

Mom's asking her questions and she answers them without a beat of hesitation. This goes on for a few more seconds until Attie gets a text from who I can only assume is one of her parents. She excuses herself from the room.

"Well, she seems like a good girl," Mom finally says. "I've only just met her but I already approve of her."

"Thanks," I mutter. Was I expecting my mother to like her? Truthfully, I didn't expect anything.

Mom focuses her attention on Derek. Thank goodness the spotlight's off of me, even if it's only for a few seconds. "I can't wait to meet whatever girl you decide to bring home, hun."

Instead of Derek's face turning red and a lackluster response, my brother's face turns pale, he looks away and doesn't say anything. I can hear an alarm ringing in my head because this isn't usual for him.

Something's definitely off with him. Derek never acts like this. Ever.

"Woo," he laughs, swiping the back of his hand over his forehead. "Is it getting hot in here?"

Before I can counter that statement, Attie walks back into the room. "Sorry about that, but I have to get back home."

In an instant, Derek jumps up from his spot. "I'll drive you back!"

"Shouldn't her boyfriend be driving her?" Mom asks.

Derek grabs Attie's bag from the floor and practically shoves it to her. "I need to pick something up from Jason anyway. I won't be long."

I can barely get another word in before he ushers Attie out of the room—his room, to be exact. She manages to call out, "it was nice to meet you! I'll see you tomorrow, Ian!"

I wave back, even though I can't see her anymore. What the hell just happened?

"Was Derek acting weird on your end?" Mom asks me. "Or was that just on my end?"

I nod without looking back at the screen. Even for Derek, that was weird. I was right earlier—something's off with Derek. He's keeping something from us—I'm the least judgemental person he knows, aside from Jason. I don't see why he needs to hide.

One day, I'll get it out of him but that day isn't today.

Chapter 26

"R emind me, again, why I agreed to this?" Chase mutters to himself as he, Ethan, and I watch our tight end, Brockman, fall into the tub. It's the day that I—along with half of the team–been dreading: dunk booth doomsday. All the seniors are lined up by a wall right outside the courtyard and by the looks on our faces we might as well be headed to the royal chambers.

If I wasn't taking part in this, I'd be laughing. Hell, I can see Derek and Jason coming up and laughing their asses off.

When Sophia announced it to the whole school this morning in the announcements, I didn't expect there to be a line of students seeking bloodlust by dunking us in a tub of water.

We've worked through about five of us so far, which isn't a lot but there were a lot more people throwing multiple baseballs at the red and white target with less force than required. What did we do to them?

"Ethan, you're up!" Rue shouts.

My friend groans in question and wipes the palms of his hands on his jeans. "Wish me luck," he tells us before stalking off to the tank. Yep, marching to his doom.

Okay, this is a little funny and I can feel a small laugh slip out.

"How are you the only one enjoying this?" Chase scowls. I know he's joking because the guy just had an edible when lunch began.

I turn to the booth, where Ethan isn't even sitting on the little platform above the water. He's with Rue, attempting to flirt. That doesn't catch me off guard—Ethan has a shitload of failed attempts at getting with Rue and I will occasionally shove them towards each other—but the girl standing across from them sort of does as soon as I notice her red hair.

This makes the whole thing even funnier.

"What?"

I point to the girl holding the baseball. I recognize her as one of Attie's friends and almost forgot that she's Ethan's sister. If I thought that plain, regular students had a bone to pick with the football team, then it's nothing compared to the relationship between a brother and his sister.

"Is it some crazy ex-girlfriend? I had one of those."

I turn to Chase. "What?"

"Yeah." He shrugs, as if it's no big deal. "We weren't exclusive or anything but she was pretty paranoid."

I don't see how paranoia is such a bad thing but then again it's Chase. Even before his injury, he was a classic surfer dude who just went with the flow and thought everyone else was the same.

My eyes move on their own accord and the next thing they find is Attie and Jason, standing by the table Sophia and Rue are occupying. Jason stands with his girlfriend and tries to make conversation while Attie stands close to Sophia. They must have made up at the party because I don't sense any animosity from the two. Rue, on the other hand, is basically ignoring the others, scrolling on her phone.

It's also not long before the baseball hits the target with a loud smack, causing Ethan to fall into the vat of water below him. I had almost forgotten that the whole thing was still going on.

"I'm gonna get another joint," Chase announces. "Wanna join?"

I shake my head. "I'm up next."

He holds three fingers up in the air, whistling a somber tune that I'm not familiar with before walking away. Either the effects of whatever edible just hit or this is how Chase acts sober.

I haven't seen him sober in a year. It's hard to remember old habits once you've flushed them out of your system.

I remove the letterman jacket from my person and place it on the fold-up table before me. I still don't have my hoodie, since the only one I currently own is in the possession of the dark-haired girl next to me.

Since I know what's going to come from sitting above the water, I remove my glasses and hold them out to Attie. "Do you think you can hold this for me?" I ask.

She grabs them from my hand and shoves them in her pocket. Meanwhile, Jason slams a fiver onto the table. "I'll take five, ladies."

Without a word, Sophia hands him the first baseball as I set myself up on the metal trapdoor. The way it's supposed to work is that if the baseball hits the target with enough force, then the trapdoor should open, allowing the victim to fall right into the waters.

"What do you think, sis?" Jason turns to Attie while tossing the ball in his hand. "Three tries?"

She scoffs. "I don't think you can hit it hard enough to get him to fall."

"Wanna bet?"

Attie crosses her arms over her chest. "I don't need to bet. It's physics."

"So you're actually learning something in Mr. Ali's class?" He snorts.

"Just throw the damn thing, Ryder!" A random voice shouts from the line. And he does. I nearly duck my head because there's no barrier to protect me. If Jason didn't have such a good aim, then I would've broken my nose—and that's not an experience I would wish upon my worst enemy.

The first two balls hit the target, but not with enough force to push me off.

"Third ball," Sophia announces.

"Please let this be the one," I mutter to myself. Sure enough, Jason throws it hard enough and I find myself falling into the clear tub with a loud splash. All the noise is drowned out in the few seconds I'm submerged into the water and I had forgotten how much I liked swimming. And the water's clean—no chlorine whatsoever.

I reach the surface and hop out of the clear tub with ease, reaching for my backpack to grab the towel I had packed inside. I dry my face and hands before turning to Attie, who steps away from me while holding my glasses out for me to grab.

For a moment, I'm almost offended until I remember... "It's just regular water, princess."

She hesitates for a second before relaxing herself a bit—I'm just assuming she's tense—before taking a couple more steps closer. Attie then rests my glasses on top of my nose and her close proximity causes my brain to short-circuit, since I wasn't expecting her to do something like that.

"Did you just sniff me?" Attie laughs.

Did I? Huh, I didn't realize. "That was a little embarrassing."

"No, I thought it was adorable."

"Ugh, Attie," Jason groans. "No guy wants to be called adorable."

"Is that true?"

I shrug, seeing as how I haven't really heard anything like that before. Might just be a Jason thing. "I don't really care, princess."

"Hey, I still have two more balls." Jason grabs two of the baseballs and holds them out to his sister. "Why don't you give this a try?"

She pushes them away. "I'm not sure."

"Come on, Attie. It'll be fun."

Attie faces me, waiting for a response. "You do what you think feels right." I take a step back from the tank, putting a bit of distance between me and her. Any more time in her proximity and I'm not so sure I could take responsibility for my actions.

"Yeah, I'll do it," she responds. "Do you need to get back up there?" She gestures to the booth.

I shake my head. "And thank God I don't."

Wait, where's—

"Is it my turn yet?" Chase's raspy voice calls out as he strides towards the booth. His eyes bounce to me and then Attie, settling on her much longer.

"Hardwick, where did you go?" Sophia scowls at him—her disdain for Chase Hardwick isn't a secret—and she's not the only one. If looks could kill, the glare coming from Jason could set Chase on fire and get the entire student body of Santa Barbara High, well, high.

But what nearly has my heart racing is the hurt look on Attie's face. Her blue eyes are wide and she's frozen in place. Her fingers are gripping tightly onto the ends of her sleeves and I get a confirmation that she's still alive once her eyes start blinking.

None of this fazes Chase as he walks over to the dunk booth and—with the help of Rue—helps himself up on the little platform. "Let's do this!" He hoots, a permanently relaxed smile on his face.

I can't say the same for my fake girlfriend, who is petrified from head to toe.

Jason places a baseball on the palm of his sister's hand before saying something to her that I can't make out. He takes a step back from Attie and places his hands in the pockets of his jeans, tapping his left foot. He's only ever done that when he's anxious.

Something's definitely up.

"Come on, Athena," Chase says. "Hit me with your best shot. It's not like you can hold one in, anyway." He follows that with laughter.

Okay, so he's definitely familiar with Attie. That much I know. As of now.

"You heard him," Jason shouts, although his tone is almost murderous. "Hit. Him."

She rolls up one of her sleeves right to her elbow and narrows both eyes at the target. Almost instantly, Attie throws the ball at her target.

It elicits a gasp from the crowd that has formed around us.

It's not the ball completely missing that surprises me. It's the sickening crunch that follows after the ball makes contact with Chase's face. I wince and clutch my nose as if I'm feeling the pain second-hand.

I've played football long enough to recognize the sound of bones breaking.

Chapter 27

Each passing second, my mind is overflowing with one thought:

Did I just do that?

Another beat passes.

Holy shit, I just did that!

Now, in my defense, I didn't think baseballs were that tough. I'm not a violent person so I threw the ball with the thought that it would only touch Chase's face. But the blood gushing from his nose is not an indicator that baseballs are part metal but that I threw it a little too hard.

This is the first time I've ever broken a bone—and it wasn't even mine!

I place both hands over my mouth and slowly walk backwards, until I'm far enough away from the tank to just turn around and start running back inside the main building. And I don't look back to find the shock on Jason's face, or the disappointment and confusion on Ian's.

"Just let her be, man," I hear Jason say from a distance. "Give her space."

What is he doing? I don't exactly know for sure but I keep running.

All those years of jogging with my family are starting to pay off because I run like I have some blessing of Hermes surrounding me. I barely make it to the computer lounge, where I had left my stuff when lunch began earlier, with time to spare.

Mr Ali glances up from the computer. A phone in hand and a puzzled expression on his face. Maybe he's just wondering why I'm panting but he doesn't say anything—just resumes his conversation. He's not speaking in English—at least, not entirely. I only hear a few recognizable words.

"I know, Winnie, but I can't skip today. It's important..."

I stop listening after realizing how personal the conversation is and just take a seat by the computer closest to me. I bury my face in Ian's hoodie and just let it out. All the months of anger and sadness escape me in the form of tears that get smeared all over my cheeks.

No one else walks into the computer room for the rest of lunch and I'm left there with no one but my physics teacher and my thoughts.

Not even the one person I actually want to walk through that door, the same way he had when I accidentally left that note in his locker.

"You should have seen it Amy!" Jason howls with laughter as he, Kelly, and Amy walk me to detention once school ends. "I shit you not, it was crazy."

"Let me see if I got this right," Amy says. She had a meeting for her yearbook class that went overtime and all she saw in the lunch aftermath was Chase with a broken nose, and me walking away from the courtyard with a shit ton of eyes following me. "You"—she points to me—"threw a baseball at Chase Hardwick's face for no apparent reason, and broke his nose?! What did he do to you?"

Jason and I share a quick glance at each other. That son of a bitch knows what he did but refuses to say that it was wrong. Do you know how much of a dumbass you have to be to not realized how fucked up it was? As stupid as Chase Hardwick is tall—and he's basically a skyscraper.

"I was trying to aim for the target," I lie.

"The target was two feet away from his face," Kelly points out. You're not helping!

"Who knows, Kels," Jason says. "Maybe she needs glasses like her boyfriend. Or a new brain."

"This was the last thing I'd expected you to get detention for," Amy admits. "A guy? Scratch that, I never expected you to get detention, period."

Yeah, I didn't think about detention when I broke Chase's nose. Anger had consumed me until I was seeing red that an hour later, I was called to Amy's dad's office and issued a detention. My first one.

"I thought Jason would've gotten detention by now, not you."

Jason whips his head towards Amy in shock. "Do you think so little of me, Tiny?"

"No, I don't. You're just more likely to get detention than Attie." She's got a point. "Attie is like a good girl personified. You are the—"

"Heartbreak prince," I interrupt. Without a doubt in my mind, the song Blank Space is also one hundred percent about Jason. Got a long list of ex lovers, they'll tell you I'm insane.

"I was going to say rebel." Amy winces. "That works too. Sorry, Kelly."

Kelly just shrugs. I don't think that's the first time she's heard that about Jason. Even though he's heard the things people say about him, he doesn't look like he gives a shit. If only I had that attitude. "I thought you would have gotten suspended for something like that."

I shouldn't have let Chase's proximity affect me in that way. God, I hate that asshole and a part of me almost feels guilty for it.

Almost.

I begin rubbing the sleeves of the dark blue hoodie. Ian's hoodie. I still can't get over seeing the look in his ocean eyes when I broke Chase's nose. Once the veil of anger was lifted over my eyes—not completely—I realized that maybe it wasn't exactly the best thing to do. But the damage had been done. All I can do now is go from there.

The four of us finally arrive at the detention room "Guess this is my eternal punishment," I sigh dramatically.

Jason rolls his eyes. "Your eternal punishment is going to be what happens when Mom and Dad find out."

I groan, wondering what levels of pissed our parents are going to be. Mom and Dad are usually pretty chill when it comes to things like dating. Until today, Jason and I never had to deal with the possibility of getting in trouble at school since we're pretty decent people.

"Wish me luck," I tell them.

"Praying for you," Amy calls out as I enter the computer lab. Luckily, I'm not the only person who got detention today. Today must have been an off day for the entire student body if almost all of the seats in the computer lab are filled, and if Mr. Ali is the one in charge.

I chuckle to myself. Man, did that young teacher get unlucky. He complained earlier today about still being called "fresh meat" after three years of teaching here and I guess that's coming back to bite him in the ass.

I take a seat next to a girl with strawberry blonde hair who doesn't look as scary as the rest of them and log onto the computer. Detention is about to start and I might as well get a project done.

"You are not allowed to use the computers for the next two hours," Mr. Ali calls out.

Two hours? Ugh, might as well be forever.

"Attie? How did you get detention?" A familiar female voice asks.

I turn around to the girl on my left. No wonder her hair looked so familiar! It's because I recognize Lydia Keller from my math class. She doesn't sit near me or Sierra but we've talked a couple of times. She's on the cheer team with Sophia and Rue but doesn't sit with them, either.

"I should be asking you that," I responded. "How did you end up here?"

She rolls her eyes. "I came late to Ms. Fowler's class and I got detention right then and there."

I wince. "That sucks." I don't have Ms. Fowler but I've heard of her reputation when it comes to attendance. You could easily get in trouble for coming in a second after the bell rings.

She waves a hand. "It's alright. But what about you? I would've been less surprised to see Jason sitting here."

I snort. "Would you have been less surprised to see Jason break someone's nose?"

Her eyes widen. "What?"

"Quiet back there!" Mr. Ali calls.

Lydia lowers her voice to a whisper. "You are explaining later."

I don't want to even think about it so I just pull out a blank piece of paper and try to pass the time by sketching my favorite cartoon characters. Okay, one of my favorites. I wouldn't be able to choose one even if Jason asked me.

"That looks so cool," Lydia says, looking down at my sketchbook.

Just then, I hear a chair pull up and a familiar yet bone-chilling voice say, "yeah, she's really talented."

Again, those chills go right to the bones. If anyone else had said those words to me, I wouldn't feel instant white-hot anger. In fact, I would have probably turned red and muttered a thank you in response. That's not the case since that voice unfortunately belongs to Chase.

Don't look at him. Do NOT look at him, Attie. He doesn't deserve a spare glance.

But my body unfortunately doesn't listen to my brain and I look up slightly to see the disheveled look he's currently sporting. He's definitely sober—that's a first—and the bandage on his nose, accompanied with the swelling under his eyes, are more of an indication that lunch wasn't a fever dream.

I really did hurt him. Almost like he had hurt me.

Refusing to make even a sound, I turn back to Lydia. "Thanks, Lydia," I whisper.

"I can barely draw a stick figure myself, so I'm easily impressed by this."

A phone begins to ring just as I'm about to open my mouth. That's definitely not my phone. Lydia checks her phone and shakes her head. Everyone's turning their heads to see who's phone it belongs to. Except Mr. Ali, who just places his hand inside his front pocket. His eyes widen at the screen. "I'll be outside for only a moment. Don't make any noise while I'm gone."

He taps his thumb on the screen and presses his phone to his ear while simultaneously running out the door like the Minotaur is at his tail. We're all silent for a moment before chatter erupts.

Lydia looks over my shoulder and winces at the sight. "Well, I guess I don't need to ask any more questions." I swear if one more person asks me about the dunk tank at lunch, I'll plotz. Or if I had actual lightning bolts, I'd zapped them out of existence, Zeus-style.

"It's not broken, Keller," Chase mumbles.

"I didn't say anything like that, Hardwick. Calm down."

He rolls his eyes at her before focusing back on his phone. I work on my cartoon of my take on a classic Disney character. A tall, blond, teenager with bright blue eyes and—

Wait, am I adding glasses? He doesn't have glasses.

I squeeze my eyes shut, clench my fist, and smack my forehead. What am I thinking? I shouldn't be drawing Ian at a time like this. He's my fake boyfriend, god dammit!

If he's not your real boyfriend, then why are you drawing him? You only sketch cartoon versions of the people you care about, my brain nags.

Shut up, brain.

"Psst, Athena," Chase whispers.

I ignore him. He does it again. It's a whole patter of him whispering and me ignoring him to the best of my ability. Until he touches my shoulder. It's a light touch, his finger briefly pressing my shoulder and I nearly snap. "Leave me alone Chase," I hiss.

"But this is important."

"Then it can wait a couple more hours." I go back to my drawing, only for Chase to start tapping his pencil at me. It's something he's always done, even when we were seeing each other last year. He would use the eraser end of his pencil to poke me and I found it just a tad annoying then.

That hasn't changed now.

A guy sitting in front of me swivels around in his chair to face me. He's wearing a baseball cap but even so, his dark hair falls over his eyes. "Is he bothering you?" He asks, jabbing a thumb in Chase's direction, earning him a scowl.

"She doesn't mind it. Fuck off, Alvarez."

The baseball-cap-guy scowls right back at Chase without a beat of hesitation. "See, I wasn't talking to you, asshole."

Some of the chatter around us has died down and a few of the students have started watching this. I just want to hide underneath the desk but that would draw the attention towards me so I continue to keep my head down.

The guy repeats his question, emphasizing each word in that sentence. "Is he bothering you?"

I'd prefer to pretend that this whole interaction isn't happening right now. If I could turn it all off, I would. But no matter what, I can't ignore what's in front of me so I muster up as much courage as I can to only utter these three words.

"Yeah, he is." I just want this whole thing to be over.

Baseball Cap turns to face Chase with a pointed glare. "I don't want to say this again but leave her alone." He then swivels around, the back end of the chair facing us.

Chase looks like he's about to protest but, luckily, Mr. Ali storms into the room before anything else can happen and everything goes silent. This, I can work with. Silence is calming. As much as I love blasting music as I work, I could sit in complete silence—no drop of a hat, or breeze brushing past—and feel peace.

"It's always the people you least expect," Lydia mutters from beside me.

I try to focus on sketching with only my mechanical pencil at my disposal, tuning out the rest of my surroundings and it doesn't feel like twoo hours have passed by before the clock strikes five-thirty and I am free.

Now I need to figure out how to face my parents when I get back home.

Jason took the car so he could take Kelly out on a date and Amy went home with her dad so I'm basically left without a ride. I can't really ask Ian either since I've been avoiding him and everyone else since lunch.

Honestly, I think I just need some time alone. Just to collect my thoughts and think about how I'm going to approach this whole—

"Athena! Wait up!"

I quicken my pace and keep my head straight so that I don't look back but even so, I still hear Chase's footsteps follow after me. Ugh, why can't he just drop it?

I barely make it outside of the building before Chase grabs my shoulder and spins me around to face him. I almost lose my footing because of it but once again, he keeps me steady when it should be illegal. Then again, getting drugged by someone you trusted is illegal, and Chase Hardwick is known for pulling off illegal shit and getting away with it.

"What now?" I hiss.

"What do you mean 'what now?'" He . "What was that all about?"

"I didn't want to talk," I respond. Doesn't he get the memo? "It's not worth getting in more trouble than I already am."

He waves it off like it's no big deal. "Mr. Ali wouldn't have cared."

"Well, I would have. Did you think about that?" How is it that I've lived on this stupid planet for a little over sixteen and a half years and still don't know how to end a conversation?

I swear, being around Chase these days is like breaking a worn out hair tie. There's only so much that can happen before I snap and right now, Chase Hardwick is stretching it real thin.

"What did I even do to you?"

I clench my fists that rest in the pocket of Ian's hoodie. Keep calm, Attie. Don't cause a scene. It's almost impossible not to since practice for just about every fall sport has let out and there are a bunch of students in the parking lot now. Some of them are possibly watching this shitshow unfold.

"You know exactly what you did," I bite out.

He runs a hand through his dark hair. "As far as I know, I didn't do anything wrong."

"Well, if you can't admit that what you did was wrong, then you don't deserve to speak to me. You broke my trust that night at Ethan's party. And I can't trust myself to be near you, never mind speaking to you for a minute." I take a deep breath before letting out my next words. "Do me a favor and never speak to me again."

And with that, I turn around and walk in whatever direction. Since I didn't even bother to call for a ride, I'm just choosing to walk the distance between school and home. I don't even like exercising but I guess it gives me time to stew over this whole thing.

It gives me time to breathe alone. And maybe that's what I need right now—to be alone.

Right now, for the foreseeable future—that's up for debate.

If I wasn't walking right now, I would go stand in a corner and think about what I had just said.

Chapter 28

I'm the last guy out of the locker room so when I do leave, it's to find BJ and Sophia waiting outside. Not just standing around in boredom, however. They choose now of all times to make out against the brick wall.

I should be used to this—they've been together for about a year now—but it's still a little uncomfortable walking into your two friends and a very intimate session of PDA.

"Someone saw my eyes off, please," I mutter mostly to myself.

Much to my surprise, the way-too-happy couple in front of me pulls apart to find me standing a good ten feet away. They're in a position that I know all too well and considering that my best friend has walked in on me before, I can't decide whether to make fun of them (I choose to wait until later to do so) or keep silent and just walk to my car.

But curiosity gets the best of me, and I ask, "BJ, what are you guys still doing here?"

He clears his throat. "Can you give us a ride?"

"Is your car in the shop again?"

Sophia nods and I try my best to hold back an eye roll. We all know the stereotype about boys being knowledgeable with cars, right? That doesn't apply to Braiden James. In fact, I think Sophia might hold more knowledge about car maintenance than her boyfriend—and she doesn't have a license.

"Come on." I motion for them to follow me. Not that they need to, since their designated parking spot is right next to my own. "Who are we dropping off first?"

"BJ," Sophia answers. Why do I even ask when I already know the answer?

Once we all get settled in the car, I drive off in the route opposite from my house. During all that, chatter erupts.

"What was up with your girl, anyway?" BJ asks from the backseat.

I glance at the rearview mirror. "What are you talking about?"

"The dunk tank, how she broke Hardwick's nose." He doesn't look up from his phone once. "Everyone on the group chat's talking about it. Didn't you see?"

I raise a brow, though he can't see my face.

Realization dawns on him. "Right, you're not on the group chat."

I could have been. It's not monitored by Coach Wells at all—we have a separate chat for that—but I don't use my phone as often as most. Sure, I answer calls and texts when needed but I don't exactly enjoy the hassle of responding to multiple people at once.

I am curious, though. Chase has pissed off a fair amount of people in the past. Attie didn't strike me as someone who would even know him, never mind hate the guy's guts.

"Sophia, you've been awfully quiet," I point out. "Nothing to add? No playful insults?"

"Did you say something?" She must have zoned out.

"Cas, are you okay?" BJ asks.

"Yeah, I'm fine."

"And by fine you mean..."

"Fine," she bites out. "I'm all for Attie breaking that asshat's nose. Someone had to do it."

"He's not that bad," I say.

Her jaw drops. "Bad? Ian, he drugged a girl at a party last year. No one that bad—wait is that Attie?"

"What?" I turn my head to the right and, to my surprise, Attie is storming off in the same direction that I'm driving. She still has her backpack with her and wears my hoodie.

It's getting dark as hell—why is she walking?

I don't know what comes over me but in the next second, I'm placing the car into park and hopping out to catch up to her.

"Attie!" I call out. She either doesn't hear me or is trying to ignore me.

I get my answer when I notice her pace quicken, so I increase my own.

I manage to catch up to Attie and I grab her wrist, slowing her down. "Hey, why are you walking this late?"

Her back is still towards me and I get no response. Maybe her shoulders are shaking a little—which is odd since she's wearing my hoodie—but no words out of her mouth.

Attie's pacing eventually comes to a stop and walk around to the front of her. "Hey, what's wrong, princess?"

Her head is bent down, long dark hair spilling over her face. I tilt her chin upward to face me and therein lies the problem. Tears are welled up in her beautiful eyes and she's attempting to hold them back.

"Shit," I mutter low enough so that Attie doesn't hear. I pull her into my chest and hold her in my arms. Attie's tense at first, probably surprised, but it only lasts one second before she relaxes in my arms and starts sniffling.

I don't even know what she's crying about because there's a whole range of emotions. Maybe she's frustrated with someone, or she's just listened to a sad song—I've been there—but regardless, I hope it's not because of me.

God, I hope it isn't. I wouldn't be able to forgive myself if that's true. The only thing worse than seeing her cry—hearing in this case—is being the reason she does in the first place.

"It's my fault," she says but her words are muffled in my jacket. Three words that she repeats and I don't understand what she's talking about.

I pull her head up to face me and wipe some of those tears away with the pad of my thumb. "You don't need to explain what's wrong, not yet. But I will not let you walk alone to your house at this time of night."

Attie removes her head from my chest and looks up, her eyes a little red from all the crying. "It's not that far, Ian. I'll be fine."

"Princess, it's dark." I stand my ground on this. Fake girlfriend or not, I will not risk Attie's safety in any way. "I don't care how relatively safe the area might be. You are coming."

"But—"

"My car's not far from here," I assure her, not letting her finish that sentence since I know she'll bring out that stubborn side to her that she doesn't let out that often.

"Ian—"

"Please." I don't care if I'm begging or if people are watching. Her safety takes priority over my current lack of embarrassment.

Attie closes her eyes for a quick second to let one last tear escape before nodding softly. "Okay," she whispers.

I brush the tear away with the pad of my thumb. "Better?"

She shakes her head. "No more tears."

At that moment, I nearly let out a sigh of relief. That's my princess. There's the Attie Ryder I know.

But I brush that thought out of my mind as I wrap one arm around Attie's shoulder and turn us both around to the direction of my car. She clings on me like I'm the most comfortable blanket in the world and I think to myself: who needs circulation? I'd take this over blood flowing through my body anyday.

We finally reach the car and Attie opens teh door to the back and squeezes in with Sophia, who wraps both arms around her without hesitation. "Hey, are you okay?" I hear her ask.

"I'm fine," Attie answers.

"Are you sure? You didn't look so good." Attie doesn't respond but I don't think Sophia cares. "Whatever. Just know you can always talk to me."

"Hey, me too," BJ adds, which almost makes me laugh.

"Also, the baseball was hilarious!" Sophia laughs. "Someone had to put Hard-Ass in his place. I've been wanting to break that guy's face for so long, Attie. You have no idea."

I glance at Attie through my rearview mirror. She notices and nods, a tight smile on her lips. She's trying to keep her brave face on, a smile that is almost identical to her real one. I know better, though. She's hiding something but it's not my place to ask her about it.

"What made you break his nose, anyway?"

It's Sophia's, apparently.

When we reach Attie's house, she grabs her stuff and says her goodbyes. Before she closes the door, I watch her tell Sophia something. My car is kind of crowded, since there are two tall football players taking up half the space inside so I can barely make out the words, "that rumor you heard? About him? Well, just know it's actually true."

I have no absolutely no idea what that means but it must be bad if it leaves Sophia in complete and utter shock.

"What is she talking about?" I ask.

Sophia shakes her head, her eyes still wide. "Oh. My. Gosh. It-it's not my place to say."

I don't push any further, but as I watch Attie slowly disappear into the house, I can't help but wonder.

Chapter 29

I'm in trouble.

No, I don't just mean getting grounded for breaking Chase's nose with a baseball—because I'm definitely in trouble for that too.

Honestly, I deserved the grounding. I'm not trying to kiss anyone's ass whatsoever—I save that for all the teachers so I can get stellar letters of recommendation—I'm just saying it's warranted.

On account of getting detention, Amy's dad had called my parents to inform them about the whole baseball ordeal. Mom was pissed with good reason. I mean, come on, I broke a guy's nose. I was provoked, yes, but that doesn't change the fact that I broke the bones on my ex's face. Surprisingly, I don't regret doing it. And I'd do it again if it didn't mean getting in trouble.

Dad, however, laughed when I explained that I thought baseballs were hollow inside.

That night, I was so thankful that Jason was home because he witnessed the whole thing. If it wasn't for him, I would've been grounded until I reached the underworld, but it only got shortened to a week.

There's only one problem: being grounded is SO FUCKING BOR-ING.

I'm only three days in and being alone in an empty house is not exactly the most ideal on a Saturday afternoon. I can't call Amy because she's helping her aunt with some sort of baking thing. Jason is hanging out with Derek and he took the Jeep since he knows I can't drive it until my grounding is over.

To top it all off, my parents are on some sort of day-long date. Which means I really am alone in the house.

I'm starting to get tired of my routine of basically waking up and doing absolutely nothing before going back to sleep. I've never craved spontaneity in my life but I guess there's a first for everything.

That's not even the icing on the cake. What really has my head in a bit of a spin is realizing that I'm not in love with Derek anymore. I actually don't think I ever was—now that I look back on the past four years.

I don't exactly know why my brain came to that conclusion when I was twelve. Maybe it was because I just felt the need to crush on a guy back in middle school since everyone was doing it and since I was around Derek a lot, he was the first boy I thought of.

But then again, Ian was also around. Maybe I got them switched up at some point.

Why can't liking boys just be less complicated?

Three o'clock quickly approaches and in that time, I've somehow managed to finish all my homework for the weekend, add any last minute details to the decals on my walls, and ponder over my Halloween costume and why I even bought one in the first place.

I'm supposed to be Taylor Swift from her 1989 World Tour. The whole cute blue two-piece that she also wore on the Eras Tour. It's my favorite outfit of hers and even though I don't plan on cutting bangs anytime soon—or ever, really—I think I look bad-ass in the clothes. If only I knew of any Halloween parties happening away from the beach.

Now I sit on the floor of my room, laptop open, editing a powerpoint presentation that has absolutely nothing to do with school. Taylor Swift blasts on my phone, my mug of hot coffee is now lukewarm, and yet I still take sips as I continue to type.

I'm starting to go slightly crazy just sitting here. Closing the laptop, I stand up and stretch my body before grabbing what's left of my lukewarm coffee and downing it before heading back downstairs. I could text Sierra but she's probably busy with Caleb, since they finally started dating.

Ian comes to mind but I immediately shut that idea down. There's no way that I'm going to just text him out of the blue. Almost every time we've texted, he's been the one to initiate conversation since that day I was making friendship bracelets.

But if I did, he wouldn't judge me, right?

He's the least judgemental person that I know—when he's around me, that is. I never found a reason to feel embarrassed around him. Maybe it's the amount of time we've spent around each other increasing significantly this past year but I'm starting to feel more comfortable around Ian.

Can you believe that? I get easily embarrassed around my parents and other relatives but not with my fake boyfriend. I find myself saying things without thinking when I'm with him.

Almost like everything just flows easier with Ian, and I'm not sure how to feel about it.

When I was walking home and Ian found me, he didn't chastise me or make me feel guilty. He did the same thing at the party too—when I kissed him. And earlier that same day, with the note he put in my locker.

It's something about him that makes me feel safe when he's around.

Wait...could I be falling for him? That doesn't seem right, does it?

It shouldn't be. Maybe I had a small elementary crush on Ian when I first met him but that's all it was. We're grown now—as grown as teenagers in high school can be—and emotions are completely different. Jason told me once that our bodies completely change every seven years so those emotions are in the past.

Pushing those thoughts aside, I wash my mug and switch to a soda before heading back upstairs. I don't know how long it's been before I start to hear a light thud from my bedroom window.

Odd, there's nothing near it. No trees, nothing. It's not even raining out.

Unlike Jason's room, my bedroom is on the other side of the house, outlooking the backyard. Nothing unique about my house, really. It's just like any other house in the suburbs of a beach town. It doesn't have a trail that leads to the nearest beach, or a swimming pool. It's just plain and simple but it's home.

I shrug off the thud and go back to my laptop.

Thud.

Okay, anymore stones thrown at my window and it will begin to look like the aftermath of that scene in Animal House. I slide my laptop under my bed and hop on top of it to slide my window open. I look out and my jaw nearly drops out of shock.

Because standing right outside my bedroom window—in my backyard nonetheless—throwing pennies at my window, is none other than Chris Evans in a pair of square-shaped glasses.

I'm just kidding, it's Ian. But he does look a little like a nerdy Captain America. I don't care if it's unintentional—it's still a bit sexy.

I barely get my head out the window before a penny hits my forehead. "Ow," I mutter, rubbing the same spot on my forehead.

"Sorry, princess!" He shouts. "Did I break anything?"

"It's a penny," I shout back. "You can't break my skull with a penny." Though I won't lie—it does sting slightly.

What is he doing here? Why is he here? Better yet...

"Why are you using pennies?" I ask. It's almost hilarious.

He shrugs. "You don't have any stones laying around."

I take a deep breath and hold back any and all laughs that attempt to escape. "And it didn't occur to you to maybe—I don't know—text me?" Actually, I don't have my phone since my parents took it away as a part of my punishment.

"Are you busy?" He runs a hand through his hair, which looks a little darker from this distance due to it being damp.

"No, why?"

"Come down from your tower, princess." Just as the words leave his mouth, he winces. "That sounded way better in my head, I swear."

"I can't leave," I tell him. "I'm grounded, remember?" I had left a letter in his locker yesterday that explained why I couldn't attend last night's game.

"Are you parents home right now?"

I shake my head dramatically.

"Then what they don't know won't hurt them."

I look down from the window and my eyes widen. Yeah, almost every thought of sneaking out of my house disappears without a trace.

Almost. Even if I don't thrive off social interaction like the rest of my family, I still can't handle staying indoors for so long. When the pandemic hit a few years ago, I was nearly driven to the brink of insanity.

So the idea of sneaking out seems a bit enticing, especially with Ian. That doesn't mean it feels right.

Still...

I close my eyes for a moment and just hope that this isn't some sort of lucid dream because I'm actually considering this. "Where are we going?"

A smile forms on his face. "Bring a swimsuit and towel and meet me by the driveway in a few minutes."

I do just that and in the next few minutes, we're getting into his little get-away car and driving away. I'm tempted to stick my head out the window but I don't have a death wish, so I just stick to hijacking the aux, shuffling all my liked songs on Spotify. In the next moment, Olivia Rodrigo's Ballad of a Homeschooled Girl starts playing.

"And here I thought you only listened to Taylor Swift," Ian teases.

I scoff. "Oh, it's not like you hate it."

He shrugs, leaving me with nothing but the lyrics playing through his speakers and a small smile on his soft lips.

I smile to myself. Yeah, I'm turning him into a Swiftie. He just doesn't know it yet.

"Dead Man's Land? Really?" I ask.

Not to my surprise, Ian and I ended up at Hendry's Beach. Or what Jason and I like to call, Dead Man's Land, due to all the times I nearly died learning how to swim.

The struggles of having a severe chlorine allergy are real. At least I can swim—it would be a major disappointment if I didn't know because that's a literal requirement of living in a beach town.

Ian switches the engine off and turns to me. "I wouldn't exactly call it that, per say."

I raise a brow at him. My past self would say otherwise.

"I mean, I haven't died yet."

I roll my eyes. "Yet."

Ian scoffs as he unstraps the surfboard from the roof of his car. It's a big, white board with a red outline and it basically towers over the both of us. I like to think I'm somewhat tall for a girl but being in the proximity of that surfboard, I start to understand why Amy wears heels all the time.

"Yeah, I'm definitely about to die," I mutter to myself.

He laughs while grabbing a few more items from the trunk of his car. "That answers the question I was about to ask. You lived in a beach town your whole life and never learned how to surf?"

I shake my head. "Swimming seemed a lot more dangerous than this."

"Isn't that a requirement?"

Why does everyone think that? I know a ton of people who can't surf. It's the typical California stereotype—live in SoCal? Oh then, you must definitely know how to shred some waves.

But as Ken from the Barbie movie pointed out, "shredding waves is much more dangerous than people realize."

I raise a brow at Ian. "Really?"

"I take that back. But you were never curious?" Ian's glasses are a bit askew on top the bridge of his nose and sensing that, he fixes them.

"Nope." I remove the cover-up I placed over my swimsuit. "Is it safe?"

"Princess, I can assure you that you will be fine. You're not dying on my watch." He places the surfboard onto the ground and slips on a black wetsuit. Hey, I may not know how to surf but that doesn't mean I'm completely clueless.

I stare at the surfboard by my feet.

"Just hop on it," he says.

This was the same spontaneity that I was craving only ninety minutes ago? I glance at Ian, who watches me as I step onto the board. It's a little sticky, which surprises me—not in a good way—and I immediately jump off. "Why is it sticky?"

Ian burst out laughing at my reaction. I narrow my eyes and cross my arms over my chest as he attempts to catch his breath and fails. Asshole.

Very hot asshole but still...

It takes him longer to catch his breath than it should but his laughter dies down and he wipes a single tear from under his glasses. "Sorry but I've never seen anyone react that way to jumping on a surfboard."

"Then why the hell is it sticky?!?" I shiver just thinking about it.

Ian hops onto the surfboard, not even looking fazed before holding out his hand. "Come on."

I reluctantly grab his hand and step onto his surfboard. It takes every little muscle in me to hold back from jumping off like I did last time and manage to stay on like a pro, though I'm nowhere near becoming one. It's not only because of the mysterious stickiness that covers the surfboard.

When I grabbed Ian's hand, I felt this weird, tingly feeling shiver up my left arm and down my spine. Part of me thought it was a breeze but while a breeze passes through the body only briefly, the little butterflies floating around in my stomach linger.

Yet I'm still standing. The grip he has on me kind of helps.

"It's wax," he explains. "Waxing the board helps us stand without falling. At least, that's what BJ said."

"Did he teach you?"

Ian nods. "A couple years ago. I was not as good as I am now. The first time I stood up on a board, I wiped out on the shore before I could catch a wave." A small smile appears on his face, exposing a set of dimples I never knew he had. "Not my best moment."

Fuck me, he has dimples. Why does he have dimples? Couldn't he just have a normal face like every teenage boy?

"Well, that's reassuring," I mutter.

"You'll definitely do better than I did." He lets go of my hand and steps off the board. I was so used to the warmth that was radiating from his body that I didn't realize how chilly the surrounding atmosphere is. "See? You haven't fallen off yet."

"Yet," I enunciate.

He playfully rolls his eyes. "Who knows? Maybe you won't fall like I did."

In which way? My mind wonders. Because it's a yes to both. I will definitely fall off the board at the first time.

As for the second type of falling? Shit, I think I'm already there.

Chapter 30

I wouldn't call myself an expert surfer bum but I'm familiar enough with the basics. Probably not the best instructor on this side of Santa Barbara but definitely the most willing.

I got Attie to lay on the board, stomach down after a lot of convincing. "Okay, now you need to pop up," I instructed.

Attie raises a dark brow.

"It means to stand up on your board."

She nods and gets up to her feet slowly.

"Okay."

"What did I do wrong?" she asks. "I know I did something wrong."

I shrug. "Nothing."

"Ian, I looked and felt like a floppy seal. Just tell me what I should do."

"Just put your dominant foot forward when you pop up," I advise. "It helps you stay on the board." Ironically, I don't exactly know the physics of it. I'm only taking AP Physics because there was no astronomy class. Sue me.

It takes about Attie an hour to get a full grasp on the basics before I deem her ready to take on the water. Since I don't have an extra surfboard and don't want to cause a hazard, I keep my feet on the shoreline and watch as she grabs the surfboard and steps onto the shore.

"You got this princess!" I shout, cupping my hands over my mouth like a megaphone.

She tries her best to hold onto the board and prevails. Probably isn't the best time to catch some waves but this is the last chance I'll get to go surfing this year. In the two years I've known how, I've learned that October is when the crowds die down and the tides are still great. The water's warmer and it just felt...right.

Attie eventually hops onto the board and starts paddling.

"Don't go too far," I call out.

"I won't!"

Maybe I can do this as a hobby—teaching young kids and tourists how to surf—if this evening goes well. She hasn't been wiped out yet, so I have some hope.

Attie stands up on the board as soon as a small wave starts to form behind her and she falls back into the ocean.

Shit.

I'm about to dive in and start swimming when her head pops out. Her hair is stuck to half of her face but she pushes away before swimming towards my board and paddling towards me.

"Surfing is a lot harder than it looks in the movies," she admits.

"Are you okay?" I ask, checking for any scratches and bruises she may have acquired from that fall.

"I'm fine," she laughs "Was I supposed to turn around?"

I nod, laughing.

She passes the surfboard back to me. "Let me see how you do it."

"Today is your day," I say, passing it back to her. "Don't you want to try again?"

"Maybe later but right now, I choose to see how the pro surfs." She pushes the surfboard back into my arms with a sly grin. "Come on, four-eyes. Show me your skills."

"I will when you stop calling me four-eyes, princess. And I'm not a pro."

Both of her brows fly up her face. "Oh really?"

"Yeah." I don't know what I'm getting myself into at this point.

Attie glances at the horizon, where the sun barely begins to set before giving me those sad, puppy-dog eyes. "Please?"

"Fine," I concede, removing the bracelet off my wrist and handing it to her. "Do you mind holding these?" I ask, removing my glasses and switching them out for the surfboard.

"Why? Can't you keep them both on?"

I shake my head. "I rely on my glasses more than contacts. As for the bracelet..." I lightly tap a red bead. "This special girl made it for me, and I don't want to lose it."

Her cheeks turn red and just the realization that I can make her blush like that causes enough adrenaline to surge through my veins and run towards the shore, so I can catch my last wave for the season.

I paddled and paddled until a wave started to form in front of me before turning around so I could paddle away and stand up. The only disadvantage of not wearing my glasses while surfing is not seeing the look on Attie's face when I keep myself balanced on my board. I'm almost as blind as a bat without them or my contacts on.

I almost fall off but manage to keep myself steady until the wave I'm surfing dies down as I get closer to the shore and I dive off the board. It's that same elated feeling I get whenever I help score a touchdown or the time I caught my first wave.

"See?" Attie smiles with triumph as I reach her. "I told you so. Pro."

All I could do was smile at her. It's one thing to be proud of yourself but when someone you deeply care about tells you? It just makes all these weeks worthwhile.

She is worthwhile.

Attie and I were at Hendry's Beach until the sun had set and when she finally managed to not fall off the board is when she called it a night. I was damn proud of her—still am, to be honest—but I was starting to get hungry.

So we drove up to Suze's, which is this quaint little diner on the boardwalk and sat down at a booth in the very back of the restaurant. We just ordered our food and Attie is completely surprised by the sandwich I ordered—I settled for a vegan burrito while Attie ordered a soup and salad.

"How are you a vegan?" She repeats for possibly the fifth time. How my diet is a surprise to her, I have no idea.

"Vegetarian," I correct. "I saw a video in middle school that traumatized me."

She laughs. "A video traumatized you."

"In my defense, it was the Supersize Me film they showed in health class."

Attie mock gags at the memory. "I get it now."

That film was burned into my twelve-year-old brain and I can't look at a cow without picturing the guy in the movie getting surgery.

Attie starts tapping her nails on the table. "Lesson learned: never assume anything about Ian Bale. You are just full of surprises."

"In a good way?" I ask.

She smiles. "Of course." Next thing I hear is the Indiana Jones theme song and Attie pulls her phone out from her purse. Her eyes widen at the screen. "I'm so sorry." She stands up from the booth and heads over to the patio to answer it. She talks animatedly but I can't hear a sound.

It's not long before she comes back to the booth. "Jason just got home and I had to beg him not to say a word to our parents."

"Must have been hard," I joke.

She snorts. "Nah, I just had to remind him about how I saved his ass last night and he was silent."

"Do I want to know?"

She shakes her head instantly. "It's best if you don't. Let's just say I'm glad the walls aren't thin."

Our food arrives a minute later and the food on our table gets demolished. Throughout that, we get into a small game of twenty questions and I'm learning so much more about Attie. I had remembered a lot about her before—that she adores the color blue to the point that most of her wardrobe is that color, her favorite artist is Taylor Swift, and that she dreams of being an animator—but that is all just surface-level stuff.

She had just finished telling me the story of how she dyed her hair blue and failed miserably.

"And that was when I learned that Jason should never become a hairstylist in the future," she concludes, taking one last bite of her salad.

"You really went through a lot with that guy, didn't you?" I had noticed that a lot of her "horror" stories involved Jason.

She nods. "Of course. We're family. We grew up with the same parents, in the same house. Hell, we're in the same grade. Wouldn't you be close with Derek if you guys were twins?"

I polish off my burrito and wipe my hands with the napkin in front of me as I ponder that question. I don't exactly know. Derek and I are close in age, sure, but that doesn't mean we're close.

But I try to phrase my answer in the best way I could. "Derek's different. Not all siblings are close the way you and Jason are. Honestly, I don't even think my brother and I are that close with each other."

Her brows furrow. "What do you mean?"

"He's been acting pretty weird lately," I explain. "Jason doesn't notice, which is weird because he's hella observant. Remember when you met my mother?"

Attie nods. "He seemed perfectly fine. Maybe in a bit of a rush when he dropped me off that day."

I sigh. "It doesn't seem like it, but I'm kind of worried about him. He's not that closed-off but still..."

Attie reaches over and places her hand on top of mine, where it rests palm down on the table. "Maybe he's stressed about something completely irrelevant. If he's just stressed, then it probably has nothing to do with you. Don't worry about it." Then, a small laugh escapes her lips. "Wow, that just came out of my mouth."

Yeah, maybe. I always tell myself to worry about it later but when it comes to the people I care about, it always comes around to bite me in the eye.

No, I don't mean the ass. The eye would be much more painful.

Chapter 31

After paying for the check, we walked out of Suze's and just started walking. No set destination, really. Just walked and talked until I spotted no line at Monty's Ice Cream Parlor and insisted that we grab a scoop.

He chose Suze's, so I'm choosing ice cream. It's only fair to end off what just happens to be one of the best nights ever with one of the best sweet treats to exist, right?

Besides, he can't pull out the vegetarian card—he can still eat ice cream.

Afterward, we sit right on the hood of his car in a mostly empty parking lot. With him, munching on a cone of peanut butter chocolate. I chose this mango-vanilla flavor that's really popular.

We're eating our ice cream in silence since I think we've gone over everything we could possibly talk about. I'm looking up at the night sky, playing a game of Connect the Dots in my head with the stars I see, since I don't really know of any constellations—except Pisces, but that's a given.

"What's on your mind, princess?" Ian asks.

A realization dawns on me. "Why do you call me that, anyway?" I question.

"What?"

"That nickname." I turn to face him. Some of the streetlights are on so I can see his face clearly. "I don't even remember the last time you called me by my actual name."

"Can't I give you a nickname just because?" He asks. Are his cheeks turning red? I'm not imagining this, am I?

I shake my head, remembering Jason's words. "I like to think that there's always a reason."

"Just don't judge me."

I chuckle. "Why would I do that? You've never given me a reason to. Unless..."

"It's not inappropriate, I swear," he clarifies, cheeks turning a light shade of crimson. "But remember those games we played back in elementary school? When Derek and I first moved here?"

I nod. Whenever Mom forced me to hang out with the boys, there were always games involved. Specifically, freeze tag, hide and seek, just to name a few. Why boys love alternate version of lacrosse and tackle football, I will never understand.

"I remember how there was always some sort of situation that ended with me saving you from getting in trouble," he continues. "I would tell my mother about it and she would say that I was some sort of knight in shining armor, ready to rescue his princess."

I giggle.

"Hey, I'm just quoting my mother," he protests.

"I know," I reply. "But I'm realizing how much of a mother's boy you are." It's pretty adorable, especially since I know how alike they are.

"Nothing wrong with it."

"I didn't say there was." I rest both my hands at the back of my head and lay down, one leg crossed over the other. Perseus was a mother's boy and he got a happy ending—then again, his father was a deadbeat olympian. I love both my parents equally and will always be grateful that I still have them both in my life, under one roof. Sometimes, I forget that not everyone is lucky.

Take Amy for example. I don't know what happened to her mother because she refuses to ever talk about it. I just assumed that she was dead because it can't be that hard to talk about your mother if she was alive, right?

"It's crazy that there are so many stars up there," I say, looking at the sky. "There's endless patterns. Shapes and sizes."

"And we have yet to find them all," Ian finishes. "Never fails to amaze."

"Never pegged you for a stargazer."

He chuckles. "Oh, I'm more than that." Ian points up to a star with his free hand, tracing a pattern. "If you look closely, you could find the big dipper."

My eyes follow his finger and the pattern he repeats. "I'm a little lost. That just looks like a big pan."

He laughs, the sound so melodic I almost tune out everything else around us just so I could keep that sound on a loop in my brain. "That's what everyone says. I don't exactly remember what it's supposed to be—only a greater part of an animal."

"Why?" I ask. "Why couldn't it just be the entire animal?" Or a bear? Bears are significantly less difficult to draw than just part of a dog.

"I don't know what to tell you, princess," Ian says. "I don't know the meaning behind the stars, or their names. I just know how to find them."

"But how?"

"Is this a game of twenty questions?"

I shake my head. "I'm only curious. I don't know anything about the stars and you just happen to know a lot." I turn to my side to face him. "What could have turned you into a little starboy?"

Ian then turns to the right and he's so close that I can feel the warmth of his body bounce off to me. "Starboy?"

"Yeah." Though I did not really think this through. "You're a boy who happens to know a lot about the stars. Hence, starboy."

He thinks about it for a moment before shrugging. "Well, it's better than four-eyes."

I smile in triumph. "That's right, starboy. Now, answer the question."

Ian raises a brow at me.

"Please?" I ask politely.

"You want to know the little sad story?"

I want to know more about you, is what I want to say. But I hold it back. Instead, I nod. "It can't be that sad, right?"

Ian looks back up at the night sky with a melancholy sigh. "It's a little sad. Before I moved here, my parents were struggling. That's as nicely as I can put it. My parents were fighting a lot before settling on divorce. I couldn't fall asleep and every night for an entire summer, I would sneak out to the backyard and lie down. Kind of like what we're doing now." He runs a hand through his hair, letting himself breathe before continuing. "When your parents are going through a divorce—especially at that time of your life when you're finally adjusting to everything—it's hard. I couldn't help but wonder if their divorce was my fault and being the Catholic boy I once was, I would pray and ask God what I did and how I could fix it."

"But it wasn't your fault," I tell him. "Your parents' decisions have nothing to do with you."

"That's not what I had thought back then." He polishes off the rest of his ice cream cone. "I found more comfort in finding constellations than people because it's somewhat soothing to realize that from up there, problems like that are so insignificant. We could be struggling to figure out if the guy or girl we like feels the same way about us and up there? It doesn't matter because we're just smaller than a speck of dust. Up there... you're free."

Am I going crazy or is there some sort of implied meaning to all of that? I knew that his parents were divorced—it seemed that way when I met Ian's mother through video call—but I didn't realize how badly it affected him.

Does he not like his status in school? Or to have everything handed to him on a silver platter? Ian never shied away from the spotlight when it was handed to him but I realize now that he didn't want it in the first place.

"Wow." I don't know what else to say. I'm sorry your parents are divorced? I can't act sympathetic because I'm not familiar with what he went through.

"The view here is a lot better, by the way," Ian marvels. "Eight years and I never got tired of it. I'll always miss Texas but I'm glad I moved here."

"Because of the view?" I tease.

He shakes his head earnestly. "Well that too. But also because I met you."

I laugh, slightly cringing on the inside due to the cheesiness of that sentence. "If I had a nickel for every little corny thing you've said in the past month, I would have been able to pay you back for dinner tonight."

He shrugs. "It's all true, princess. And don't think I'm letting you pay me back."

"We'll see about that." I sigh as I bring my knees up, resting my chin on top. "So that's your little story? The big secret?"

"I wouldn't call it a secret," he says. "But sure. What about you?"

"What about me?" I don't know. I like to think I'm an open book—to a certain extent, that is. "I'm not really that interesting, Ian. So ask away, but I guarantee that you'll be disappointed."

"I only have one question."

I look down at my nails. The white polish was already chipping off so I might as well continue to pick at it. "Go ahead."

"What happened with you and Hardwick?"

I feel myself freeze up at the question. Shit, I walked right into that one, didn't I?

Chapter 32

Truth be told, I had more than one question running through my mind but I was worried those would scare her away so I chose the one that seemed the easiest to answer.

I didn't ask the right question, did I? Because I've gotten nothing but silence on Attie's end since I brought up Chase. Curiosity got the best of me.

My hand softly touches her now stiff shoulder instinctively. "Should I have not asked?"

She shakes her head, still not facing me. "I told you to ask away, didn't I?"

"Yeah, but—"

"I'm just not sure if you want me to answer that question," she tells me. "I don't want to change anything."

"Between us?"

"Between you and Chase." She brushes her hair over to her other shoulder. "I mean, you guys are friends, right?"

"Meh." Hardwick and were good friends while he was on the team, sure. However, when he left, so did all the other reasons to hang out with him. Football is pretty time-consuming and now we just greet each other in passing. The dunk booth was the only exception.

"I won't lie," Attie adds. "It would change your outlook on me, too."

My hand moves from her shoulder to her knee. I give it a small squeeze. "Nothing's going to change how I see you, princess. I promise."

Attie finally turns to face me and takes a deep breath before explaining. "You might want to rethink that statement after I finish telling you the story. Last year, I was trying to get over this huge crush I had."

"The guy you wrote the letter to?" I ask.

She nods before continuing. "Anyway, I had thought to myself, 'what's the best way to get over a guy? Date someone else.'"

She visibly cringes at the sentence falling out of her mouth. I don't blame her—if I were in her shoes, I would have felt the same.

"I knew Chase from an encounter I had with him at the school library. He had that injury that stopped him from playing football. And I thought he was cute so I decided to make a move on him—by that I mean, I asked him to watch my stuff, he took a peek at my sketchbook, and started a conversation about one of my sketches." She pauses for a moment. "I swear, I'm getting to the point."

I wave a hand in dismissal. "Take your time, princess. There's no rush." I could listen to her talk for hours and still not tire of the sound of her soft voice.

A small smile appears on her lips for a mere moment before disappearing, in a blink-and-you-miss-it kind of moment. "One thing led to another, and I found myself stealing any chance I could get with him. He had almost all my firsts. Those two months were a good distraction. At least, until they weren't."

"Almost?" That was a thought that should not have left my brain. Ugh, stupid mouth just won't cooperate.

"Chase wanted to move things a little faster and I wasn't ready, no matter how many times he begged or tried. So at Ethan Haynes's party—it was actually a year ago today, now that I think about it—we met up." She absentmindedly brings one hand up to her left knee, tracing circles on my wrist before resuming. It's a little soothing—I won't lie—but this might just be a warning to not freak out and kick a palm tree. I can't make any promises. "I can recall the moments before disaster all too well. He fetched me a beer and I drank the whole thing without even thinking, while Amy played a game of seven minutes in heaven. All of a sudden, I had this really bad headache and I went to go lie down somewhere. I wasn't paying attention to my surroundings before I passed out and woke up in my bedroom the next morning."

I don't say anything for about a minute because I'm trying to wrap my head around it all. That was a lot of information to take in all at once.

"Ian, your hand's a little too tight."

I soften my grip on Attie's knee, but keep my hand there. "He did this?" I cannot believe what I had just heard. Attie didn't say it outright—but the symptoms...

That rumor you heard? About him? Well, it's actually true.

This explains so much. Okay, it's not like Galileo discovered a whole new comet or anything but it might as well be.

Last year, there was a rumor spreading around about what Hardwick did to some girl at a party, just before homecoming. I was at that party and didn't notice anything sketchy. Then again, my mind and body were a bit preoccupied that night.

I didn't believe that rumor for a second when it first started spreading because I had thought him to be a decent guy. The entire cheer team believed the rumor, my brother believed it, and there were a few others but that was about it.

I really hope, for the sake of both of us, that Attie's kidding. No one—and I mean no one—should have to go through something like that.

Unfortunately, she nods with her head hung low. "I should have been more careful about what was in that cup in the first place. I always knew I was a lightweight—it runs in the family—but when Jason told me that it never happens to him, that's when I knew."

"Jason knows?"

"He was the reason I woke up in my own bed instead of somewhere else."

This actually explains his behavior. Sophia wasn't the only person hostile to Hardwick—Jason didn't like the guy either. I thought he just didn't like the guy in general. Hell, I wouldn't even be surprised if he got a punch in when it happened.

Not many people are lucky enough to have a sibling that would do anything for their sister. Attie is surrounded by people who love and care about her to that extent. I would do anything for that girl. Even if it meant punching the daylights out of Hardwick.

No friend of mine would do anything like that to anyone, nevermind Attie Ryder. It almost feels like a betrayal of sorts.

"Wait a minute," I say, as a realization dawns on me. "Did you just say that you should have done something about it?"

Attie nods, tears welling up in her eyes. "If I was more aware of what was happening, of his real intentions, then I would have put a stop to it. I shouldn't have to spend so much time fawning over someone who doesn't really care. But I did, and look where it got me."

"No, this has nothing to do with you." I cup both of my hands to each cheek. "None of this is your fault, princess. Do you understand? None of it." I can't emphasize that enough.

"But—"

"I know you're probably going to say that it is for some other reason," I continue, interrupting her. "But that's all on Chase. He made that choice himself. I'm not trying to defend him in any way. You can't let someone put you down like that." I just hate seeing her look so defeated. A guy did something stupid, and for some reason, the blame is placed on her.

"Besides, you technically did do something about it," I point out in an attempt to brighten the situation. "You broke his nose."

Attie sniffles and wipes a tear that escapes her eye. "I did. It was a good taste of his own medicine. Now that I think of it."

I raise a brow. "Maybe I'll get a turn at socking him next time I see him."

Her eyes widen. "Please don't. It's not worth getting you in trouble."

Not like I haven't gotten into trouble already. "It's not like Jason didn't punch him the first chance he got."

"He didn't."

That catches me by surprise. "Your brother. The over-protective, extremely sarcastic, slightly aggressive, twin brother didn't punch Hardwick?"

She shakes her head, twirling a piece of dark hair between her fingertips. "He almost did, but I stopped him since it wasn't worth getting suspended for."

Shame. If it was up to me, I would have knocked his lights out. Repeatedly. And not feel a single ounce of remorse before giving Jason a turn.

"You should have let him, princess," I chuckle.

"Maybe when we graduate high school," she says. "If not, then I'll get him a punching bag for Christmas and stick a picture of Chase's face on it."

We look at each other as the thought of it settles into our minds before we burst out laughing until our lungs can't take it. It's good to see her smile after confiding in me about something so personal.

"Maybe I'm overthinking everything," Attie eventually says. "Should I just stop thinking?"

"Not completely," I say before cringing. "That came out wrong, didn't it?"

"What do you mean?"

I almost punch myself for even answering the question. That alone didn't feel right but I couldn't stop myself. "Can I start over?"

She nods.

I think carefully about the words I want to say for a few seconds before I start talking. "Maybe you're not letting yourself feel. The way you're phrasing it sounds to me like you're a head-over-heart kind of girl, princess."

Attie starters at me for a minute. "You should be a therapist."

I shake my head, suddenly feeling a little shy. Nah, I'll stick to analyzing space over people. "Maybe try doing something without thinking about it."

"At all?" Her eyes widen.

"Right now," I nod. "Unless it requires thinking."

Attie hesitates, allowing herself a moment to dwell on it. It's dark out and all the light is coming from the moon beaming at us from the night sky and the street lamps but even so, I allow myself to gaze upon her.

This girl is so fucking beautiful and she doesn't know it.

"Okay," she finally says. "One more thing."

"Sure."

"Please don't hate me for this."

I'm a little confused. "Princess, why would I—"

I can't even finish that sentence because, in the next moment, Attie pulls my face closer to hers and kisses me. It happened so fast that my brain couldn't regulate it until I feel her pull away. My eyes open slightly and she stares at me with her wide blue eyes, as if to ask, is this okay?

The moment her soft lips press onto mine again, I could taste her mango ice cream that she had eaten not that long ago almost instantly and I'm hooked. I pull her closer until there is almost no space between us because I just cannot get enough of this.

When her arms wrap around my torso, I get the hunch that she wants more from this moment. From me. From us.

And neither of us wants it to end.

But it had to end. The moment we both came back up for air, I had no other choice but to drive her back home so she doesn't get caught sneaking in. We don't really talk for most of the ride. I can't say why Attie's silent, but I can't lie and explain that I was focusing on the road in front of me.

I don't think I've ever felt more relaxed around someone the way I've been around Attie in just six hours.

That high doesn't leave me when I kiss her goodnight, or the entire drive back home. And when Derek looks at me weirdly and asks what drug I took, I ignore him and head straight up to my room.

I remove my glasses and place them inside the top drawer on my nightstand when something blue and sparkly catches my eyes. A wax seal with the letter R capitalized.

Huh. Truthfully, I forgot that it existed. There were a bunch of letters from Attie that I've kept in my locker. This one—the one she'd left in there by accident last month—is the only one that hasn't been opened.

I haven't read it but right now, it's basically chanting in my ear: Open me, Ian. Open me.

The temptation is strong but I fell as if I'm invading Attie's privacy just by opening the letter and reading what's inside.

The two halves of my brain are conflicting with each other but I close the top drawer anyway.

Shoving that thought away, I change out of my shorts and shirt and shower, washing the smell of salt water out of my body and before I can dive into the bed, my hands move on their own accord and I find myself opening that same drawer again.

If anyone wants to know how it feels to have a fucking piece of paper taunt you to no bitter end, then let me just say: it's a pain in the ass.

In other words: do as I say and not as I do.

Curiosity overpowers whatever resistance I have and I find my arm reaching inside the open drawer for the letter.

Just one little peek at the letter shouldn't hurt, right?

Only two words.

Chapter 33

I close my locker door immediately before turning to face Sierra. We decided to meet up along with our secretary and treasurer to discuss the details regarding tomorrow's club meeting. Even though the end-of-the-year project is underway, there's the matter of finances and scheduling...technically everything else. Since the beginning of the month, we've been laser-focused on our little animation project. It's nothing crazy—just to help newcomers adjust to how the next semester will work—but I'm excited to see the end product.

"So, there's still the movie night we're hosting before winter break," Sierra says. "Do you think the ICC department will let us stay past sunset then?"

I shrug. "We have to talk to Cameron about that."

The meeting goes off without a hitch but I feel like everyone is speaking at a sloth's pace. Possibly because my mind drifts off to Saturday night more than once. I still fill in little details and ask questions but that's about as much as I can handle. Sierra's more active in these settings than I am.

To say that Saturday was possibly one of the best days I've ever had would be pretty damn accurate. In my sixteen years of living on this planet, I've never snuck out of my house.

I can only describe it in one word: invigorating.

From learning how to surf to telling Ian about what happened with Chase—and even kissing him? I kissed him. Not the other way around. I didn't have a reason to kiss him nor did I need one.

No dares.

No audience.

Just me, him, and the shining stars above us. I swear I could hear them clapping when it all happened.

I couldn't tell Amy about everything as soon as I got back home because I technically wasn't allowed to use my phone since I was and am still grounded. Even now, she's blissfully unaware of that night.

If so, then why don't I care?

I play with the mouse headband I took off at the beginning of the meeting. Today marks the first day of homecoming spirit week. Also known as today, this theme requires us to dress like animals. I don't know whose idea it was to do this but I like spirit days and don't mind dressing up, so I borrowed Jason's old Mickey Mouse ears from our one and only trip to Disneyland and wore all brown to look like Jerry the Mouse.

The clever mouse from Tom and Jerry. I used to love that show when I was a kid.

"Attie?" Sierra's voice brings me out of the little bubble of thoughts. I look up to find four pairs of eyes staring at me.

My cheeks heat up. "Yeah?"

"Did you want to present the project?"

Oh, right. I'm usually the one who comes up with the original idea before the rest of the club members either tweak or add to it. If things go accordingly, the project will be done by spring and can be entered into a short film competition.

I reach into my backpack and pull out a piece of scratch paper that I drew on for the meeting, as I had no time to go to Michaels and buy a new sketchbook.

You know, being grounded and all.

Mrs. Johnson, our club advisor, chimes in whenever needed and we wrap up a few minutes earlier than planned.

Thank the gods for that because I am so hungry that I could eat a fucking Trojan horse.

I wave goodbye to the rest of the board members before heading in the direction of the cafeteria. There should be enough time to grab lunch but I don't think I can finish it before math.

Just as I reach the doors, a hand pulls me back and I let out a yelp. What is it with my arm? It's not a stupid doorknob.

Just as I'm about to say something along the lines of that, I find Ian's ocean eyes on me and almost instantly, my heart starts pounding right out of my chest. If I was in an animated movie, you would see the hearts in my eyes.

Sounds embarrassing but true. I hadn't seen him all morning. Not including the lack of text messages—again, no phone—I haven't been able to spot him in the halls. You'd think a six-foot-two blonde with square-shaped glasses would be a breeze to find.

You'd be wrong.

"We need to talk," he tells me.

Those four words send a small shiver down my spine. Not in a good way. Though the last time I heard those words come out of Ian's mouth, in that exact order no less, nothing bad came from it. However, I can't say the same again.

The tone of Ian's voice was laced with...hurt. Wait, what? How is that possible?

And my mind is going another hundred miles per hour just dissecting this little gesture.

I take a deep breath. "Okay," I reply.

Ian leads me to the only empty classroom close enough to the cafeteria, which takes a little longer than usual, considering that we've reached that time in the semester when students would sit in teacher's classrooms and eat their lunches while studying.

We may or may not have walked into a club meeting but in my defense, it was for a chess club—they weren't as loud as all the others.

Ian closes the door behind him, the movements are not as fluid as usual, and it almost scares me. Is he okay? Did something bad happen to his family?

Shit, I hope I'm just overreacting again.

"I won't lie," I begin. "You're kind of scaring me right now, Ian. Are you okay? What's going on?"

"I'm fine," he answers. "Just answer me this. Do you think I'm a decent person?"

I nod.

"And you trust me?"

"What's with the twenty questions?" I ask. "I'm not being recorded, am I?"

He shakes his head. "Please, princess. Just answer the question."

"Yes, I trust you." What is going on here? "Why would I not—"

"Then why didn't you tell me about Derek?"

I almost didn't hear Ian ask the question until he brought up his brother and all the noise falling out of my mouth runs dry. One-half of my brain wonders how he could know about Derek. The other half?

Well, it's afraid. I'm scared to ask, knowing that he probably did.

I thought he wasn't going to do it!

"Oh my gosh," I mutter to myself in disbelief before raising my voice loud enough for him to hear. There's no one else in the classroom for some odd reason—what is with teachers leaving them unattended?

"You read the letter, didn't you?" I implore.

Much to my horror, the guy doesn't respond. His eyes are hesitant and I wonder to myself why I even asked the question.

His mannerisms are enough of a response.

I should have known that he was going to read it. It was inevitable given that he held onto that letter since September. Multiple thoughts fly around in my head but only one that sticks out like a sore thumb in this very moment:

I thought I trusted him.

"I wouldn't have said anything," he says, "I'm just a little offended, to be honest."

"Why?" I feel tears in my eyes but refuse to let them fall.

"Because I thought you trusted me!" He breathes in and exhales, holding back frustration. "I've told you so many times that I wouldn't make fun of you for anything. I would never intentionally hurt you. I'm not hurt that you didn't write the letter for me, Attie."

The name. It's a rarity, hearing my real name fall from his lips but I didn't think it would hurt so much.

"I'm hurt that you didn't think you could trust me," he finishes.

"I don't know what to think! Okay?" I finally blurt. Those words were a long time coming but they needed to be said. And the tear finally falls. "What was I supposed to say to you? 'Oh, I thought I was in love with your brother but surprise! I'm not?' Like that's even believable."

"You could have told the truth." He heavily emphasizes those last three words. "That's all it takes."

"Would you have believed it?" I question, looking straight into his eyes. How I manage to not stray from his ocean eyes without crying, I will never know. "Would you have trusted me to tell you the truth?"

Ian doesn't answer right away and therein lies an answer.

I scoff. "That's what I thought."

"Attie—"

"That was something I thought I could trust you with," I continue, ignoring his protest. "I'm starting to regret trusting you with that letter." I grab my backpack from the floor and start walking towards the door of the classroom, which is now slightly ajar.

Ian grabs my hand and I spin around to face him. "No, Ian," I beg. "I can't do this anymore. All of this." I gesture to the space between us. "The lies, all of it. I'm done. I just can't. We don't even need to do it."

Without another glance, I walk straight out of that classroom as the bell starts ringing.

There will be no more pretending. I should feel lighter, somehow. No longer feeling guilty of lying to everyone else. So the question I'm asking myself now is why do I feel burdened?

Chapter 34

"Dude, what's up with you?" Derek demands as he enters my room. No knocking, no alerting me that he would be entering. Nope, he just charges into my room.

"Man, can you just leave me alone right now?" I don't want to talk to anyone, especially Derek of all people.

"No." And he doesn't. "Do you know how bad you have to be acting for BJ to ask me about you?"

Pretty bad, I have to agree. My best friend isn't exactly known to be the most observant—except when it comes to Sophia.

"You didn't even go to practice today!" He exclaims. "What happened, man?"

"I wasn't feeling well," I lie.

I try my best to tune him out by focusing my attention back on my phone. Instead of my brother taking the hint, he just snatches it up. "I'm not leaving until you answer me."

"Frickin nuisance," I mutter.

"You call me that for a reason." And he's fully owning up to that nickname. On any other day, I wouldn't have given a shit but the cosmic being that is currently watching over this house must despise me right now.

I narrow my eyes at Derek, who places my phone away in the back pocket of his jeans. "I'm not even scared right now," he says. "You couldn't look angry even if you tried."

"I am," I say.

"Then talk about it."

"I am not subjecting myself to a therapy session."

"Suit yourself." Derek's phone starts ringing, startling the both of us. "Okay, I wasn't expecting a phone call." He reaches into his front pocket and brings his phone up to his ear. "What's up, Jason?"

Oh, shit.

"Dude, can you calm down? I don't want permanent hearing damage." Derek's brown eyes widen and turn to me. "Oh shit. You're kidding." A beat of silence follows. "Uh-huh. Yeah, I'll make sure to tell him. No, Jason. He is seventeen—why would he have a will written?"

What the hell?

"I'm trying, man! He's acting like a stubborn ass right now and won't say shit. No, you're not driving over here. Because I don't want to clean up all his blood before Dad gets home, that's why!"

"He can hear you," I murmur.

Derek holds up a hand, telling me to be patient. "Calm down, man. You talk to her, I'll try to talk to him, and we'll convene later. BYE." He hangs up the phone and punches my left shoulder. Hard.

"Ow!" I rub my shoulder. That hurt more than I thought it would. "What the f—"

"You broke up with Attie?!" He shouts, interrupting me.

"You don't have to remind me. I was there." It's on the tip of my tongue to correct Derek—she was the one who ended it all when she stormed out of that classroom without a second glance—but I hold back.

Derek pinches the bridge of his nose to conceal how annoyed he is with me. "You are—and these are Jason's words, mind you—the 'biggest dumbass I've ever met.'"

He got one thing right. I am a dumbass for not seeing that Attie had feelings for my brother the whole time instead of me. I wouldn't have agreed to the whole thing if I knew. There's a whole lot that I wouldn't have done if I knew.

Would you, though?

My head is pounding because of that one question that has been on my mind for the past six hours. Because...I don't know. Looking back at it now, it would have seemed reasonable.

"Ian, at least tell me what happened." Derek makes his way over to the other side of the bed and sits down, eyes not straying from my own. I think.

"Do I have to?" I move my eyes from Derek and towards my nightstand, where the letter that's been taunting me all day rests right under my glasses. Glittery blue wax seal and all.

Derek's eyes must have moved to the nightstand as well because he hops off the bed to grab my glasses and the letter. He first holds out my glasses for me to take—which I hesitantly do so—and holds the letter up. "Is this a break-up letter?"

I put my glasses on and the blob in front of me transforms into my younger brother dressed in all brown, freckles on display, and fake antlers on his head. "You're not going to leave until I answer you, aren't you?"

"What makes you think I was even going to leave at all?" He raises a brow.

I sigh in defeat. "That's the letter from September."

His eyes widen, like a deer in the headlights. It fits, since today is the first day of Spirit Week and the theme was Pets vs.Wildlife. "Wait, the one that landed in your locker?"

I nod.

"The one that Attie said she knew where it was from?"

I nod again.

"Are you going to answer me with actual words?"

I shake my head in response.

"And you call me a nuisance," he mutters, lifting the seal off the paper.

"No, wait! Don't—"

"What's so bad about this letter that it broke you two up..." his voice trails off as he starts reading. His brows fly off his face before settling back down only a few minutes later. "Oh." His eyes move up to me before moving back to the letter.

"Are you done, yet?" I murmur.

"No way, man. I'm almost done."

I have to wait two more minutes before Derek folds the letter and hands it to me. "Did you read the letter?"

"Yeah, I did."

"But did you read it?"

Why the hell is he asking me this? I read the letter. Is there anything left to say? I don't think so.

"Derek, I read the letter." I run a hand through my hair aggressively. "I know what it is. She wrote a love letter for you—"

"It's not a love letter."

That stops me in my tracks. "What do you mean? Do you not see the heart there? It's a love letter." And love letters are not meant for Ian Bale.

"I see the heart, man," Derek acknowledges. "I also read the first sentence." Much to my dismay, he unfolds the letter and points to the first paragraph.

Before you continue reading, I just want to make this clear: I'm not begging for anything. I wrote this so I could get it all out of my system. Specifically, to get you out of my system.

"Did you actually read the whole thing?"

I hang my head. Okay, maybe I didn't read the whole thing. Just the first two words. Specifically, where it reads: *Dear Derek.*

"I'm glad this isn't a love letter," Derek says. "It would be embarrassing for both of us."

I raise a brow at him. "Why would it be embarrassing to you?" Derek's never fazed by anything.

"First of all, it's Derek's sister. That would break the bro code." Well, that's obvious. Technically, I broke the bro code but Jason has yet to punch the daylights out of me. Not for faking a relationship with his sister—if he even knows about it, which is likely—but for ending said relationship over a piece of paper.

Sticks and stones can break my bones but I didn't think words would hurt this much.

"Wait," I say just as my brain comes to a full stop. "You said 'first of all.' What's the second thing?"

"What?" I've never seen Derek's face so pale in my life, which says a lot since he's naturally kind of pale.

Oh my God. He is hiding something. I was right all along.

"I won't judge, man," I assure him, holding both hands up as if I'm holding white flags. "I'd never judge you."

His eyes focus on me, almost like he's trying to figure out if I'm telling him the truth. Aside from the letter and the fake relationship, I've never given Derek a reason to think otherwise.

He takes a deep breath and pinches the duvet between his two fingers. "I guess I'd have to tell you at some point. It would have been embarrassing because..."

Cue the subtle drum roll.

"Because I'm gay."

Derek squeezes his eyes shut while waiting for my response. I'll be honest—I didn't know what reasoning he was going to give me but it certainly wasn't this. But who the fuck am I to judge?

"How long have you known?" I ask.

His eyes slowly open, and when he notices the lack of surprise on my face, his body loosens up. I had once thought that it could be a possibility but I didn't let myself dive deep into that train of thought because half of the time, my gut instinct is wrong.

"I guess I've always known," he finally responds.

"Even in middle school?"

He nods. This explains more than I thought.

"Okay."

Derek. "That's it?"

I shrug. "What? I'm not going to make a big deal out of this. I mean, I'm glad you trusted me enough to tell me something so important but you're still the little brother who threw a butter knife over my head when I was five. Who or what you like doesn't change that."

My brother lets out a breath of relief and laughs. I remember that day all too well, while he doesn't. I still take every chance I can to remind him because it's just funny to me. And to Mom, who witnessed the whole thing happen.

A realization dawns on me. Actually, I'm brought back to another, more recent memory...

"Is this why you dodge Mom's questions about dating?"

Almost immediately, his smile drops and he nods. I can start to see his eyes get a little glassy. Immediately, I wrap my brother in a hug. I don't try to understand what he's going through—hell, he just told me something majorly important to him—but the best I can do right now is comfort him. I don't know what it's like to be in his shoes.

"You know how Mom reacted when you introduced her to Attie over the video call the other day," he sobs. "She was so happy for you. I know she wants that for me. Happily married to a woman who cherishes me. I just don't want to see her disappointed if she finds out."

"When," I correct him. "Derek, Mom just wants you to be happy. Regardless of who you love."

He pulls away to wipe his face. "I don't know if she'll be happy for me if I told her."

"She will." I rub his shoulder. "Mom loves you so much. And if she doesn't accept you, then it's her loss. You shouldn't have to spend so much time over somebody who doesn't truly love you."

As soon as the words leave my mouth, Attie's voice appears in my mind. I shouldn't have to spend so much time fawning over someone who doesn't really care.

I shouldn't be thinking about her right now of all times but my mind sure loves deceiving me.

Derek must sense something because now he's patting my back. "Alright, bud. Enough about me. I doubt that letter is the only cause of your moodiness. And you're telling me everything."

"Everything?" I whine. I know I'm whining about this but my love life (lack thereof, in most cases) is not one I prefer to talk about. I'd rather bring up the Roman Empire and I know jack shit about that.

"There's not much to tell," I lie. To me, there isn't. It's just a deal I made with Attie. Did it evolve to more? Possibly. Did I forget about the deal for longer than I should have? Maybe.

"Um, yes!" Derek exclaims. "Of course there fucking is."

I can't deny it any longer, can I? At some point, my brother would have found out one way or another.

"No, there isn't," I refute, taking a deep breath. Okay, here it goes. "Because none of it was real."

See, in absolute Derek-Jackson-Bale-nature, I would have expected him to burst with questions. His mind is probably doing exactly that but instead, with a demeanor so calm it's almost terrifying, he simply just coaxes me into explaining what I had just told him.

And so I do. I tell him everything. Okay, not everything but I manage to get the important details out in the air.

"This is a lot to take in," he finally responds after mere minutes of silence. "But I see why she's mad at you."

"Oh great. Exactly what I want to hear."

My brother tilts his head. "Is that supposed to be sarcasm? Because you're not very good at it."

"Just tell me why," I urge him.

"Alright, alright," he complies. "Pushy. Were you supposed to read the letter?"

That's where he got me. Instead of responding, my eyes wander around my room, a small confined area that I'm more familiar with than the rest of this house.

"I rest my case," Derek announces. "She didn't want you to read it but because you did, she felt betrayed. Granted, this whole breakup could have easily been avoided had you not opened the letter—"

"You don't have to remind me, Derek," I interrupt. "I was there."

"You're not entirely to blame, if that helps." He pats my shoulder. "In my opinion, at least. I can't read Attie's mind so I don't understand why she did that but it wasn't right to cut you off like that."

Do I agree with my brother on that? I'm not sure. On one hand, I do wish that she let me speak. I wanted so badly to but never got the chance. On the other hand, I don't completely blame her, knowing what I do. I crossed a boundary when I opened that letter.

Sadly, I'm not the first guy to do that with her.

"How do I get her to trust me again?" I ask with defeat. Let's face it—I might need some help.

Derek shrugs. "You'll need to talk to her. One day, when this all blows over and she's not steaming mad, you talk to her."

"One day."

He nods. "Yes. Right now, however, you are going to take your mind off of the girl you love—"

My eyes widen.

"Oh stop denying it," he teases. "You wouldn't be like this if you weren't in love with her. It's painfully obvious."

I'm a little hurt, mostly confused. That much is certain because all of this was sudden. The "break-up" and her outburst. The revelation that she didn't believe she could trust me with something.

Is it really possible that I could be in love with her? Could that be why it hurts so much?

"But you can't sit around like that forever, though," Derek continues. "I'm not saying to rebound but you have to keep moving. Physically. One day, you can apologize and make things right for the two of you. But right now? You need to keep your mind from floating around in a depressing-ass cloud."

He's right about two things:

Firstly, I got to keep my head on my schoolwork and football for the rest of the week, assuming I can hold onto that promise for long.

The second? I wasn't wearing some rose-colored glasses or seeing things that weren't there. I just didn't see what was there from the beginning. It was painfully obvious. Just not for me.

I didn't see that, all this time, I was in love with Attie Ryder.

Was? Who the hell am I kidding—that never changed.

Chapter 35

"At-Bat?" Amy's voice breaks through. All day, I've been hearing muffled voices similar to the adults in Charlie Brown. Just muffled, off-key, trumpet noises.

I look up from the instructions. We're doing a two-week long lab in physics today and me, Jason, and Amy decided to pair up and build our rocket for our projectile motion unit.

Yes, that's a thing you get to do in physics. The artist in me would have been excited if I wasn't so distracted.

"Did you hear anything we said?" Jason stares at me the way I would observe any of the cartoon paintings on my wall.

I blink at him and shake my head. "Sorry, what did you guys need?"

Amy looks over the table and reads the instructions. "So we need to decide what shape the top should be."

"Easy," Jason says. "A cone." He then turns to me. "Right?"

I barely hear him but I nod anyway.

"Attie?" He snaps a finger in my face.

I turn to him and glare. "Rude."

"Well, what are brothers for if not to be rude?"

I roll my eyes at him, which causes a soft smile to appear on my brother's face. He did that on purpose. Jason doesn't do things without a reason, which says a lot when his ADHD is taken into consideration.

I try to focus on the work in front of us but at this point, every little thing reminds me of Ian. He's in the class after mine, probably doing something similar to this. Hell, I swear I saw someone with a dragon pin on their backpack and immediately thought of the one I drew on his arm a couple of weeks ago.

It's not right to think so much about the boy who broke my heart but I can't help it.

This is why I chose to not get wrapped up in relationships! After what Chase did my sophomore year and what Ian had said–or hadn't said—to me...

And what I said to him...

I just don't think my head or my heart could handle it.

But I took that jump and landed headfirst on a rock that broke me. Not literally, but it might as well given how much it hurts. I let myself out of my head and look at what that led to.

The bell rings and we pack up our things. At this point, Mr. Ali is going by each group and checking on our progress. Luckily we managed to finish building our rocket before he finally approaches our table.

"Looks like you guys are ready for next week," he observes.

Jason and Amy pack up their things but I'm still sitting down and barely moving an inch. It doesn't hurt to move—come on, I'm not that dramatic—but I don't want to go to the cafeteria.

"I'll wait for you outside," Jason tells me before he and Amy walk out of the classroom. My best friend has to meet with her dad every day during lunch so it doesn't bother me that she leaves without a word.

"Attie, are you okay?" Mr. Ali asks.

"I'm fine, Mr. Ali," I lie.

He shakes his head, clearly not believing me. "No, you're not. It's so obvious."

I raise my head to look at him. He's a pretty tall guy—around six feet if I had to guess—with curly jet-black hair, medium-dark skin, and sleeves of tattoos on both arms. Mr. Ali also has the equivalent of a male resting bitch-face which has me wondering how this guy could know what goes on inside the mind of a teenage girl, despite being on the younger side of the age spectrum.

"I have a sister your age who's been through this," he clarifies. "Sort of."

"I thought your sister was older than you." He talks about his sister a lot in class. Okay, not a lot but when someone goes off-topic, he'll occasionally bring up his sister and some weird story.

He smiles softly. "I have two sisters. A blessing and a curse." Mr. Ali sits on top of the desk next to me. "Not to turn this into a therapy session but recently, we found out that my mother is probably not going to make it. When we got the news, it felt like the world was ending."

"What makes you think that it's the same as how I'm feeling?"

"I observe a lot," he tells me. "I was sixteen not that long ago. I understand what heartbreak feels like."

Okay, so maybe he does know what I'm feeling. It's still two different types of heartbreak.

"How did you get over it?" I ask softly.

He hops off the desk and grabs the rocket off mine, keeping a firm grasp on it. "I'm really not. I got the news only a week ago but I'm trying to handle it the same way I did when she was first diagnosed." He takes a deep breath. "Heartbreak is normal but no matter what, all you can do about it is take it one day at a time."

I tilt my head. "Does that work?"

My physics teacher shrugs, carefully twirling my rocket in both hands. "I'll let you know when I start feeling better."

That's totally assuring.

"It's not great advice—I leave the therapy stuff to my younger sister—but it's the best I can do," he tells me, placing the rocket back onto my desk.

It's only been two days since everything happened with Ian. How long would it take to erase what was probably the most thrilling and amazing month of my life?

"I'll think about it," I say.

He nods before heading back to his desk.

"Hey, why don't you mention your little sister?" I ask, just out of curiosity as I begin packing my things.

My teacher hesitates. "I'm not sure it's appropriate for me to answer that question."

I take my time packing my things up before exiting the classroom. Just as he has promised, Jason's standing by the door. Only now, he's not alone.

Either I was in that classroom longer than I had thought, or Amy's meeting with her dad didn't consist of much because I find my best friend and brother conversing with pinkies hooked.

"What's with the pinkies?" I ask.

Almost immediately, they let go as if either one had contracted cooties. "Nothing, why?"

"We were just trying to think of a cool handshake," Amy blurts, with Jason narrowing his eyes as if to think, seriously?

"It took you eleven years to realize that?"

"Yeah, yeah, we're eleven years late, whatever." Jason rushes through the whole thing before grabbing my arm. "Come on, we're going."

"Where?" Amy and I ask simultaneously.

"Out."

Uhhh. "Jason?"

"Yeah?"

"You do know that none of us can leave campus, right?" That's a privilege only allowed to seniors. The three of us, however, are juniors.

My brother shrugs. "Well, what our parents and Amy's dad don't know won't hurt them." He drags us towards the big glass doors that lead to the student parking lot. "Besides, Kelly's not here and I promised a friend we'd go somewhere for lunch."

Before I can ask who we're meeting up with, Jason pushes on the door almost aggressively and we're now outside.

And the inventor of the door rests happily in his grave.

"Finally! What took you guys so long?" A familiar voice calls out.

I look out to the student parking lot to find a tall figure leaning on the passenger side of the Jeep. At first, I feel my heart rate speed up like crazy, thinking why Ian could be there.

Until I notice the lack of square-shaped glasses and blond hair. I breathe a little easier knowing that it's Derek and not his older brother.

When we approach the car, Amy blurts out, "Why are you here?"

"Amy!" I scold.

She shrugs. "What? You were thinking it too, Attie."

Usually, the thought of hanging out with Derek would make butterflies flutter around in my stomach but I haven't felt any bouts of nervousness in the past month. But even just one thought of his brother makes my heart drop.

A lot has changed in the past month.

As if he's reading my thoughts, Derek holds his hands up, as if he's holding up two white flags. "I'm just here because I can't wait another three hours to leave campus."

Jason unlocks the car and we all pile inside, with me and Amy taking the backseat and Derek and Jason up front. I hold onto the handlebar as soon as I close the door.

Jason buckles up before looking at the rearview mirror and rolling his eyes at the sight. "Nice to know you have faith in my driving skills. And here I was about to hand you the aux."

I instantly let go of the handlebar and hold out my hand. "Please?"

Jason plugs his phone into the long charging cord and hands it to me. "Just don't play the ten-minute version of All Too Well again."

"Fine." After clicking on Spotify, I search for some random playlist and hit shuffle. The four of us sit in silence as music plays through the speakers of the car.

"Jason?" Amy asks after one song finishes and the next one starts playing. "Where exactly are we going?" I hope it's to get smoothies.

"To Michaels."

Wait, what? "Jason, you hate going to Michaels," I point out.

"So?" He shrugs, pulling into the parking lot. It's odd for me because anytime I need something from Michaels, Jason takes any excuse to stay behind, like faking a headache or being behind on homework.

All four of us exit the car as soon as Jason turns off the engine. "We meet back here in fifteen minutes. Sounds good?"

We all nod as we approach the craft store entrance and split off in multiple directions.

Chapter 36

I spent the past five minutes wandering around Michaels with no set destination until I find myself in the painter's aisles. I scan each shade in front of me, grabbing one bottle after the other before placing it back on the shelf. There are only so many colors on display.

"Are you going to buy any of that?"

I turn away from the display to find Derek standing across from me in the aisle. "Maybe." It's the first time in a while that we've hung out without either one of our brothers interfering. "What happened to Jason?"

He shrugs. "I lost him."

I laugh. "You lost Jason in a Michaels?"

Derek nods, a blush creeping onto his face. "I know, I know. How irresponsible of me."

This makes me laugh even harder and Derek follows suit. We both know my brother all too well. The reason he's hardly ever alone isn't only due to how social he is—it's because he's like a dog without a leash. Let the leash go, and you lose him.

Don't keep an eye on Jason, you will lose him. It's easy to lose track of my brother. It makes me wonder how we're even twins. Until I am reminded of the home-birth video Mom showed me and all my doubts get thrown out the window.

"Did you check the exit?" I ask in between laughs.

He nods. "Wasn't there." He laughs for a little longer before sobering up. "Honestly, I kind of just wanted to talk to you. Without Jason."

"Kind of?"

"It's important." He looks down both sides of the aisle, likely checking for anyone nearby. "It's about Ian."

Right then and there, my head and heart drops. Where is Jason when you need him? I do not want to talk or think about Ian at all. Especially now, when my heart feels more sore than my shoulder would after a tetanus shot. Or any stunt pulled in Phineas and Ferb.

"What about Ian?" I turn away from Derek and force my attention on a big bottle of titanium white paint. "We broke up. The End. There's nothing to talk about." No one lived happily ever after.

"He told me everything."

"He did?!" My voice cracks loudly and I slap my hand over my mouth. That was embarrassing.

I clear my throat and lower my voice. "I mean, he did?"

"Yep, on Monday." Derek runs a hand through his dark hair and I only notice how similar he is to his brother. Sure, they don't look alike but their mannerisms are the same.

I shouldn't have let Jason invite Derek along. Hanging out with one Bale brother after breaking up with the other isn't helping me overcome any feelings I harbored for Ian. Then again, I've spent the last two nights watching the All Too Well Short Film and listening to the designated heartbreak album: the Tortured Poets Department. Who's to say I'm completely numb? At least I can feel something whilst watching the film and listening to music.

"I'm kind of glad it wasn't a love note but—"

"Doesn't matter," I interrupt. "It's over between me and him."

Instead of shutting his mouth, Derek silently watches me for a minute before asking, "Is it?"

Yes! "Why are you asking?"

He shrugs. "I'm just trying to get a grasp on the whole "fake relationship" thing because it's kinda odd."

I focus my attention on the red bottle of paint behind me because I don't want to think or talk about this. I did need some paint because I ran out of titanium white acrylic last night when I was avoiding my weekly physics homework but I could use some more colors.

The possibility of coming back here after school is slim to nothing, since the store closes early and my grounding doesn't end until later tonight.

"I mean, why start a fake relationship? It's a little stupid," Derek continues.

"I ask myself that all the time," I mutter to myself before speaking back up. "Derek, why are you here? No offense but I don't see why you're doing this."

"None taken," he responds. "I just wanted to ask why."

"Your brother told you everything," I grit out. Not to sound rude now but this whole interogation session going on is starting to get on my nerves.

"He told me his side of the story." Derek grabs the bottle of paint out of my hands and places it down, causing me to look up at him. I don't feel a single ounce of emotion. Other than annoyed but that's a given. "I want to hear yours."

"What makes you think there's another side to this?"

He shrugs. "There always is." Derek looks away for a moment, gazing at the multiple colors of paint, the canvases behind him, and the brushes before wandering his light brown eyes back to me. I used to swoon over his eyes.

Now, I feel nothing.

"In my experience, no side is completely identical to the other," Derek explains. "No colors end up the exact same." He then chuckles. "Hell, not even twins have completely identical DNA. There's always one outlier. One little minute detail that separates them."

I furrow my brows at Derek. "You are surprisingly mature for a sixteen-year-old boy."

"You don't learn all this suddenly." He shakes his head. "Enough about me. Let's talk about you. Lay it on me, young Ryder."

I roll my eyes, holding back from correcting him. Because—for some odd fucking reason—I actually want to tell Derek everything. Amy doesn't know the full story because I could only tell her so much. It's not normal of me, to hold back from explaining everything to my best friend.

"This stays between us?" I ask wearily.

He nods, and that's the bit of assurance I need to continue.

I take a deep breath before finding the right words. "Back in Septembe r..."

At first, I was hesitant. This is Ian's younger brother—some details are not meant to be heard by a girl who is not only confused about her feelings towards said brother but regretful about her actions.

Fear of oversharing shouldn't be a problem when you're asked to tell yout side of the story, shouldn't it?

I do manage to hold back a couple of details.

"And now we're here," I conclude, gesturing to the piant supplies around us.

Derek reflects on the story for about a minute. Enough time for me to grab a large bottle of titanium white paint and decide to pay for it when I reach the front.

"You think he hates you because of this?" Derek guesses.

"I know he does," I correct him. The words I threw right at him still haunt me.

I'm starting to regret trusting you.

Just remembering those words causes tears to form in my eyes. I sniffle and wipe the one tear that escapes. Why am I crying over this?

Derek places one hand on my shoulder. "Seems like there's more to this that I don't know about. What I do know is that he doesn't hate you."

"What makes you believe that?" He seemed angry in that classroom before I left.

"Attie, I know my brother. It takes a lot for him to develop hatred for somebody. Even so, there is a fine line between love and hate." He shoves his hands into both pockets of his jacket. "Personally, I think it's both of your faults that you got into this mess."

"What a way to make me feel better," I mutter.

"I wasn't trying to."

I furrow my brows. "You are starting to sound a lot like Jason."

Derek rolls his eyes in response, cheeks turning red. "No I don't."

I gesture to his face. "See? You even roll your eyes like him."

"Here's something Jason would say if he knew all of this, then," he laughs quickly before sobering up. "It's not that you don't trust Ian—maybe you just don't trust yourself."

Five words that I didn't expect to render me speechless.

"I don't know why that's the case," he continues as if the statement didn't cause a sort of big bang in his head like it did for me. "All I can tell you is to sit on that for a minute. Talk to Ian. He'll understand. I, however, have to go find your brother."

Derek wanders away from the aisles and I'm left alone with the revelation.

He's right about one thing: I don't trust myself. At least, to an extent. With my artwork and schoolwork, that's simple enough. I'm confident in my talent because that shit took years. People, however? Not many of those are allowed in my tiny bubble of trust. I'm not exactly one of them, either. How did he know all that simply by the information that I gave him?

I'm left with two other thoughts consuming my brain:

Firstly: would Ian really understand?

Secondly: Derek should be a therapist.

Chapter 37

I don't know how the conversation led to that topic but one minute, my mother was all sunshine and rainbows, hay bale and horses—all that kind of stuff.

The next minute, she's just about ready to throw a metal horseshoe at my face. Or, more realistically, the screen.

"How did I raise such a stupid son?" She mutters, removing her glasses from her face to rub the bridge of her nose.

"Oof," Derek whispers in my direction. "You know you fucked up when Mom does that."

I elbow him on his left side.

Mom takes a deep breath in and exhales. "Boy, you better win her back."

"Mom, what makes you think that's possible?" Although I've spent more than half of my time focusing on my studies and training for the big game tomorrow—a game that my dad might actually show up to—the rest of the time has been spent thinking about Attie.

It's been a breeze avoiding her because of football but all I wanted to do was find her and tell her everything. But I know that even without all my commitments to football, Attie would actively avoid me.

"I've told you this before, Ian. And I will say it again," my mom explains. "You do not come across a girl like that very often. Someone as sweet and independent as her. I don't know what happened—and frankly, I don't want to—but a girl like that is a girl you better hold onto for the rest of your life." She places her glasses back on her face and crosses her arms.

"I'll try, Mom," I respond with, just to shift the topic.

Her eyes move to Derek. "You see to it that he does, hun."

My brother snorts. "Already a step ahead of you."

She hums. "That's my boy. Enough about your brother's mess up—"

"Hey," I complain, but she ignores it.

"How about you, Derek? Anyone special?"

That's my cue. I look down at my phone and widen my eyes. "Sorry to cut this short, Mom. But there's a team call that I need to be a part of. I have to go." I stand up from the floor and before I can turn around, Derek pulls on my shorts.

"Where are you going?" He whisper-shouts.

I gesture to my phone and shrug before heading out of his room. Once I'm out of sight, I shoot my brother a text.

Me: You've got this, bro. I'll always be in your corner. No matter what.

Derek told me on Wednesday that he was going to come out to Mom at our next video call with her. I'm keeping that door of opportunity ajar before it slams shut. The only thing that's been stopping him from taking that step towards being his true self has been our mother—apparently when he told Dad, it wasn't as much of a surprise.

Since Monday, his mannerisms and attitude are a lot more relaxed around me and I think that maybe it has lifted a weight off of his shoulders, one that he shouldn't have been carrying in the first place, if you ask me. Maybe talking to Mom about it would ease the rest of it off.

After heading downstairs, I walk towards the kitchen and barely open the fridge door when a rhythm of loud knocking is heard. I don't need to look through the peephole to see Jason standing there because he's the only person I know who doesn't use the doorbell. Either he arrives with Derek or bangs on the door in some random rhythm that I can't figure out.

I grab my Ginger Ale, close the fridge door shut and make my way over to the front door and unlock it without hesitation. Sure enough, Jason stands there looking down at his phone, probably talking to his girlfriend.

I'm holding back any laughter at how stupid he looks. Spirit week is still among us and Jason still dons his outfit from school this morning—or in his case, this afternoon. Jason came in during lunch, wearing a t-shirt with the Iron Man logo sprayed on and sunglasses, despite the sunset not shining in our direction.

Worst experience ever.

Imagine spending eight hours walking around while people whistled and shouted, "now that's America's ass!" To say that I've never been happier to go home is an understatement.

"What are you doing here?" I ask, though my question is aimed more towards Amy than to Jason.

Jason is the one who answers. "Derek invited me."

"You know that doesn't answer my question, right?" Jason comes here so much that he only needs to leave either one of us—me or Derek—a text. The only problem is that he hates texting for reasons I can't understand.

He shrugs. "Oh well, too bad. Can I come in?"

I gesture for him to enter and he walks straight towards the kitchen to open the fridge and grab a can of Dr. Pepper. This is basically a standard routine whenever Derek's not down to greet him.

"Jason, what are you doing here?" I repeat. "Not that we don't want you here but—"

"I know it's a surprise," he interrupts. "But this couldn't wait any longer."

Now? His posture is straight and his hazel-green eyes hidden behind sunglasses brighten like a neon sign with nothing but determination.

I'm almost afraid to ask. "What couldn't wait?"

Before Jason can answer my question, the sounds of footsteps are heard and Derek finally bounces down the last step and onto the floor. Thank fucking God because someone needs to play mediator between these two, and it's sure as hell not going to be me.

When I turn around to thank Derek, I notice how upright he is. His shoulders are usually slouched and he walks around like he's carrying something. Now, his face is brighter and he looks...lighter, for lack of a better word.

An indication that his conversation with Mom went well.

I smile to myself. Thanks, Mom. The most important thing someone can do is just be there for them and though our mother is hundreds of miles away, it's good to know that her support and unwavering love for us will never die.

"What's the game plan, guys?" He asks, with a bright smile on his face.

I shrug. "Can you tell me?"

My brother turns to Jason. "Nothing, man?"

"We just got here, man. Not all of us can improvise on the spot."

"Says the guy who pushes off all his essays until the night before," Derek retorts back, which ultimately shuts Jason up.

Damn.

"Someone please tell me what's going on!" I finally exclaim. This is like middle school again, when I was playing mediator at one of their stupid arguments. They weren't anything crazy, just about trivial things such as

The guys stop talking and turn to me. My brother raises a brow and jabs a thumb at Jason and asks, "did he really not tell you?"

"I was about to before you came down," he chirps before saying to me, "we're helping you win my sister over." Then, he shudders. "That doesn't feel right saying out loud."

I snort. "Good luck with that." I can't even get Attie to look at me, even if I tried—and my outfit decisions from earlier today can testify to that. Honestly, it hurts to know that she's actively avoiding me.

"It shouldn't be that hard," Derek ponders. "Can't you just talk to her? Be persistent."

"Maybe if she wasn't avoiding me, then I'd actually have a chance," I shoot back.

His eyes widen. "Still?"

I nod. "She hates me for what I did, guys. There's no going back to that." I breached her trust when I read that letter. Passed a boundary, crossed a line I shouldn't have—take your pick, I got more.

The worst part about this is that I'm not the first one to do so. Chase did this a year ago as well. I know I shouldn't compare myself to him because I would never in my life stoop as low as him but I can't help but remember how Attie is still hurt from that

"Then, let's talk to someone she isn't avoiding," Jason suggests.

"I'm talking to you," I point out.

He shakes his head. "Not me." Jason then reaches into his pocket and pulls out his phone. He then quickly taps on the screen with his thumb before ringing is heard. Who could he be calling at this time?

At the confusion on both mine and Derek's faces, he answers, "yesterday, Amy and I were discussing this whole thing. If there's anyone who can help us with this, it's her."

"But Amy doesn't know about the fake relationship," Derek says.

Jason waves a hand. "She knew the whole time it was happening."

For some reason, that doesn't surprise me. I think if there was anyone she would have told about this, it would have been her best friend.

After about two more rings, she answers the phone. "Jason, why are you calling me? Shouldn't you be at Ian's right now?" Her voice is heard clearly from the phone.

"I am," he responds. "You're on speaker right now."

"Seriously?" She hisses. "Attie could hear me right now."

"Where are you?" I inquire, mostly out of curiosity.

"We're at my house right now. She needed to stop sulking over you so I had to drag her away from her art supplies." Amy lets out a breath. "A lot harder than you'd think."

"Isn't Attie a little suspicious about this?" Derek asks.

"If she's curious then it's not enough to care. We're getting ready to watch a movie but if I have to rewatch the All Too Well short film one more time, I'm coming over so I can pull Ian's hair out for doing this to her."

"See, Ian?" Jason laughs. "The fate of your hair rests on this."

I roll my eyes so hard that I have to close them for a few seconds before focusing back on the phone call. "You can pull my hair out another time, Pierce; right now we need your help."

"I don't have much time right now," she warns. "But I'll try my best."

"At this point, we'll take anything," Jason mutters, mostly to himself, but the guy isn't exactly known for being quiet.

"Just give the phone to Ian."

"Amy, you're on speaker," Derek reminds her.

"Oh, right. In that case, leave him alone. We technically don't need you two brothers hovering over this conversation."

The boys complain about this, with the more prominent one being about how Jason needs to hold onto his phone. For someone who has lost track of his phone on multiple occasions—one of them being at a donut shop on some unfortunate date—he really is protective of it.

After assuring Jason that I won't lose his phone, he gives in and both he and Derek exit the living room. I appreciate their desire to help with this but Amy does have a point—this all falls on me.

"I know they mean well but in the end, it all lands on you," Amy says.

"How's she doing?" I ask.

She sighs. "Honestly? Last time I saw her like this was a year ago and it kind of hurts because I don't know what happened then and couldn't help her."

Amy doesn't know about Chase? That's interesting but I choose to keep that tidbit of information to myself, knowing that Attie will tell her best friend on her own terms. Either that, or Jason will slip up.

Both options are bound to happen.

"But," she continues. "I am partially to blame here and Jason isn't so I guess this is my redemption arc." She snorts.

"What do you mean by that?"

Amy laughs awkwardly at my question. "My aunt and I may have been the ones to suggest that she write a letter to her supposed crush and slip it in his locker. I didn't think it would end up in yours but here we are."

Yep. Here we are.

"What a month," I agree.

"Wait, it's only been a month?" She sounds baffled on the phone. "It feels like it's been forever, with everything that's happened." I hear shuffling on the line for a minute before Amy's voice fills my ear. "Sorry, I had to take care of something really quick. Anyway, I only have one question to ask you."

"Ask away," I say without a bout of hesitation.

"How much do you care about Attie?"

I was expecting this question to come more out of Jason's mouth than Amy's but I'm not surprised, regardless. "I'm asking you for help to win her over." That says a lot, doesn't it?

She clicks her tongue. "Dude, that's not an adequate enough answer."

"What are you asking me to say?"

"Just the truth," she answers nonchalantly, her voice low in volume. "Don't bullshit anything."

"I am not someone who enjoys lying, Amy. I hate it more than anything but I spent an entire month lying to everyone else I knew with Attie because I wanted to save her from feeling embarrassed when she didn't even need to feel that way. In that entire month, I've never felt more comfortable around a person than I have around her."

"Okay—" she begins to intrude but I'm not finished yet. The words keep falling out but I'm not building a dam to stop them.

"It kills me to think that I'm doing this to her."

"Okay, savior complex," she mutters sarcastically over the phone. "But you don't have to feel obligated."

"I don't, Amy," I tell her. "That's the thing. I've never once felt obligated to do anything when it came to Attie." Not once in my seventeen and a half years of life. "I don't know how much she told you—"

"Everything," Amy fills in.

"But just know that none of it was done because I had to do it. It was a choice on my end and I would do it again in a heartbeat."

"Because you love her, don't you?"

I sigh, repeating the words. "Because I love her. So much. And I don't know what to do about it."

A moment of silence passes by between us and it's not until I'm sure that Amy hung up that she speaks up. "Well, that's pretty simple, now isn't it?"

Those words did not make sense to me whatsoever. "I'm not following, Pierce."

"You tell her. Everything that you just said to me right now, you tell her."

"What if she doesn't want to listen to me?"

"She doesn't exactly have to listen." I hear the sounds of clashing pans, followed by a curse that I can't transcribe. "Crap, I have to go. Just tell her, okay?"

Before I can ask her what she's talking about, Amy hangs up, and I'm left with a black screen on Jason's phone.

What the hell is Amy talking about?

After heading back upstairs to Derek's room, where I hand Jason back to his phone, I wordlessly trek back to my room and plant myself onto my bed, face down on a pillow, and let out a groan of frustration.

I've got nothing. Abso-fucking-lutely nothing in mind. My mind is almost never blank with random thoughts—how I'm going to finish an essay due next week, college applications, to name a few—but in this situation? I'm drawing blanks.

How is it that my brain shuts down when it matters the most? Does this only happen to me?

When my brain starts to hurt from all the overthinking—how Attie doesn't get headaches from this, I will never understand—I open the top nightstand drawer and remove my glasses. Maybe if I sleep on this, then a great idea will come to me in a dream.

Right below my glasses case, a slip of paper peeks out. Lifting my black carrier case, I reveal the letter. The same one that started it all.

She doesn't exactly have to listen.

And, like an asteroid towards Earth, it hits me.

Placing my glasses back on, I rush out of my room and next door to Derek's, where he and Jason are watching a horror movie. If I had to guess, knowing Derek and by listening to a girl scream bloody murder, it's safe to assume that the movie in question is probably the Halloween film franchise since he always forces Jason to watch it when the holiday is near.

Derek's eyes are pinned to the laptop, while Jason clutches a pillow for dear life, squinting as if Michael Myers is going to poke his head out of Derek's laptop and murder him.

Jason's eyes veer off from the movie and find me standing by the doorway. "Enjoying the show?"

"It's Halloween," I say dumbly. Personally, I think the movie is stupid. "I have a favor to ask of you."

He raises a brow. "Both of us?"

"Just you and Amy," I assure him. "Make sure you get Attie to tomorrow night's game. I'll take care of the rest."

A smirk appears on his face. "Ah. I'm on it." He does a two finger salute and I head downstairs to retrieve my keys. I definitely need to grab a couple of things for this.

Just like Amy said, Attie doesn't exactly have to listen.

Chapter 38

School ending this early in the day only means one thing in October. Homecoming week is coming to a close.

I'm just coming out of my sixth period—in which we did absolutely NOTHING—and decided to meet Amy at my locker so we can walk over to her aunt's car. The plan was to grab smoothies and watch as many Disney movies as humanly possible before getting our nails done.

Even after everything with Ian happened, Amy convinced me to attend homecoming. I had bought the ticket, my dress, and shoes, so it would go to waste if I didn't use them.

Amy has a big smile on my face when I approach her. "What's with the face?"

"What face?" She asks innocently, the smile not disappearing.

I point to her smile. "That. Is Carter able to come after all?"

She shakes her head, curls hitting her face. "No. I'm just excited to see you, that's all. Can't a girl be excited to hang out with her best friend for once? Especially since there's a chance you're spending the night at my place this time."

"That's still up for debate." I know that my grounding sentence is over but I'm still unsure about spending the night there. The last time I did, we accidentally caused a small fire because I lit a candle close to a bouquet of poppies.

Since then, I haven't touched a burner or anything that can light fires. Like matches, lighters, or even holding a glass at a certain angle to the sunlight and aiming that ray at an inanimate object.

"Come on, At-Bat. It'll be fun! Mary's testing out a new recipe for Dad's birthday on Tuesday. You love being a taste-tester for her recipes, right?"

I don't say anything as I enter the combination to my locker and open it up. I notice a book I knew wasn't there when I checked earlier this morning. It's not from my bag because I haven't gone back to my locker during the pep rally that I was forced to attend and in between classes.

I pull it out and notice the cover. A sketchbook. One without a cracked spine and a faded cover. But the pages are crisp and clean. I open it halfway only to find blank pages and close it before turning to Amy. "Did you put this in here?" I ask her.

She shakes her head, indigo eyes wide. "I don't know what you're talking about."

"Ames..."

Amy holds her hands up. "I swear! I didn't buy anything but washi tape and a box when we went to Michaels the other day. Maybe Jason put the sketchbook there."

That's not possible. It could be some sort of prank, but our little prank war has seceded since I placed the fake spider under his duvet earlier this month.

"Who knows?" Amy says. "Maybe it's an early Christmas gift or something. I say: don't question it."

I look back down at the book in my hands. Jason and Amy are the only two people who know my locker combination. I believe Amy when she said that it wasn't her and I know my brother would not give out a gift so early—he waits until the month before. Yeah, he's pretty particular about things like this—so how could it have possibly ended up in my locker?

Maybe...

No. That's not possible. I shove that thought to the back of my mind and place that book into my backpack. "You know what? Let's head over. Maybe we can sneak in some leftover frosting."

She loops her arm around mine with a playful smile on her face and pulls me towards the exit, alongside the multiple students escaping to their freedom that awaits. Since today was only a half-day, we were released from school at noon and there isn't a student that hangs back just because they miss spending time here until three in the afternoon. "That's the spirit, At-Bat."

As we make our way towards the beat up sedan, I hear a voice call out our names. Amy looks behind her shoulder and I swear I catch an eye roll. My best friend may be the confrontational one in this duo but the girl hardly ever rolls her eyes. "Hang on, your brother's about to pass out."

I spin around to find Jason, not out of breath actually, but standing upright and breathing properly. With the added addition of his middle finger aimed at Amy. "What did I ever do to you?"

She chuckles. "You make it so easy."

"How??"

"What is it, Jason?" I ask, putting this little spat to a stop. As much as I love their banter, I'm not in the mood to witness it today. "I thought you and Kelly were going out before the game."

He holds up two fingers. "Two things. One, you left all your overnight stuff in the Jeep so you need to grab it."

"Oh."

"Secondly," he continues. "I just want to check and make sure you two are going to the game tonight, since none of Kelly's friends are and I know she would want to see you two."

"I'm down," Amy answers. "Kelly's a sweetheart."

Jason nods before turning to me. "What about you, sis?"

As much as I would enjoy hanging out with Kelly—I genuinely think that this relationship will make it past two months—the idea of going to the football game, especially tonight, has any excitement buried six feet under, with no sign of life.

"I should grab my stuff," I announce. "From the Jeep." I drop my bag in front of the car and head towards the Jeep, thankful as ever that it's blue and stands out from all other black, gray, white, and red cars that are parked. Jason follows after me.

"Seriously?" Jason implores. "You didn't answer."

"Why is it so important to you that I go?" I pull on the car door only to remember that I was the one driving this morning and locked it. "Can you unlock the door, Jason?"

"Can you answer my question?"

"Ugh."

"Attie, it's the homecoming game," Jason insists. "The one and only football game that you are not allowed to miss."

"Says who?" I ask.

He scoffs. "It's the principle of the thing. Everyone knows this. Everyone but you, apparently."

"I'm not going to the game because I don't want to," I tell him. "That's all."

My brother wants to argue this but I shoot him a look that has his mouth closing shut. He reaches into the pocket of his jacket and presses a button on the key fob, unlocking the car. I grab my overnight bag, which is really just an old backpack that I don't use anymore, and close the door.

"Is that the only reason you don't want to go?" Jason calls out as I start walking away.

Of course he knows that it isn't. But I refuse to say anything on the matter.

I don't respond and walk back to Amy's car. My best friend tilts her head and I know her indigo eyes are filled with worry but I'm not acknowledging it. However, Jason isn't letting this die because he follows me back to the red sedan.

"Is she okay?" Amy asks him as I open the trunk and place my stuff inside.

"Nope," Jason responds. "But she doesn't want to go to the game."

"Because of Ian?"

"Please," I beg. "Don't bring him up."

"It is." Amy makes her way around the front of the sedan to meet my eyes. Her indigo eyes are filled with concern. "Isn't it?"

The tears I've been holding back finally escape and Amy brings me into a hug and I start to cry. Given that I'm taller than her, it's a little weird hiding my face in Amy's shoulder but I manage as I wrap my arms around her in response. "I really messed things up, Ames."

My best friend pats my shoulder. "You didn't, Attie."

"I did!" I cry, pulling back from the hug and wiping my tears. They're black, on account of my mascara. "I pushed him away, Amy! He's been actively avoiding me since then and I know it's all my fault. So yeah! He's the reason why I don't want to go because I can't stand to be in the same area as someone who hates me."

"Attie." Jason comes around and pats me on the back. Again, he's not exactly a hugger. "He doesn't hate you."

I sniff. "What makes you think that?"

"Because I know you," he insists. "So does Ian. Look, I don't know how much you told him but I figure it's enough to understand that you're terrified of trusting another guy after last year."

"Excuse me," Amy interjects. "But what happened last year?"

So Jason didn't slip up and tell Amy. Honestly, I was expecting that. Not because Jason has a hard time keeping a secret but because my best friend is a stubborn mouse. She wants information, she'll get it.

I wave it off. "I'll tell you later."

"You better," she insists before entering the car. I guess she sensed that this conversation needs to rest between me and Jason only. Amy's good at setting boundaries so I shouldn't be surprised, even when she puts her phone up to her ear.

I focus back on Jason, crossing my arms over my chest. It's not that cold, right? Then again, I am wearing a thin sweater and overalls so it could just be my fault for not preparing for the unexpectedly chilly autumn weather.

"Look, Attie. I know Chase ruined whatever confidence you had left in you. But Ian and Chase are two completely different people. And despite everything that happened between you two, he still cares about you, I know it. Enough to give you space when you need it, to be there for you."

I stand in silence, fidgeting with my fingers and tracing circles on the hood of the car, allowing my brain to absorb what my brother is saying.

"How do you do it?" I ask quietly. "How do you manage to go from one girl to the other?"

Jason inhales through his nose. "Because I would rather jump in head-first and not give a damn. Life's too short to have regrets about what could have been when I could focus on the present."

"That seems easier said than done," I mutter.

"I may have regrets but at least I know that I didn't fuck things up in that moment," he says. "And I try to not let those regrets consume my head because that could instigate a migraine."

I wince because I've seen Jason when he has a migraine and it's not pretty. Luckily for me, I've never experienced one and I never will.

"But I fucked things up with Ian," I counter.

"Then fix it," he suggests. "It's never too late to fix it and I know that Ian will hear you out no matter what. Promise me on that." Jason holds out his pinky, and with that seemingly miniscule gesture, I know for certain that he's not bluffing.

I hook my pinky with his. "Fine. I'll go to the game. Now, go hang out with your girlfriend."

My brother chuckles before walking away, leaving me with the promise hanging above my head. Do I feel lighter on my feet? Not just yet because there's still the major obstacle at hand. I'll come across it.

I'll talk to Ian.

One day, I'll set things straight.

I'm just not sure if today's that day.

I should be finely adjusted to standing in the middle of a rowdy bunch of teenagers in school gear but after the multiple games I've gone to in the past month...let's just say that being around a whole bunch of sweaty bodies is not and never will be my forte.

The sheer volume of school spirit bouncing off the rails of the bleachers is intense enough for me to feel a little uncomfortable but I'm trying to focus on anything else besides the game in front of me. I don't know how far along we are into tonight's game and though even just glancing over at the scoreboard could give me the answer, I still refuse to glance in front of me.

Why the hell did I agree to coming tonight?

Then, I hear Kelly screaming when our team scores, followed by a load of giggles and remember that I have friends who actually enjoy these games. Friends that I enjoy being around. Friends that I'm completely certain don't hate me.

Oh, and Jason too.

Should I make an attempt to enjoy this game? Or have fun, just like everyone else around me? This might be the last game I attend for a long time so maybe I should enjoy it while I can.

Maybe I don't exactly enjoy standing in silence whenever the student section goes off in a chant that I don't know. I also don't enjoy being surrounded by couples—present company included—acting all gushy and adorable. God, why can't I have that?

Actually, I could have. I still want that relationship—the kind where everything just fades away and the only people standing

I also know who I want that with.

But there's no way in Dante's Circle of Hell that sentiment is neutral. I just know it because if I was in his position, I would hate myself. It seems inevitable.

So did Ian reading that letter. Ugh, I need to stop thinking about that.

I know that I shouldn't be thinking about Ian right now but it's impossible since he's out on the field, leading our team to what is possibly another win. To not think about the one guy I shouldn't is like taking away my sketchbook—I'll somehow find a way to draw without it.

But there's a whole other level of pain when you can't have the one thing you so badly want.

A horn sounds loud enough for the rest of the stadium to hear, signaling that the quarter is over. When I finally gather enough courage to stop swiveling my head around and keep it in one position, I find the rest of the football team heading off the field and the marching band taking their place.

It must be halftime.

Two of the football players stray off from the rest of the team and make their way off to a small group of people in formal outfits. Right, I almost forgot that tonight's the homecoming game for a minute. They don't crown the homecoming king and queen until halftime. All of the nominees are seniors and from my view, two of them are cheerleaders, two are seniors I'm not familiar with. One of them is BJ.

The other is Ian.

I could have mistaken him for any other blond on the football team but it's not only the number eight on the back of his jersey that differentiates him.

It's the tattoo of all eight phases of the moon on his calf that I can pinpoint clearly, even from this distance, where they look like black specks or even moles. All of his tattoos are etched into my brain.

When he turns around, his eyes instantly connect with mine in the crowd and my heart stops. Almost as if all time stopped around us and we're the only beings not affected by it. But I can't breathe, blink, or move. I'm fucking paralyzed down to my toes.

Before either of us can act on it, the announcer's voice breaks through that sound barrier and jars me back into reality. I let out a shaky exhale and turn to Amy. I can't do this anymore.

I need to get out of here.

"Ames," I begin. "I forgot something in your car. Can I grab it really quick?"

She studies my face for a minute, then briefly reaches into her tote bag and tosses me the keys. "Don't take too long, At-Bat."

I grasp tightly onto her keys and sprint down the steps and out the stadium faster than the roadrunner from Looney Tunes.

What a good friend I am for ditching her. At least I'm not planning on driving away—I may be crazy but I swear that I'm not stupid.

Once I slip into the passenger's seat of Amy's car, I flick the light on and reach for the sketchbook, only to find some thick, blue piece of paper sticking out from the side.

"What the..." I pull on the corner of the paper to reveal what is actually an envelope. A blue envelope with my name on the back. Scribbled in chicken scratch that I've seen only once before. Jason's handwriting is very distinctive and though his love language is acts of service, something in my heart tells me that this isn't his doing.

Curiosity gets the best of me and I find myself opening that envelope and reading the letter inside.

Attie,

I know that no amount of verbal apologies is going to sway you, so I thought that maybe a written one would work. You've written me many letters in the past month, princess, so it feels right that I return the favor. Writing isn't my strong suit like yours but I'm trying here, so please bear with me.

Firstly, I'm so fucking sorry. You have no idea how I wish I didn't read that letter but it's not for the reason you think. I'm sorry you didn't think you could trust me enough to tell me. I get that. Honestly, I really do. I was very hesitant around people when my parents were first divorced and my dad moved Derek and I here.

Besides the point, I know you've been burned before. You have scars from what Hardwick did to you. I may not be him, but I refuse to make that mistake and hurt you in any similar manner.

You asked me why I like studying the stars so much last week and I didn't tell you the entire truth. Here it is: In their darkest moments, stars always shine. Even when they don't notice. I may always call you princess but in reality, you're a star to me. Always a bright spot in the darkest places and that's how I've always seen you. That's why I love stars so much.

That's why I love you.

It's crazy for me to write those words on a paper but it's true. I am deeply in love with you, Athena Eirene Ryder.

I'm not expecting a letter back or really anything else. All that I wish for you is that one day, you'll trust me again. Or even yourself because I have so much faith in you. Always have, and forever will. I won't hesitate to write it in the stars if it means you'll truly believe me.

Ian.

I reread the final sentence over and over again. No exact reason as to why I'm doing that, since it's already etched itself into my brain. The sketchbook was from Ian?

He doesn't hate me? All this time...

Oh.

My.

God.

I still can't believe that he remembered how much I needed a new sketchbook. Wiping the tears from my face, I place the letter back in its envelope and sit in silence, the loud cheers from the stadium dulled out.

Shit, this really hurts. How is it that Ian is still one of the kindest people I've known, especially to me?

He should be mad at me! He should hate me, for crying out loud. But nope—he loves me.

He fucking loves me.

Resting my head on the car seat, I close my eyes and count to three in my head. Allowing myself to collect my thoughts and instead, think more about this logically but it's damn near impossible because only one of those thoughts stays at the forefront of my mind.

I need to talk to him.

I check the time on my phone. Halftime is definitely over by now and the game is back on but I can't bring myself to enter the stadium. There's no way I'll be able to grab his attention at this time, with him still playing on the field. I'll just wait.

Once the game is over, I'll find him.

I will set things straight with Ian. One way or another.

Because I can't let the guy I love walk away.

Chapter 39

The homecoming game is always the easiest game of the season. A secret that not many people outside of high school football will reveal is that almost all homecoming games are played against teams that can easily be defeated.

That's why I'm allowed to sit at the bench after the third quarter of the game while my backup QB, Marlow Jackson, goes up and takes his spot. We're up by thirty points because we're playing Barin High yet again and they do suck but at least they're trying.

I head over to the cooler, grab a paper cup, and fill it with water. The day of the homecoming game always feels like the longest for me. Fridays just feel long during football season in general.

Like Father Time just enjoys torturing me.

When the fourth quarter begins, BJ sits back down next to me, wearing the homecoming king sash. They announced the winners during half-time and though I was nominated, I didn't win. I'm not pressed about it because I still cannot fathom how I even got nominated in the first place but I'm happy for him and Soph.

I am. Even if I seem the opposite. There's just a lot going on in my mind right now.

I glance behind me at the bleachers. Jason texted me before the game to tell me that his sister was standing in the student section with him and the others but as I scan the crowd, I struggle with my attempt at spotting the familiar pair of overalls or long dark hair. I still hold onto a sliver of hope. Maybe she went to grab snacks or something.

"Did you see her yet?" BJ asks.

I shake my head.

He winces. "Sorry, dude. Maybe she's seated farther back."

I shrug. "Maybe." Earlier today, I had filled BJ and Sophia in on what I planned to do. Technically, I only told BJ but my friend tells his girlfriend everything, so Sophia knew by default.

Right now, my only hope is that she got the sketchbook. The first part of the plan was to slip it inside her locker when she wasn't around, then apologize and practically beg for another chance. If I didn't fuck up the way I had, tomorrow would've been the last day of our fake relationship.

Come to think of it, I don't know why we had started one in the first place.

The game is over and though it was an easy win for the team, I still feel a little tense. Not even a shower does anything for me. All my thoughts are consumed by Attie. She's not even nearby right now and even still, I can't stop worrying.

Did she read the letter?

Where is she?

Once I high-five the back-up QB as I exit the locker room, I head straight for the bleachers to find her. During halftime, I spotted her in the student section—where those decked in school spirit cheer to their heart's content.

No sign of her. Amy's standing there, with Jason, Derek, and Jason's girlfriend. I march over to them and practically demand, "where is she?"

They all stop whatever conversation and turn to me. Amy's eyes are wide, Jason tightens his hold on his girlfriend, and Derek stands still without flinching. "You need to calm down, man."

"I don't know," Amy says. "I told her to come back because she needed to grab something from my car but that was during halftime."

"Halftime was an hour ago!"

"I realize that!" She snaps and I take a small step back from. It's always the short people that are the scariest. She probably means well but in all honesty, I'm a little terrified of Amy.

"You two need to calm down," Jason interjects. "She's not crazy enough to drive away with Amy's car so she's probably still here."

"But where?"

He shrugs. "You tell me. Do you want us to look for her?"

As nice as that would be, I shake my head. "I'll do it. Thanks, anyway." I head back down the bleachers and search the crowds to find her but it's a little difficult. With the marching band, cheerleading team, and vendors packing up for the night, it's almost impossible.

Just as I take that last step and onto concrete, I run into someone and manage to both steady myself and catch them before either one of us falls onto the ground.

"I'm so sor—" I'm about to say when I look into a pair of wide, pale blue eyes that I've never been more thankful to see.

Oh thank fucking God I found her. Totally broke a commandment there with that but I can't give one iota of a damn about that. All that matters is that she's here.

In my arms, right where she belongs.

I'm not sure how long it's been—because time basically stopped the moment Attie fell into my arms—before she scrambles off me and straightens up. "Sorry," she mumbles.

My mouth is slightly open but no words are coming out. Why is it that when I plan an entire speech inside my head, it all disappears as the moment arrives? I spent hours rehearsing what I would say to her on the off-chance that she approached me first. Now, it's as if I never thought about it in the first place.

But I don't want to assume anything. So I nod over to the bleachers. "Jason's still up there."

Shaking her head, she says, "I was looking for you."

"So was I." I clear my throat after realizing I said that out loud instead of keeping it in my head. "I mean–I wasn't looking for myself. I was—" Here I am, turning into a stuttering mess.

I'm normally not this awkward but I guess there's a first for everything.

"I know what you're trying to say," she assures me, wide-eyed and barely moving.

It's now or never, Bale. Now or never. I count to three in my head before opening my mouth but she kind of beats me to it.

"Can we talk?" We ask simultaneously.

By then, the crowds are dying down, and the bleachers are almost empty. I swear Jason and the rest of the gang are watching this extremely awkward interaction and for the first time ever, I feel a tiny bit uncomfortable.

I nod and grab her hand. "Probably not right here."

I lead Attie over to this dimly lit area under the bleachers. Just as the both of us sit down on the patchy spot of grass, her shoulders sag and she covers her face. I'm about to ask what's wrong before they start shaking. On instinct, I wrap both of my arms around her and pull her into my chest.

"I'm so sorry," she cries into my chest. A little muffled but I can hear her just fine. "For everything."

"Princess, you don't have to apologize."

"Yes, I do!" She lifts her head off my chest and wipes her cheeks. "I'm the reason this week has been a mess."

"Well, I understand why you're upset." I run a hand through her soft, dark hair. "And this goes both ways. If anything, we're both to blame for what's happened. Just breathe with me, right now, okay?"

She nods and rests her head on my chest again, taking a few deep breaths. After exhaling the last one, she adjusts her head so that she faces me. I don't know if she's aware of how close our faces are in this position, or maybe the erratic beating of my heart. Probably both but I shove those thoughts to the very depths of my mind and focus on her.

"Better?" I ask.

She hesitates before nodding. "How are you not mad at me?"

"What?"

"After Monday, and what I said to you..." She grimaces at the memory. "I just thought that you would hate me or something."

"I don't hate you," I tell her.

"I know that now but you should."

"I should hate you?" I repeat. "You're kidding, right? Because that's impossible for me."

She squeezes her eyes shut and a single tear falls down her cheek. I wipe the tear away with my thumb before tilting her chin up so her eyes meet mine.

"I could never, in my life, hate you."

"I know, but your life would be easier if you did hate me."

I shake my head. "Too bad because I don't want it to be easy. I just want you in it."

She sniffs. "Really?"

"Really."

Attie wraps both of her arms around my neck and pulls me into a hug so tight that it almost consumes me. I don't hesitate to hold her back because I don't want to let her go. Not at this moment.

Not ever.

"I'm sorry for lashing out on you, Ian. I really am."

Is this a good time to bring up the letter? I should probably ease into it, right? What if she didn't even read it?

Nope, I'm not going to bring it up. If Attie read the letter, then she would bring it up first, right?

"I'm sorry for reading the letter," I respond. "We need to work on our communication."

She chuckles. "Yeah, we definitely do." Much to my dismay, she pulls back from the hug. "So, what now?"

Oh shit, that was not a question I prepared myself for. "What do you want?"

She sighs. "I'm not sure. Because I don't think we can go back to how things were before this all began."

"I don't think we can, either," I agree. "All we can do is move forward."

"I'm not sure I can," she admits, her voice wobbly.

"We have to move forward. As painful as it is, it's inevitable." One useful bit of knowledge I learned during my parents' divorce that sticks with me, even now. "You're not doing it alone, Attie." I rest my hand on top of hers, which lies on her knee, palm down. "I'm right there with you."

About five seconds pass before her head comes to rest on my shoulder. Her hand that rests below mine is turned over and she starts squeezing it.

"I know," she whispers. "Can I ask you something?"

"Anything."

"Did you really mean it? The letter?"

I don't even hesitate. "Every single word."

She lets out a small gasp and I turn my head slightly so as to not move hers. "Even..."

"Yes, princess. Even that." I'm waiting for the rejection to hit. For her to tell me that she never felt the same way or that she still has feelings for my brother.

But it doesn't.

"How long?" She asks, lifting her head off my shoulder.

I shrug. "Since the beginning? Maybe even before that? I lost track of time."

Another beat of silence passes, and I grow more anxious waiting for her response.

"Oh, thank God!"

Wait, what?

I turn to face her, a baffled expression on my face. Huh?

With cheeks turning red, she explains, "I may or may not have felt the same way for about the same amount of time."

See, I knew we needed to communicate more but I didn't know how bad it was.

"Seriously?"

She nods shyly. "It took me a while to figure it out. I thought I messed things up terribly until I read the letter you wrote and knew I still had a chance."

"But you never lost it," I correct her.

"It felt like I did. Honestly, Ian, my head is filled with nothing but chaos, cartoons, and Taylor Swift lyrics and I don't feel like my brain's about to explode whenever you're near. It's like you know what to say to keep me at bay and I didn't realize how much I needed that until I lost it." She clears her throat. "Or, I thought I lost it."

"That leads us to the day-old question," I ponder.

"What do we do now?" She repeats.

What indeed? I don't need to ask myself that question because I already know what I want. It's a matter of whether or not, attie wants it as well. Part of me is confident that she does but it doesn't hurt to ask.

"I have a proposition," I suggest out of thin air. "We move forward."

"I don't think that—"

I hold a hand up. "Can you let me finish, please?"

Attie wordlessly gestures for me to go on.

"No time constraints, no rules. Just keep going as we have been this past month and let everything happen as it should."

Her bright eyes light up like a kid on Christmas. "Like, an actual relationship?"

"Sounds like it to me."

She gestures to herself. "With me?"

I chuckle. "Yes, princess. With you."

A knowing smile stretches across her face. "Of course, Ian. I'll do it."

Before I can respond or make a move to kiss her, she beats me to it, pressing her lips to mine and kissing me gently, to which I reciprocate. After she pulls back, she buries her head in the crook of my neck, holding on tightly. I close my eyes and allow myself to savor this moment. She's here, in my arms. And she's mine. No rules, no ruse. Nothing is stopping me from squeezing her as tight as I can without cutting off her air supply.

It's a moment made even better when she whispers five words into my ear: "I love you too, Ian."

Epilogue

5 months later

"So, you're getting on a surfboard willingly?" Amy asks as she observes the surfboard half-buried in the sand next to Ian.

It's spring break and today, Amy, Ian, and I are at Hendry's Beach yet again. Amy needed a break from something and decided to join us. I wasn't exactly sure about her joining because I didn't think she'd want to be a fifth wheel—BJ and Sophia are joining us later today—but she was insistent about not staying at home for the entire day.

"He's going to attempt to teach me," I correct her, flipping off my sandals and placing them near her tote bag. I take a seat next to her and untie my hair from the elastic. "Again."

"To have a mediocre surfer as a boyfriend," she sighs dramatically. "How ever can I relate to that?"

I wrap an arm around her shoulder. Since what happened with Carter a few months ago, Amy has sworn off dating. My best friend claims that she's doing alright but I can't always be sure. She's usually a closed book about these things. "Don't worry, Ames. You don't need to date a surfer. Besides, Ian can teach you."

"I don't have a death wish, At-Bat. You won't ever catch me near a surfboard." She perches her sunglasses on top of her head and lays back down on the beach towel. "Land is a whole lot safer."

"Hey, it's not that bad," Ian chimes in, wrapping one arm around my waist. "Just get through the first couple of wipeouts and you'll be just fine."

We burst into fits of laughter. It's crazy to me that after these past few months, Ian still decides to stick by my side. To love someone who can manage all the good and the bad is someone worth keeping.

I just wish I'd seen it a whole lot sooner than this.

"Last I remember, I hardly had any wipeouts," I tease, perching my chin on top of his shoulder.

He responds by kissing my forehead. "Well, that's just beginner's luck, princess. You're not a beginner anymore."

"Okay, you two lovebirds." Amy begins to shoo us away. "Go be lovey-dovey somewhere else."

I ruffle her blonde curls before taking Ian's right hand in mine. He holds his surfboard under his left arm and squeezes onto my hand tight.

"You ready?" He asks, handing me the surfboard.

"Let's do this." I take the surfboard in both hands and move along towards the shore. Really, I'm waddling because of how big the board is. I don't surf enough to get my own board so Ian and I agreed that it would be better if we shared his.

"You got this, princess!" He shouts, grabbing the attention of a few tourists and locals. My cheeks heat up to epic proportions but the water spraying on me as I move deeper cools me off slightly.

As someone who gets embarrassed easily, I can't help but feel giddy when someone shows confidence in me because I'm not used to it. An odd concept it is but I digress.

Luckily for the both of us, I remember most of the basics from back when he first taught me in October. That doesn't mean that I'm a master because my first attempt in five months is not something you'd find in Surf's Up or something.

Once I start wobbling, I know for certain that I'm about to fall off. Trying not to resist, I let my body take its course and fall back-first into the water and come back up laughing. Though it was only the first wave, those five seconds of standing were invigorating.

I don't have a choice but to swim towards the shore, since that's where the board drifted off to. Back to its rightful owner, who stands there with a shit-eating grin on his face.

I grab both hands on my hips. "Okay, you can just let it all out now. I can handle the laughter."

"I'm not laughing," he counters.

"But you want to," I observe, gesturing to the grin on his face.

"It was more of a graceful fall than a wipeout."

"Ian," I laugh, shaking my head. "I'm anything but graceful."

Shaking his head, he pulls me into his arms and kisses my smile. I can seriously never get enough of him. His fresh scent that reminds me of clean linen, the softness of his lips against mine—everything.

Before either one of us breaks it, I unwrap my left arm from his torso and grasp onto the surfboard.

"Hey!" Ian laughs as I race down the shore, with him following just behind. Since he's a lot taller and takes longer strides than I do, it's a bit of a challenge. Luckily, I reach the shore before he can.

"I'm gonna try again!" I announce.

"Fine, but if you wipeout again, it's my turn!"

"Deal!" I call back. I start paddling farther away from shore until my arms get tired.

Sitting back up on the board, with my legs dangling in the water, I watch for any incoming waves, which doesn't take very long.

My eyes widen when I take notice of the size. Oh boy, that's a big one.

Instantly, I turn the board around and start paddling for a few more seconds before standing back up on the board.

I manage to keep myself steady on the board and get a glimpse behind me. "I can do this," I tell myself repeatedly. Keep my chin up and breathe.

Eventually, the wave dies down and I'm still standing. Once I've made it to shore, I hop off the board and exhale a breath that I had no clue I was holding. Holy shit!

I didn't even wipe out.

I'm still in shock when Ian runs over to me and lifts me in his arms, spinning me around.

"I fucking did it!" I cheer, holding on tight to my boyfriend.

Once I'm on my feet, I press my lips to his and I swear he dips me. "I'm so proud of you, princess. I knew you could do it."

"Oh, please," I joke. "You were just waiting for me to wipe out."

"No way. I had a lot of faith in you."

I stand on my toes and press a kiss to his cheek. "I know you do. You won't let me forget it."

He turns around to face me, sincerity lacing his ocean blue eyes. "I'll tell you everyday if I have to."

"And I'll believe you every time." I take a step back so I can grab the board from the sand and hand it over to him. "Are you still able to surf with this on?" I gesture to the right side of his neck. The day Ian turned eighteen, about three weeks ago, he went straight to the tattoo parlor and got himself his third tattoo.

I was there when it all happened. He claims that it didn't hurt compared to his previous tattoos but I'm still not sure if that's entirely true. My ears are pierced—twice actually—but I don't know if I could ever get a tattoo myself.

From a distance, it looks like a blob of ink but the details are much clearer close up. The replica of the wax seal just below his ear always makes me smile. The little heart in the middle of it all is just another reminder of how I fell in love with him.

"I should be fine," he answers. "The second skin should protect it well enough."

"Okay. Be safe."

He chuckles, removing his glasses and handing them to me. "I always am."

It's still crazy to me how far we've come. These past five months have really been some of the best I've had in a long time. Not just because of Ian—trust me, he's definitely a contributing factor—but because I've learned to not hold on so much. That's what I've been doing. Even though I'm still finding that balance between holding on and letting go, I can confirm that it's getting a whole lot better than it was when junior year began.

Especially with my hair, which I cut to a shorter length back in January and dyed back to one color—my natural hair. But that's besides the point.

I watch Ian stand up on his board, doing a much better job than me. Twirling his glasses in my hand, I observe the other surfers around him. This would make for a great sketch. I should grab my phone and take a picture.

Heading towards the beach towel, I reach into Amy's tote bag for my phone. "Hey, can I borrow some—" I look up from the tote bag and see nothing. I'm not kidding. The beach towel where Amy was resting only a moment earlier is vacant.

"Ames?" I call out, scanning the area. That's weird. I look into her bag again. Everything except for her phone and wallet are accounted for. She couldn't have just run off like that, could she?

"Taking a break?" Ian jogs over to our stuff and sits down on the towel.

I frown. "Just trying to figure out where Amy is."

"Can't you check her location or something?"

I shake my head. "She doesn't have an iPhone."

"Not on Snapchat?"

I shrug. "She doesn't have an account." When I asked her about it once, she claimed that it was practically a waste of time.

"Well, she'll be back," he assures me. "All of Amy's stuff is here. She doesn't strike me as someone who would just abandon everything for no reason."

"Right." I take a deep breath and rest the back of my head on his lap. "She'll be back."

Ian smiles softly. "That's my princess."

I laugh lightly. I don't think I'll ever get used to him calling me that. A nickname that he reserved just for me. How did I get so damn lucky? Out of all the guys on this planet, Ian just happened to be the one who chose me.

Written in the stars, he would say.

I don't need stars to voice what is already true.

"What's with that smile?" He asks, cheeks turning pink.

"Oh nothing," I say nonchalantly, lifting my head off his lap. "Just remembering how much I love you."

He then pulls me up onto his lap and hugs me. Though I love his kisses, nothing beats hugs. When Ian Bale hugs you, it's with every fiber of his being. His heart, his soul—you can feel his love through his hug.

"I love you too, princess," he mumbles in my ear. "And I'm so glad you found your way to me."

www.ingramcontent.com/pod-product-compliance
Lightning Source LLC
Chambersburg PA
CBHW060759210726

48292CB00013B/713